T.

Diana Nicosia

THE CARAVAGGIO CONTRACT

DIANA NICOSIA

Merrimack Media
Cambridge, Massachusetts

Library of Congress Control Number: 2015948405

ISBN: print: 978-1-939166-78-4

ISBN: ebook: 978-1-939166-77-7

Copyright © 2015 Diana Nicosia

All rights reserved. No part of this book may be reproduced or transmitted in any form or by any means, electronic or mechanical, including photocopying, recording, or by any information storage and retrieval system, without permissions in writing from the copyright owner.

This is a work of fiction. However, certain public figures and incidents in this book are inspired by actual events. All other characters described in the book are imaginary.

Published by Merrimack Media, Cambridge, Massachusetts
Septmember, 2015

To my husband,

Arthur Bauernfeind

Contents

Prologue	ix
Capri	1
Amalfi	25
Capri	91
Naples	97
Rome	141
Acknowledgments	222

Prologue

TUSCANY, JULY 15, 1610

His harsh cry pierced the quiet slumber of the small harbor. He was a young man, a black flailing figure against a huge red sun ball half-set on the horizon. Running, gasping for breath, he hurled himself off the beach onto the dock, his feet skidding on the worn, slippery wood. At the end of the dock, he stopped abruptly and almost tumbled into the brackish water. Staring intently out to sea, he stood still for a moment and tried to breathe. Caravaggio, the most important Baroque artist in Italy, had been reduced to a pauper after bribing his way out of the frontier prison. Seeing his future sailing away in the felucca, a small boat, he became desperate. He shook his fists, screamed, raged against the disappearing boat. His head sunk to his chest.

Caravaggio began his career in a blaze of light; he portrayed radiance on simple subjects of natural beauty. He moved from his impoverished childhood home in Milan to Rome hoping his painting skills might prove useful to the rich and powerful. He was so poor that many times he traded his paintings for scraps of food.

He was saved by his magical power of capturing light and shade when one of his early paintings caught the eye of a famous art patron, Cardinal Francesco Maria Del Monte. The cardinal encouraged his career, obtained important commissions for him and eventually included Caravaggio in his household. For the first time, the young artist had a refuge and could create paintings of wonder and enchantment.

But all his life, Caravaggio was plagued by a sense of abandonment, a constant theme in his paintings. As he grew more famous, he seemed to grow angry and had frequent arrests. He fled Rome after he was accused of murdering a local gangster, and a *banda capitale*, a death sentence, was issued. This brutal sentence meant that anyone, in any place, could carry it out. He had been on the run from the authorities ever since.

In the spring of 1610, Caravaggio returned to Naples, where he had been offered sanctuary by the Colonna family. He enjoyed a lavish lifestyle, feted by the noblest Italian families, but was always in danger, hunted by the Knights of Malta and, perhaps, by the Spanish. While he awaited a papal pardon, he prepared several paintings intended as gifts of tribute to thank his benefactors in Rome. Some of the paintings were small so that they could be packed and carried easily. He took a separate studio and began his last, great paintings in a frenzy of production. Finally, the death sentence was commuted by Pope Paul V and Caravaggio believed his future was once again secure. He immediately departed for Rome. Caravaggio thought he was only days away from a comfortable household when his boat made an unexpected stop.

The small two-masted felucca needed fresh supplies and had put in at a tiny port, Palo, little more than a fortress castle under Spanish rule. Caravaggio most likely intended to disembark here and continue to Rome by land, but misfortune struck. The Spanish authorities of the fortress detained him to check the validity of his papal pass. Perhaps, the commander of the Spanish fortress mistook Caravaggio for a bandit they had been alerted to detain, but then again, perhaps it was simply bad luck.

Caravaggio was still locked in the frontier prison as the felucca prepared to set sail. With a storm approaching, the boat could not wait for one passenger. Her captain decided to leave Caravaggio behind, to abandon him to his captors, and sailed on to Porto Ercole, away from Rome, farther up the coast of Tuscany.

Caravaggio was desperate to retrieve the fortune hidden in the hold of the felucca. Chasing after the boat was futile so, driven to despair, he concocted a mad plan: He resolved to walk to the next port and, with the last of his funds, hire a faster boat. Caravaggio set off on a determined march on the scalding beach separating the two towns. He had left on impulse, poorly prepared to walk alone in the forbidding territory surrounded by a disease-infested marshland. By now, Caravaggio was weakened from his old wounds and was delirious with malaria. The sad, lonely painter collapsed midway on the desolate beach from fever.

It was a miracle that a stranger found the semiconscious man lying prostrate on the beach and dragged him to the next town's tiny hospital. Caravaggio lay on his sickbed all the while raving about his lost paintings and how the pope was expecting him. He languished in the hospital, never able to answer questions about his identity.

A few days later, Caravaggio succumbed to his fever and wounds and died. The record maintained by the Brothers of San Sebastiano in Porto Ercole simply states: "On July 18, Michelangelo Merisi da Caravaggio, the painter, died of disease in the hospital of St. Mary the Helper." Caravaggio was thirty-nine years old.

What happened to the paintings?

Diana Nicosia

Capri

AUGUST 4, 1985

EARLY MORNING

"*Cattivo!*"

Fiona Appleton kicked repeatedly as she attempted to start an old, battered Vespa. She shook her head, wondering if she was angry at the motor scooter or at her husband, Sergio Celesti. After whisking her away from their home in Rome to a summer rental on the island of Capri, Sergio had become cold and distant. Fiona was surprised and upset by Sergio's attitude as he had promised her a summer of relaxation and loving companionship. The summer-long rental on Capri was supposed to be a celebration of their two-year marriage – a renewal of their commitment to one another and the promise of more years of happiness to come.

She had expected lazy days spent sunning themselves by the sea and fun evenings at the local cafès. Instead, Fiona spent the summer dealing with Sergio's silences or his long absences away from the villa. Even when Sergio was at the villa, he was not necessarily available, there but not there, disappearing into a room made into an office for long hours, the door shut. No harsh words had been said by either of them, but Fiona felt she could no longer ignore the growing tension between them. She was saddened to realize that the marriage had failed. Fiona was determined to confront Sergio. After all, she wondered, how did an antique dealer support a luxurious villa rental in Anacapri?

With one vicious kick, the small engine sputtered to life and she wrapped her long, slender fingers around the black leather handle grips. Kicking the stand away, she revved the machine and the Vespa hurtled down the driveway spraying white gravel.

Turning quickly, she shouted over her shoulder, "Guido, *seduto!*" The white spitz looked longingly at his mistress but promptly sat down on his haunches. She was to be obeyed. The electronic gates clanged shut behind her. Fiona Appleton knew her dog was safe behind the metal gates and the beautiful day lay before her for the taking. Her plans were as bright as the sunlight in her eyes.

A tall man wearing well-cut casual clothes walked in a smooth gait that seemed to propel him effortlessly across the road toward the gates of Fiona's villa. He had been about to drop a small envelope into the mailbox suspended on a column by the gate but hesitated upon hearing the whine of the motor scooter's engine. Instead, he stopped abruptly, withdrew his hand and stood still. His eyes were almond-shaped, brilliantly blue and alert. He took his sunglasses off to polish them as his eyes swept around the street to see if anyone else was waiting for the driver of the Vespa.

The man was Arturo Monti, the legendary financier, and an old friend of Fiona's from Boston. In a seamless sleight of hand, he palmed the small envelope as he stretched his neck to catch his first glimpse of Fiona. Arturo smiled as he saw Fiona seated on her white Vespa.

Fiona had called him a few days ago asking for his advice and help. Although Arturo had been flattered that Fiona had turned to him for advice, he had been surprised to hear her dramatic plea for help. Even after so much time had passed – two years without any communication from her – Arturo agreed to help her, to save her. He only had arrived on Capri in the early morning and already was standing outside her villa. The contents of the envelope listed his contact information on the island and a note suggesting that they set up a meeting at his hotel to further their discussions.

Fiona and Arturo had been lovers while she was enrolled in Harvard's master of arts program and he was a visiting professor at MIT. They first had met at a student art show at the Fogg Museum in Cambridge. There was an immediate attraction and soon they were inseparable, but Fiona always maintained her commitment to finishing her degree, which necessitated going to Italy for a semester. Of course, Arturo understood and encouraged Fiona to pursue her passion for art. She left for a tutorial in Rome; he remained behind at MIT.

While studying Old Masters in Rome, Fiona met Sergio Celesti, an art restorer and antique dealer. Their chance meeting led to romance and an impulsive marriage. Arturo was teaching in Cambridge, waiting for Fiona's return. He had thought they were destined to be together, true soul mates, but instead he got a single letter from her. Fiona wrote that she herself was surprised by her sudden marriage; she hoped to be happy, and apologized if there were any hurt feelings.

Only one letter, not asking for a reply, as it was final. A leave-taking. Silence. Fiona simply vanished from his life. She was married and living in Rome. Until now, two years later, and here she was spending the summer of 1985 on the island of Capri.

According to Fiona, her husband had been acting mysteriously, and she could not fathom how Sergio supported their grand lifestyle. Fiona, furthermore, asked Arturo to make a few phone calls and check on her husband's business. Better yet, could he visit Capri and offer Sergio advice and counsel? After all, Arturo was a businessman investing in companies doing business around the world. Solving an antique dealer's business problems should be simple. Wouldn't it? Fiona pleaded with him over the phone and Arturo canceled business meetings, putting his life on hold to come to her aid.

He smiled despite his feelings of misgiving as Fiona re-entered his life with such an intense distress call. And to top it off, she chose the glamorous, international summer playground of Capri for this reunion. Yes, Fiona was correct in sensing trouble. Sergio Celesti was up to his neck in bad business dealings and overdue loans. Arturo speculated that Sergio must be anxious about his business affairs and on edge about where to turn for help. But was Fiona in immediate danger? Fiona presented what the Romans called a "bella figure". No matter what, it was imperative to look great, to present a beautiful image. Perhaps living in Rome all these years had gone to Fiona's head? Arturo shook his head almost as if he silently was disagreeing with himself. He trusted Fiona that her values and her character were the same as before – as rock-solid as the Faraglioni, the famous stones jutting out of the Mediterranean Sea.

Now in the summer of 1985, after two years of marriage, Fiona called her former lover, Arturo Monti, to save either her marriage or her. As he stood so very still waiting for Fiona, Arturo sensed his impatience to see her and he forced himself not to show his pent-up feeling of longing for her.

The electronic gates slid open; Fiona raised her eyes from the gravel path and looked up at the entrance. Suddenly with a flash of recognition, her eyes locked onto Arturo. She smiled grandly and waved with a free hand, all the while balancing the old Vespa. She braked the Vespa as soon as she cleared the gates and came up beside Arturo. Tipping the motor scooter to one side, she clicked the supporting stand and the Vespa stood upright. Fiona balanced the Vespa and embraced Arturo with a big hug and kisses on either cheek.

Arturo kissed Fiona and returned her hug. He laughed with pure joy to see her again. He looked her up and down and admired what he saw. Fiona had luxurious blonde hair cascading down her back, skin the color of alabaster, and violet eyes, so luminous and large that a man could see them from a great distance. With her long-limbed dancer's body and dressed as she was now, in brief running shorts with a thin, cotton, pastel top, she was dangerously attractive. He was smitten.

Fiona laughed as she squinted into the sun and found Arturo's eyes staring back at her. She saw a man in his mid-thirties who retained an aura of power – mature for someone his age. Arturo grinned back at her. She remembered how their casual romance grew slowly, blossoming into love. Fiona was a determined art student with a lofty ambition: to become a significant painter. She loved Arturo but wanted to pursue her craft. Arturo and Fiona parted amicably when she left for a fellowship at the American Academy in Rome, both thinking they would continue their close relationship. But somehow their good intentions, their love affair, were not meant to be.

Fiona told herself to stop thinking of the past and silently looked at Arturo, assessing him. How little Arturo had changed since they had seen each other, she thought. There were a few more pounds on his lean frame, but she saw he was still fit despite the long hours spent at his office. His dark-blonde, wavy hair only had a few streaks of gray and he wore it stylishly short. His cheekbones were still high and sharp, and the aquiline nose looked as though it had been carved from granite. It was a timeless face, resembling a Roman centurion. His face could be a face on the cover of an Italian fashion magazine or a face from a Renaissance portrait. It was also a face of an aristocratic origin. Arturo's blue eyes were shielded by aviator sunglasses, making him seem mysterious. Her heart hammered; she suddenly was brought up quickly by the realization she wanted to know him again and, judging by her racing heart, to know him well.

After mentally cataloging his appearance, Fiona smiled with pleasure. In a teasing manner, she said, "Arturo, I didn't know you were here. Why didn't you call me with your plans? I would have met you at the docks. Where are you staying? And are you alone?"

Her teasing ceased when she saw Arturo polishing his glasses. It was a gesture she recognized from his past. He always polished his glasses to bide time before saying something serious. Fiona hurriedly asked, "It's bad, isn't it? Much worse than I'd imagined?" She almost stammered from her agitation.

Arturo put his sunglasses on. He nodded his head,

cleared his throat and said, "Of all the places in the world to see you again and have to discuss business!"

He reached over and gave her arm a light squeeze as if to reassure her and said, "I'm here to help you. Let's move slowly, logically and review all the facts. There will be a way to proceed in an orderly fashion so that no one will be hurt."

Arturo tilted his head slightly and said in a low voice, "Are you in any danger?"

"Arturo, you're scaring me! Why should I be in danger? Do you think Sergio would hurt me?"

"I don't know Sergio, and when you telephoned me, you were in distress. You sounded agitated on the phone. I took it as a cry for help. So, here I am. Are you in danger? It's a normal question under the circumstances." Arturo continued to look steadily at Fiona.

"No. I've never felt in danger from Sergio. And Sergio's never acted as if he's been threatened by anyone, only harassed by the insurance company."

"*Va bene*, it's good. At least we got that cleared up." Arturo smiled and relaxed his stance. His eyes twinkled when he said, "I did try to reach you by telephone. No one answered, so I was just dropping off a note with my island contact information when your villa gates opened. I checked into Hotel Quisisana this morning. And I'm alone. I'm here to help if you need it. How is Sergio, by the way? Has he changed? Is he volatile?"

Arturo caught his breath when her incredible eyes misted and came to rest again on him. In a husky voice, he said, "Fiona, you look marvelous. You haven't aged." He looked at her with admiration.

Fiona adjusted her weight as she straddled the Vespa, stretched her arms and said in a quiet, measured tone,

"Arturo, you're sweet and I appreciate you. You dropped everything to help me. I don't know what Sergio's real plans are, or why we left Rome for a summer in Capri. I don't even know the state of our finances. Sergio won't answer any of my questions about his business, the fire in his restoration workshop, nothing. He's moody but not volatile. He won't talk to me." Her voice faded and she looked up at Arturo with wide eyes.

"I'm here to help. Let's not jump to any conclusions yet." He cleared his throat. "Sergio has a prominent art and antique business. You may only be reacting to his mood swings. He settled with the insurance company and decided to take a vacation. Let's give him the chance to share some information and then I can determine if I can be of any help – if any is needed."

Arturo looked into her eyes, which were clouded over, and he knew Fiona was too smart to accept his smooth explanation of her husband's sudden change of address to Capri. He didn't trust Sergio and hoped Fiona would not be caught in a scandal. He also wondered about her feelings toward her husband. Did she love a man she no longer could trust? A man who put her in danger?

Aloud, he said, "In all seriousness, if the situation is dire, if you feel in danger, I'll do whatever it takes to get you away. We need more information before any decisions can be made." He smiled and continued, "Va bene. A quiet dinner at the Quisisana. Tonight at eight?"

Fiona remained still for a moment and then leaned over the Vespa's side toward him, hugged him and said, "Thanks for understanding. I feel somewhat stronger with you here. When I first met Sergio, I told him about college life and our affair. He's heard a lot about you and respects you. He'll be surprised to see you, but somehow I'll handle it. Maybe he'll confide in you? Maybe we'll get to the truth?"

Arturo stroked her arm gently but did not try to hold onto her. Instead, he replied in a crisp, loud voice, "See you tonight on the hotel's terrace."

Fiona squared her shoulders and resumed her balancing act on the motor scooter. She lifted her chin and said, "Now, I must return to my favorite spot to catch the light. The painting is almost finished. Do you want a lift?"

"No, thanks. I left my Vespa over by your neighbor's wall."

"Va bene."

Fiona shook her fingers, giving a flourish to her wave. She revved the tiny engine and the Vespa bucked over the crushed stones and began the steep climb. She looked back and blew him a kiss.

Arturo watched Fiona as she sped away. She exuded vitality and health. He smiled when he saw the motor scooter was laden with customized Gucci canvas saddlebags holding brushes, paints and other assorted artist's paraphernalia. He later would observe that the brilliant summer morning was a metaphor for Fiona's life as she had known it. He first knew Fiona when they were both on college campuses in Cambridge; he quickly had fallen in love with the willful artist. He admired Fiona's strength of character, her enormous talent and her commitment to painting. For Arturo, his heart was taken. When she reached out to him in London a few days ago, he reassigned his work, canceled appointments and flew to Capri. Arturo somehow hoped that this was his chance not only to help Fiona, but to rekindle their love.

Then Arturo sighed when his thoughts returned to the magical time they had spent in Cambridge. Why did she not choose him? They were evenly matched. They fit together. He remained pensive, drove to the first bar and ordered a *tè freddo*, iced tea. Sitting down under a massive canopy of mimosa, the bright-yellow flowering trees, the symbol of Italian feminism, he thought about Sergio Celesti, the dubious art restorer and antique dealer. After receiving Fiona's distress call, he immediately called a private detective who was under retainer to his firm and ordered a background check of Sergio and all of his business partnerships. The detective was quick but thorough and soon had hand-delivered a thick file to his office. It was worse than Arturo ever imagined. After reading the file, Arturo lost all respect for Sergio and feared for Fiona's safety. Arturo didn't care what happened to Sergio. He doubted Sergio would try to protect Fiona from his thuggish partners. Fiona very likely was in mortal danger; Arturo's plan was to extricate her. He had to prepare her. Fiona needed an orderly presentation of the facts in the presence of her husband. Once everything was out in the open, she could make her decision. He only hoped Sergio was willing to let Fiona go. Arturo squinted his eyes in concentration. He thought of ways to get Fiona off the island and away from both Sergio's business dealings and his unsavory partners.

Fiona continued on her morning commute acutely aware of Arturo's concern about her welfare. She sensed that she might be in definite danger. She thought about Arturo and how quickly he responded to her late-night telephone call; he managed to secure accommodations in the most popular and famous hotel at the height of the season. Pretty impressive clout, thought Fiona. Almost overnight, Arturo was on Capri and back into her life. She felt the same tremor between them and knew she was still attracted to him. Did Arturo feel the same way, she wondered, or was it a memory of their personal history? Maybe, just maybe, she was grasping at memories of their idealized youthful romance? Fiona remembered how strong-minded she was as an art student at Harvard, enrolled to earn her master's degree in fine art when she met and fell in love with Arturo, the handsome visiting professor from Italy.

Fiona corrected herself, remembering that Arturo had not been a professor of economics on loan from an Italian business school. Arturo had taken a sabbatical from his high-powered job in arbitrage. He had been working in London. On a lark, and challenged by his old professor, Arturo took a temporary leave from global investments to teach a year in post-graduate finance at MIT.

Although impressed by Arturo's accomplishments and wealth, Fiona never wavered from her own dream. She remained steadfast in her ambitious pursuit of fine art. Fiona planned on having a major career in visual art. In retrospect, Arturo always encouraged her to pursue her dreams. He wanted her to experience both success and recognition in the art world.

She recalled how they treated each other with mutual respect even though Arturo was clearly way ahead of her on his career path. Their friendship grew into a grand passion; their lives and thoughts became almost as one. Memories of days in bed, spent with delicious abandon, flooded back to her and she began to recall details of the bedroom scenes ...

Fiona shook her head to rid herself of further worrisome distractions. She reminded herself that she lived in Rome and was married to Sergio, a successful art restorer and antique dealer. She had a growing career along with responsibilities to Sergio. Her loyalties were pledged to her husband, Fiona scolded herself in silence. She forced her attention back to the present and concentrated on the road.

Fiona continued her drive; she drove cautiously as the estate walls were carved out of rough stone. These ancient public roads were just as treacherous as they were too narrow for automobiles and also were bordered on each side by jagged stone.

Breezing by flowering broom and ornamental grasses, the Vespa made a steady climb past orchards and vineyards into the town of Capri. The town spills over gentle slopes beneath island-dividing cliffs. A medieval castle caps the pointed hill of Il Castiglione. Fiona left her villa in Anacapri daily to drive down to the center of the bustling town. Anacapri, on the other hand, was 'old Capri' – the land of ancient olive groves, terraced vineyards, lemon trees and myths. There were still tracts of land with working farms. The multi-tiered gardens of grapes were a design dating back to early Roman times. Separated by cliffs, the villages always have been jealous rivals.

It was grueling work, sweaty work, trying to capture the overwhelming beauty of Capri as every inch of the island was perfect. As an artist, she knew the impossibility of her task yet she doggedly pursued it. She was in love with the rich history of the island and its incredible natural beauty. Capri, the most ancient resort on earth, rose out of the Bay of Naples like a miracle of nature. She wanted to capture some of this miracle on her canvas.

Fiona came to the end of the road and veered sharply into the private parking lot for island residents. She found a slot for her Vespa and turned off the engine, leaving it standing in the sunlight.

She carried her canvases, her Julian easel and her painting supplies. Rounding the corner to avoid a big shade tree, she collided with a jogger and fell, scattering her art supplies and her painting. Fiona looked up and saw a young man, wearing longish, bottle-dyed blond hair, sporting a hot-pink silk scarf around his neck. He was muscular and, as he leaned down to help her get up, he smirked at her. Once she stood, he moved to help her brush the dirt off her clothing. Fiona felt the hair on the back of her neck rise and she quickly moved away, avoiding any physical contact with him.

He spoke in a heavy Neapolitan dialect. "I'm sorry, Signorina," he said, "I had no way of seeing you as it's a blind curve. Are you okay?"

Fiona looked into his concerned eyes and said, "I'm fine, just flustered." She looked down to dust off her clothes and bare legs.

The jogger persisted in his attention to her by asking, "You look familiar. Do we know one another?"

Fiona noticed the tone of his voice had changed; it was lower and flirtatious. She raised her eyes and saw he was leering at her.

In a clipped manner, Fiona asked, "Is this an accidental meeting?"

"Not really," the strange-looking man drawled in an exaggerated dialect. "All summer long, I've watched you paint. You walk to the end of the *via* overlooking the Faraglioni and paint. Later in the morning, you walk to the *piazzetta*, sit at a table to have un caffè and wait for a rough-looking man to join you."

"He's my husband."

The man rolled his eyes and stage-whispered, "Are you in danger, *cara*, dear?"

"Excuse me? I'm not your sweetie! Leave me alone!" Fiona was shaking in anger and screamed at the man, "*Basta!* Leave me alone."

Again, he leered at her and said, "I'll be watching you. *Arrivederla*, see you again, beauty."

She watched him jog away. The parking lot was again quiet with only the sound of fluttering leaves in the nearby olive trees. Fiona was angry and perspiring from her pent-up feelings of exasperation. She felt disoriented and tried to rein in her emotions as she examined the painting. She was relieved to see there was no damage and felt fortunate for small miracles. Fiona fought to control her mind so she could concentrate. She wanted to appear normal. She said to herself: It must be a joke. I am not in danger. But had the man threatened her? Was it some kind of warning? She shook her head trying to clear away her feelings of impending dread. Fiona forced herself to think clearly, to move ahead. Everything will be fine, she told herself. Sergio will have a simple explanation.

Fiona glided through the famous square of Capri on her way to the painting site that overlooked the Faraglioni, the dramatic rock formations of Capri.

Suddenly, she saw Sergio waving to her from a café table. She was surprised as their daily routine was to meet at the piazzetta, an open-air market that served as an informal café or meeting place for the locals and summer residents, after her painting session, not before. The square was formally named the Piazza Umberto but was nicknamed "the piazzetta" by the *Capresi*, the locals. Fiona knew their daily cappuccino break was timed by the locals — even the mysterious jogger seemed to know their schedule. So what was Sergio doing here so early?

Fiona was moved again by Sergio's striking good looks

with his strong Sicilian features. His hair was an unruly mop of dark curls. Sergio had a deep tan, round, dark eyes and the whitest teeth. When he smiled, his appearance changed dramatically, his eyes narrowed to become dark slits, and he cleverly used his smile and his laugh to his advantage. Women could not resist his attentions and men were drawn by his magnetism. It was as if a light went out in the room when he left and then light reappeared when he returned.

Sergio helped her carry her easel and supplies to the table and then ordered an additional caffè for her. Another waiter bustled over to remove the easel and bag from the crowded café space. They needed to be stored, as usual, behind the bar. Fiona turned all her attention to her husband, wondering why they were having a caffè so early in the day. She looked at him with inquiring eyes.

"I felt like seeing you today as my morning was so exceptional."

"Oh?" Fiona's hands tightened their grip on the arm of the bistro chair as she speculated whether Sergio already knew about Arturo's arrival on Capri. She decided to tell him about the parking-lot disturbance. Fiona described the jogger's strange appearance, his brassy-colored hair, deep Neapolitan accent and the odd, pink silk scarf. "What surprised me was his sudden appearance, as if he was hiding, ready to pounce on me. I should have seen him when I was parking my Vespa. It's unsettling," explained Fiona.

Sergio waited to hear her story and was a good listener. Sergio probed, "Did he call you by your name? Did you say anything to him?"

Fiona shook her head, an unhappy look on her face

and continued, "He said he'd been watching me paint, that he knew my schedule. I told him to leave me alone."

"Well, he's just a *cretino*, a jerk. Some day-tripper out for a few laughs at your expense," groused Sergio.

"It's nothing," Sergio smiled at her and was outwardly relaxed, wanting to reassure his rattled wife. But Fiona suspected he was shaken by her story.

Sergio hesitated and seemed to withdraw into himself. He shook his shoulders as if he had made a decision and wanted to move forward, albeit in a reluctant manner. He looked into Fiona's wide, still-innocent eyes and said, "As I was saying, my morning was exceptional because I want to share some business information, some paperwork with you, and why we are in Capri."

Fiona's mind went blank and she held her breath. She stared into her husband's eyes and time stood still for her. Sergio was not one for histrionics and never exaggerated the scope of a problem. She felt something terrible was gnawing at him. His eyes looked haunted as he gave a shuddering breath.

"*Carissima*, I don't know how to begin," Sergio said, uncertainty in his voice. He carefully took her hand and began stroking it as he continued, "This isn't easy to explain. There was insurance for the workshop and everything lost in the fire except for one important painting being restored for a private collector. I thought I'd have it in the restoration workshop for only a short time. It wasn't insured. My investors ..."

"Ciao, Sergio, *come stai?*"

Sergio jumped up from his chair, pushing the table away from him and looked at a tall, older man. Fiona sensed Sergio's uneasiness toward the stranger. She swiveled in her seat to better observe the man. He had a long, thin face and black hair slicked back in the style of old Hollywood glamour or as an old Hollywood gangster. Fiona had no idea who the man was, but he seemed dangerous, filled with a menacing tension.

"Fine."

"You've been missed."

The swarthy-faced man turned to Fiona and asked, "Where are Sergio's manners? I am Umberto Licciardi, an old friend and business associate from Forcella. You must be Fiona, his most beautiful and glamorous wife."

Fiona watched her husband throw back his shoulders as if expecting a blow from the coarse-sounding stranger, who spoke in the long, drawn-out dialect of deep Naples. She noticed that he was at least a few inches taller than Sergio, powerfully built but agile in his movement. His clothes were well-cut but too formal for Capri. To Fiona, he seemed a shady type of businessman taking a quick trip for the day, *una gita*, from Naples or Sorrento.

Umberto took Fiona's hand and caressed her fingers in a slight kiss and then clicked his heels without making any noise. It was a gracious display of old-world manners, and anyone viewing this little scene would be charmed. Umberto's brown eyes, however, were cold and contemptuous, almost mocking her. Fiona's body shuddered involuntarily and she withdrew her hand abruptly, not saying a word. Umberto turned sharply away from her and said, "Sergio, do not be so old-fashioned to hide your wife from your friends. Why are you so possessive? Don't you trust her? You're acting as if you're from the South. She'll think you're Sicilian! We're like family and she should know us." Umberto rolled his eyes dramatically and laughed. It was a loud, shrill bray, eerily resembling the sound of a donkey.

Sergio froze and said nothing. He hung his head for a

moment and then looked up quickly; his eyes scanned the piazzetta and came to rest on Umberto. Sergio smiled and said in a light voice, "Sorry, Umberto, I wanted to take a break from work and my routine. My wife and I needed a rest and chose Capri. We are still near Napoli but feel as if we're on holiday."

"Eh, no concerns, no worries? Just pleasure? You're too young to retire. Your business needs you. Your partners want to hear from you. Perhaps we can go somewhere private to talk? Or do you want to include the lovely Fiona in our business?"

Umberto narrowed his eyes and stared down at Sergio. Although Umberto waited quietly, his attitude reminded Fiona of a viper coiled tightly, ready to strike. Fiona remained silent, standing very still, all the while watching Sergio and Umberto. She tried to quell her creeping fright, her hands were clammy and there were goosebumps on her chilled arms despite being in the hot sun. Fiona willed herself to stop shaking.

Sergio looked over at Fiona and said quietly, "I need to deal with this. I'll go for a walk with Umberto and meet you back at the villa." Sergio escorted her to a nearby bus and watched her get on. He nodded to her, "Don't worry. Leave the Vespa in the lot. Go directly home. Don't dawdle. I'll be back soon."

The bus was filled with locals and made frequent stops on the way to Anacapri. Fiona's sandal slipped on the worn steps as she stumbled off the bus and arrived at the paved-stone piazzetta of Anacapri. She continued walking, her mind working furiously about Sergio and his strange visitor from Naples. Fiona was brought up short when she heard, "Signora Celesti, *come sta?*" It was the familiar voice of the unofficial mayor of Anacapri, Signore

Petacci. She looked over and saw he was waving from the terrace of the Saraceno restaurant. Fiona waved and walked over to greet him. Signore Petacci was an elderly, short, deeply tanned man. His face was lined with years of sun exposure, and he was bent like a twig from working daily in the surrounding olive groves. Now he was retired, exhausted from farming and spent many hours in the walled garden of the restaurant.

"I'm well, Don Carlo," Fiona replied and asked, "and you?"

"I'm an old man, enjoying the sun. But my young beauty, you, look sad. Is your husband not treating you well?" Signore Petacci's eyes twinkled when he looked at her. Fiona knew he was simply teasing and she smiled.

"No, he's fine. He's in Capri and will be home in a while. I'm sorry I cannot stay as I need to tend to the dog. Ciao, Don Carlo."

"Ciao, ciao." The old man continued to stare at Fiona as she walked slowly down the road to her villa. He shook his head and gave a sigh. *Che bella*, he thought to himself and went to the bar to get a grappa for his espresso.

Fiona turned away from the restaurant and walked down the steep paved road to her villa's entrance. She thought briefly about Don Carlo and the lifestyle of living year-round on Capri. Yes, she reflected, Don Carlo led a simple life, but he seemed happy in the sunshine at peace with his friends and family surrounding him. Although island living was quiet and the views were beautiful, Fiona knew in her heart that her future happiness was in Rome. Fiona immediately thought of her husband and his present difficulties. Her shoulders slumped with worry. She went past the garden gate, her feet scrunching on the loose stone, and stooped down to hug her dog. Fiona went into the kitchen and gave Guido some table scraps and fresh water. After changing into a linen caftan, she walked out onto the terrace and settled into a chaise lounge.

How did that dangerous man from Naples know Sergio and what business did they have in partnership, wondered Fiona, as she tried to calm her nerves by focusing her eyes on the magnificent view of the glittering Mediterranean Sea. Her scattered thoughts kept going back to the parking lot and then to Umberto. Fiona wondered about Sergio's partnership with Umberto and whether all his business associates were so smarmy. Fiona shook her head and pursed her lips. It was useless to worry until she had more information from Sergio. She forced herself to refocus on the line of the horizon.

Suddenly, Fiona felt her shoulder wrenched and immediately emerged out of her trance-like state. Sergio entered her line of vision, and she looked up at her husband. He was silent, almost subdued. Fiona saw he was offering her a champagne glass; she took the flute and watched Sergio pour the prosecco with his usual grand gesture.

"What is it?" she asked. She meant to accompany her words with a casual smile, but it did not work. Fiona was baffled by Sergio's behavior. He was acting as if he had no cares in the world.

Using a bantering tone of voice, Sergio exclaimed, "I have news! We're going to Positano. Let's pack light and take my motorcycle." The words seemed to roll smoothly off his tongue.

"Why so fast? What's the rush?" Fiona arched her back, about to spring out of the chaise but then hesitated as she continued to watch her husband.

"Be calm, cara! I know you're concerned, maybe confused by what happened in the piazzetta with Umberto. I intend to tell you everything but not now. I'm afraid we'll have to return to Rome sooner than expected. I want to go to Positano for a few days before we end our vacation. It's a short ride. I already have the ferry tickets and I left your Vespa safely parked in the lot. We'll talk at the hotel. I want to get away from here; you look too worried. It's nothing, I tell you! Just a business misunderstanding. The Amalfi Drive is beautiful, and I want to show it to you again. We haven't been back to Amalfi since our wedding anniversary party. It will be fun to visit for a few days. We'll return to Rome as if nothing ever happened except a summer spent in Capri."

Sergio examined her face for any reaction. He gathered his thoughts and continued, "We can discuss my business matters at the hotel in Positano. There's plenty of time."

Now Fiona stopped, sharply placing the flute onto the table, causing the wine to slosh onto the marble top. She had an impulse to return to Rome, alone, to her home and studio. To leave Sergio. A change had come over him. She stared into Sergio's eyes, now brilliant but empty, nothing but brown bits with a slit in them. Were his eyes meaningless, nothing to do with him? Fiona remembered an old Italian proverb about how the eyes revealed the soul. She wanted to see love in his eyes, to see what was really going on. She saw nothing, no flare of emotion, no spirit. It was as if she was looking into one of those antique metal mirrors, a hard, dull surface. Fiona felt a tension between them. Sergio was the man she fell in love with and married but they were not in harmony, not soul mates. She did not know him. Her marriage had been an illusion. The magical time was over and she was alone. The wordless shock of this realization struck her. She shook as if she was having a fit, fearing she might not be able to bear this peeling away of their lives together. She could not catch her breath, yet she was breathing fast.

"What's happening to you? Are you all right?" Sergio cried, "Did Umberto scare you? Did someone visit you here? Were you threatened?" Sergio was shouting.

"No," Fiona gasped as she inwardly cringed from his raised voice.

"Umberto is a small-time crook. He looks like the dirty hustler he is. I'm under no obligation to him! Or to anyone! I knew him from my childhood in Naples," Sergio snapped, furious at her.

Fiona felt overwhelmed by strangeness, as if in another place. She was surrounded by hostility. As Sergio yanked her arms away from her body, she felt isolated and fought for time. She could not leave Sergio yet. She would determine the truth about their married life and his business practices. But she felt an inner calm when she thought about how she could rely on Arturo. At that moment, her anxiety broke and Fiona relaxed. She wanted to make all the nastiness, the fear of deception go away. Perhaps she was mistaken. Perhaps this fear was an illusion. Fiona wanted Sergio to say everything was all right.

She took back the champagne flute, all the while watching Sergio resume pouring the sparkling wine with fanfare. She measured the extent of his discomfort. Fiona still sensed his false cheer and bravado about their impending trip to Amalfi. She desperately wanted everything to be all right, to go back to their life in Rome.

"Where are my paintings? Did you leave them at the bar?"

"They're safe and sound. I left them with Stefano the bartender. He put them in a private closet."

For a moment, Fiona fought back tears. Finally she said, "All right."

"We need to go. Presto, soon. Let's pack light. The dog will be fine with the maid. It will be a short trip away and very romantic. Va bene?"

Playing for time to collect her wits, she decided she had to pretend the trip was fine. She would go along with Sergio for now.

"This view still enchants me. It's been a wonderful summer. Every inch of this island is vibrant with color. It's almost impossible to capture the light onto canvas. And the colors of the sea are superb," Fiona whispered almost to herself.

"I told you everything would be all right. You'll see." Sergio turned his head to stare at the Mediterranean and drained his glass.

"I've always loved Positano and Amalfi. It will be a wonderful way to wrap up the summer." Fiona smiled, drank her prosecco as her mind raced. How could she get a message to Arturo?

She quickly went into her room to pack her bags. Fiona carefully moved the phone into her bathroom, called the Hotel Quisisana and reached Arturo in his room. "Ciao, Arturo, it's Fiona. I'm sorry, but Sergio insists on leaving immediately for Positano. We are booked into Il San Pietro. I don't know what is going on, but he promised to tell me all that's been troubling him by tonight. May I call you later in the evening? Va bene. Grazie. I must go. A presto."

Amalfi

AUGUST 4, 1985

LATE AFTERNOON

The horizon line was a slash of mauve in the pink light. Fiona took one parting look at the slice of sea and sky and ran to the driveway. Sergio gunned the powerful engine of the fire-engine-red Moto Guzzi, and they hurtled forward. In a short time, they arrived at the docks. Marina Grande was busy with people scrambling to get onto the hulking ferry. It dominated the harbor that was lined with tiny cliffside houses. Fiona enjoyed the ferry ride with the bracing sea air. The ferry berthed into the busy harbor of Sorrento, and they were among the first to disembark.

Fiona had read about the fearsome drive they were about to take. The route from Sorrento to Positano was known to be both fascinating and formidable, exuding beauty and danger. It lived up to Fiona's expectations.

Sergio concentrated on his driving as twisting curves with daredevil drops held a surprise at every turn. High mountains falling steeply into the deep blue sea and a winding, hair-raising road carved on the verge of the abyss proved a tantalizing distraction for Fiona.

Fiona found herself leaning dangerously close to the road's edge as she tried to see the Mediterranean. The sea bit deeply into the hills; the cliffs rose vertically. She recalled her high school Latin classes on Homer. He had placed the home of the Sirens – seductive and dangerous – on the Amalfi Coast. It would be easy to become mesmerized by this fascinating landscape, miss the turn and be lost forever. Fiona swung her body back onto the center of the Moto Guzzi as they careened around the curve. The call of the Sirens was less audible and she relaxed.

After leaving the old, worn town of Meta, the change in landscape was remarkable. No more honking horns, irritable drivers after you, no squalid tenement buildings. The road wound gently downhill. Sergio and Fiona were among quiet lemon and olive groves. There were well-maintained gardens with wrought-iron gates allowing glimpses of patrician villas. The silence was omnipresent, no small miracle. Affluence and distance can buy silence, thought Fiona. She relaxed as the sapphire-blue sky and the azure Mediterranean exerted their powers over her.

Fiona was reminded of Dante's Volume III, *Paradiso*. She recently had painted a series about this volume before her summer idyll on Capri. Perhaps they were on the road to their personal Paradise? Suddenly, her thoughts shifted to Umberto and Fiona recalled Dante's *Inferno*. Fiona wondered if they were headed to hell. She calmed her skittering mind as silence rolled over her consciousness. Fiona's eyes relaxed as she opened them up to receive all the beauty of the surroundings.

They were on their way to Positano, driving through hairpin curves. The countryside suddenly opened up as they reached the final slopes of the hill. They could see the coastline ahead as they started on the Amalfi Drive. The call of the Sirens became stronger. The wind picked up as the Moto Guzzi tore down the road.

Sergio and Fiona decided to stop for a cold drink at a café. The bar's spacious terrace overlooked the countless dips and curves in the sea. They looked at the olive trees, standing round and full. The silvery backs of their leaves occasionally puffed in the breeze. The leaves of orange and lemon trees, oaks and umbrella pines were fluttering in the wind. As the coast faced south, there always was sunshine on the water, causing the waves to flicker with reflections.

Fiona sipped her tè freddo, trying to find the right words, an opening gambit, to ask Sergio about his business and Umberto. The cold tea swirled around in the large glass, the small cube of ice clicking against the glass. Fiona put the glass down and looked directly at her husband. Without formulating a diplomatic preamble, she blurted out, "Now? Can we talk about your business and what has upset you so?"

"Let's get to the hotel, have a spectacular dinner and talk tomorrow morning. I just want to relax at the hotel before starting a long discussion. Okay?"

"All summer I've waited for you to talk. To explain why you were so tense. So nervous and on edge. I've been walking on eggshells. Please, just tell me!"

"Cara, don't worry your pretty head! I love you and only want to take care of you, of everything. I'm tired from the motorcycle ride. You've waited this long. You can wait a little more." Sergio looked at his watch as if to gauge the time to get to the hotel.

"We need to get to Positano. *Andiamo.*" Sergio shoved

the chair back from the small café table and stood waiting for her.

For a moment, Fiona fought back tears. Finally, she said, "Va bene."

Sergio took her arm and encouraged Fiona to take one last look at the magnificent view. She looked at the hillside and the blue sky. They turned away from the terrace and walked to the car park. They were silent as they mounted the motorcycle and sped away from the bar. Fiona hardly noticed the beautiful vistas as they made their way to Il San Pietro.

Sergio reserved a suite at Il San Pietro, the iconic hotel that had revived the tourism business for the Amalfi Drive area. First built into a cliff in Positano after the war, Il San Pietro became the chic address in the '60s and still dominated the scene today. The hotel was famous for its unassuming entrance, little more than a windswept flattened perch on a cliff with an offering to St. Peter in a carved niche. The town of Positano was still a fishing village, albeit one overrun with tourists during the summer season. Many of the simple fishing houses were painted white and looked like steps on the hillside. Flat-soled espadrilles were not only fashionable but also practical for serious walking on the streets of carved stone. The simple fishing town would be a good contrast to the glamorous international crowd staying at Il San Pietro.

Sergio drove fast but with skill. After a few corkscrew turns, they arrived in the parking lot of Il San Pietro. The lot overlooked the sea and had a small whitewashed alcove with a votive and an offering to a local saint.

Fiona looked around the empty lot and asked the valet, "Where is the hotel, Il San Pietro?"

The valet raised his eyes to stare unabashedly at the

beautiful, young woman, who reminded him of a ballerina with the grace of a panther. He admired Fiona as she stretched getting off the powerful motorcycle. *Que bella figura*, the valet mused.

The valet quickly tried to take control of their arrival and said in a brusque tone of voice, "Signorina, this is Il San Pietro. The elevator is here in the chapel. You enter and we take you down the cliff to the lobby and the concierge."

The valet bustled over with a flourish to grab their luggage. Not much luggage, but all expensive leather goods, just like everyone else who arrives by limousine, thought the young man. He noticed she was wearing a Bulgari starsapphire necklace with matching earrings. Her ring fingers were adorned with brilliant yellow and white diamonds.

"Grazie," said the powerfully built man getting off the bike as he handed the keys to the valet. The valet quickly averted his eyes from the young woman and shifted his attention to the motorcycle driver. Sergio looked closely into the valet's eyes, letting the younger man know that he recognized the other man's open admiration for Fiona but would brook no familiarity. "And it's signora," Sergio snapped as he walked toward the chapel.

The couple entered the elevator. Slowly, as if the elevator had a mind of its own, they were lowered by fits and starts down the seaside cliff. Upon the elevator door opening, the lobby proved to be a spacious, airy delight with well-appointed Continental antiques juxtaposed with stylish '60s pieces. It was a flamboyant interior decorated with verve. The interior walls were whitewashed with a vaulted ceiling. There was lush vegetation, and purple bougainvillea grew up the walls from oversized terra-cotta planters. The floor was tiled in an antique honey-colored stone.

The concierge confirmed their reservation and, after checking their passports, he gave Sergio the room key. Their suite opened up onto the sea and was filled with wavering light. Many of the bureaus and tables were silver-leafed, painted in a dusty blue with hand-decorated panels depicting mythological gods. The generous-sized balcony overlooked the Mediterranean. The suite promised an overwhelming sense of luxe and calm.

Sergio turned to Fiona and said, "Don't I take care of you? How's this for style?" He turned and tipped the valet. Once they were alone, Sergio said, "I want to relax and see the rest of the hotel. Let's explore and have a drink in the lounge."

They strolled into the blindingly white lounge and ordered Campari and sodas. The long room had a breathtaking view of the sapphire Mediterranean. With its white-tiled floors and all-white decorating scheme, Fiona felt she was immersed in the sea. The arched windows were without glass. The sea air was sweet. Fiona and Sergio fell silent as they gazed onto the sea and sky.

In the deep shade of a recessed corner, an older man observed Sergio and Fiona from his table in the lounge. He was in his late sixties, a large, heavy man. His hair was completely white but thick and long. He was wearing a light-wool suit with a white shirt, opened at the collar. He had the easy warmth of a wealthy businessman, and the reserve of power and privilege. The man was a Venetian count, Count Volpe, staying at Il San Pietro. He also had arrived that day but in the morning. After checking in with the concierge, however, the count stayed in the lounge as if he were waiting for someone.

My suspicions of Sergio were correct, Count Volpe said to himself. Here he is with his young wife acting every bit the aristocrat! He's nothing but a common cheat to steal from his partners. To think, I gave him his start and continued to finance him. How will I surprise him, catch him off guard and not cause him to run away? I need a private meeting with him, he mused. I need a plan: set the stage and then join them at dinner. Hmmm, here goes ...

"Now that's an interesting couple," Count Volpe said out loud to anyone within earshot. "I wonder what their story is?" He gestured to the bar man to get his attention.

"Fabrizio," Count Volpe asked, "Do you know that young couple?" The old man's eyes twinkled, feigning innocence, as he looked up.

"Sì, Count Volpe, I know them. They had a big party in Amalfi with a special ceremony in the cathedral about a year ago. They didn't stay at Il San Pietro, but I saw them walk down the grand steps after the church service. I think it was some anniversary celebration. It was a lavish affair with many people from Naples, Rome and even America. The young man has an uncle who used to be generale of the Roman polizia. You remember him, Orsini, who controlled the police throughout Campania?"

The bartender looked at Count Volpe, waited for the brief nod of assent and continued. "It was rumored he was also close to the Camorra but nothing was ever proved. Just rumors. The president forced Orsini into early retirement. Anyway, the couple stayed at Le Sirenuse and spent a lot of money."

"I remember Orsini. He was around during the Red Brigade terror. The president thought Orsini might organize a coup so he forced him out. He's a Knight of Malta, as am I."

"Do you want to meet them?"

The count pretended to consider the offer of an introduction and responded, "Perhaps, but in time."

Count Volpe posed as if in languor, but his mind was racing. He admired the lovely, young woman. A true lady, the count thought to himself. Sergio was indeed a member of the Orsini family but, as with any old family, it had numerous family branches and many accomplishments. Some not so savory. The family could not have approved of Sergio and his shady business practices. Well, he continued with his reckoning, Sergio's wife was an asset. The young woman was a stunner, and she apparently made her way through Roman society by her natural grace, good manners and generosity of spirit. After all, the count harrumphed, he had checked with some of his social connections in Rome. The count heard that Fiona came from a patrician family in Boston and was an artist of great promise. Count Volpe mulled these thoughts around in his head and he almost spoke aloud, "Sergio, you stinker, chose wisely." Sergio built upon his young wife's natural assets, her caché, to make a name in Roman society. He exploited her social connections to forge new alliances for his business operations. I wonder if Sergio ever loved her? At least she's a pretty little thing, the count mused and continued on with his silent deliberation. To do it right, to use his young, beautiful wife to his advantage, Sergio needed a big bankroll. Just how big? How much money was spent over the summer? Yes, I must surprise Sergio and force his hand. I am due for a change in fortune, Count Volpe considered as he rolled his crystal glass in his hand. And it's time to give the devil his due.

The embroidered Frette linens were tousled and draped on the floor. Used champagne flutes littered the bedside tables. The sound of a hair dryer howled from the bathroom. Sergio ducked his head into the marble and mirrored room and loudly invited Fiona onto the balcony for more prosecco.

He was gazing out onto the horizon when Fiona joined him, threw her arms around his neck, and placed a light kiss on his cheek with her mouth. Sergio felt the warmth of her breath and the natural scent of her body. It smelled of the sea, and Fiona's smile sparkled against the light of the Mediterranean.

"Your dress mimics the sky, all blues and mauves. The silk moves along your body as waves in the sea. What a vision," Sergio looked at her with approval and admiration in his eyes.

"Grazie mille. And now, amore, let's go to dinner. We've worked up an appetite!" murmured Fiona as she stroked his arm.

Sergio returned her loving smile and felt his desire for her again. "There's still time …"

"Andiamo! Let's go. I'm famished!" Fiona urged Sergio out the door, and they entered the elevator.

Sergio hesitated at the door of the lounge as he surveyed the other guests. All were staying at least several days at Il San Pietro as transients were not allowed. Nodding to several faces he recognized, Sergio helped seat Fiona. Prosecco arrived, and they toasted the beginning of their evening. Sergio turned all his attention to Fiona and was bending toward her to give her a kiss when he heard a familiar voice.

"*Scusi*, Signore Celesti. It's been a while since I saw you in Rome at your antique shop. May I say how nice it is to see you tonight and what a lovely place to be." Count Volpe looked directly into Sergio's eyes. The count's eyes seemed to be wide with innocence and delight to see him. Sergio gave a start of surprise and then quickly introduced the count to Fiona.

"Your wife is enchanting, Sergio. It's an honor to meet her. I envy your youth," Count Volpe said with genuine pleasure in his eyes.

Cajoled by such florid expressions of appreciation of Fiona's beauty, Sergio stood and gestured to Count Volpe to take a seat, which the old man quickly did. The count easily entertained them with stories about life in Venice and some of the amusing trades he made for antiques and fine art.

"Are you in Southern Italy looking for antiques, Count Volpe?" Fiona inquired.

"No, my dear, I'm hunting for a painting. An antique painting. A Caravaggio, the master of Baroque."

Keeping her voice light, Fiona exclaimed, "What a pity. No luck for the living artist! Italy is not kind to contemporary artists." She rolled her eyes in mock protest.

"You must have courage, my dear. But alas, I must go. Thank you for listening to the tales of an old man. It was fortuitous to see you, Sergio, and such a delightful surprise to run into you at Il San Pietro, away from work. But what an enchanting wife, such a prize," Count Volpe simpered. "You must guard the lovely Fiona carefully and not be all business all the time, Sergio. If you work all the time, someone could whisk her away." Count Volpe said this with mischievous eyes and then winked at Fiona. Without waiting for a response, the count air-kissed Fiona with a brushing gesture to her hand and swept off into the night.

Sergio, his eyes wide open with shock, stared at the old man's departing back and swiftly finished his wine. He shivered and then muttered almost to himself, "What odd timing."

Fiona opened her eyes wide and countered, "He's a lovely old man. Such old-world manners and charm," she effused. "I found the count delightful. Let's have dinner with him tomorrow night. How do you know him?"

"Being in the antique and fine art business, you meet every person of consequence at some point," Sergio muttered. "I met the count in Rome when I first started in the antique and art-restoration business. He's from an old Venetian family with a palazzo on the Grand Canal. Count Volpe has an unlimited supply of antiques from his family palazzo's attic. That attic must be huge," he drawled with sardonic humor. "He trades out of a dilapidated house on a small canal. The old man seems to have connections everywhere in Italy."

Fiona considered her husband's comments and assessment of the count. She sensed Sergio did not like Count Volpe. He certainly kept his guard up around the count, Fiona mused. Sergio never truly relaxed during the count's impromptu visit – he was acting a part, she was convinced. She continued her rumination: Was this a staged surprise by Count Volpe? What was it he wanted? Her attention abruptly shifted as a waiter came to their table and said, "A telephone call for you, sir." Quickly, Sergio stood up and excused himself for a moment.

Fiona watched Sergio exit the room and was surprised to see Count Volpe peer at her from the bar. He waved and walked over to her table. The count clicked his heels and asked if he could sit down for a minute. Fiona smiled at him, giggled and said, "Please join me."

The count leaned in close. Speaking quietly, almost whispering, Count Volpe said, "My dear, you are in danger. Sergio is in trouble, and his business problems may overwhelm the two of you. I feel you should be forewarned, Fiona."

Fiona gulped with sudden fright as Count Volpe's words registered. She nervously clutched her neck and looked into Count Volpe's bird-like eyes until a sudden movement caused her to break her stare and she looked away in confusion. For a moment, her thoughts froze and then she saw Sergio walking back to the table. He glowered at them, pulled his chair back with a shriek of wood on wood and sat down on the other side of Fiona. Sergio took up his napkin and snapped it loudly before putting it on his lap. He looked stonily at the count.

"What have you been telling my wife?"

In a firm voice, the count replied, "The truth. It's about time you told her." The count smoothed out the tablecloth in front of him, got to his feet and said, "I'm sorry, my dear, but the situation is volatile." He clicked his heels and left.

Fiona's back arched up and hit the back of her chair, her eyes suddenly wide with alarm. "What's going on? Tell me now!"

Sergio pulled her to her feet. "In our room."

They took the elevator to their suite and Sergio closed the door quietly. Fiona went into the living room and clicked on the lights. She sat down, clasped her hands in her lap and waited for him to begin.

"Okay, okay. Now we'll talk as I know you're worried." Sergio's eyes flashed and his voice dripped with sarcasm. He stared down at her and turned up the corners of his mouth in a tight smile. "I'm in trouble. Bad trouble. I'm out of money and I owe my partners. And they're not the type of people you'd ever hang out with, Fiona," Sergio gave her a wily look and continued, "It wasn't any of your business.

And I knew you'd worry and try to butt in. You're an artist, for God's sake! So you paint, big deal. You know color!" Sergio took a big breath while he dramatically rolled his eyes to the ceiling and continued, "You're not in any real business and you certainly don't know mine. I was overextended and took on partners. It's an old story. So what? They gave me credit, cash and I could continue operating. Then there was this friggin' fire. The insurance company became difficult. They're assholes! I gave them all the work papers, inventory lists, documents, what more could I do? The insurance company said I shouldn't have kept a client's painting at the studio while I was restoring it. I forgot to list it on the insurance rider, so they don't want to pay. They're chiselers! All these years, I've been paying into insurance monthly, but it was just a rolling value of inventory. A while ago, to save money on the premium, I chose a listed form at the advice of my insurance broker. But I had to list every friggin' item. I gave them all the paperwork they wanted, but they're crooks. They didn't settle the entire amount of the insurance claim. So, I panicked and we left Rome."

"How could you not tell me this? I was suspicious but never realized the extent of your lies."

"You're just as guilty, little girl! You looked the other way as I bought you things, expensive gifts, the clothes. What did you think I really did for a living? How did you think I managed? Did I have a money tree? You were so happy about the summer rental on Capri. How do you think I afforded such a lifestyle?"

"How was I to know if your business supported our lifestyle? You had numerous shops, restoration workshops in Naples and Rome. You had designers flying in with their wealthy clients. I thought yours was a big business."

Sergio's eyes flashed with a slyness Fiona never noticed before. "You are not just an innocent abroad. You were a struggling artist, living in a hovel of a studio. You grabbed onto me and took a brilliant lifestyle to your cold, greedy heart. How honest were you? You never wondered? Or did you just look the other way?" Sergio sneered at her. "Bah. I made money but it was not enough to support such a lifestyle. It took money, lots of it, to entertain all these people. To get ahead, we had to look the part: We had to be well-dressed, go to all the openings of restaurants. You drove me to such extremes!"

"But I led a simple life. I worked in my studio, produced my paintings and sold to dealers. I would have helped you if you had asked. You never hinted at the truth, that you were desperate. I never suspected we were in over our heads. What will your partners do?"

Sergio's face turned bright red, contorted into a freakish mask of a monster, and he struck her. He slapped her across her face. Fiona reeled from the blow and fell on the floor. She was shocked by his attack and turned her eyes to focus on Sergio. He suddenly lunged toward her and she frantically crawled away to look for a place for shelter. Sergio came forward and swooped down as if to pull her hair. Fiona felt his perspiration drip onto her exposed back. At the last moment, Sergio reined in his hands and kicked over a table, shattering the glass top. Sergio abruptly turned on his heels and left, slamming the door.

Fiona collapsed in a heap on the bed. She rubbed her face and sobbed. She fought to suppress the sharp little flashes of panic so she could concentrate. She was in danger from her husband and also his business partners. She had to think, to make a plan, to get away from Sergio as soon as possible. Fiona bolted the door and further secured it by tilting a chair under the doorknob. She moved jerkily toward a nearby wall mirror and looked into the glass. She examined her eye closely and determined there was no outward damage.

Fiona sat down at a little desk and wrote a list of what to do tomorrow. She had to get away in the morning, she kept reminding herself. Fiona grabbed her pocketbook and looked for Arturo's written note with his contact information. She found the number for Hotel Quisisana and quickly stabbed out the numbers on the phone.

The switchboard assured her they knew the room number and Fiona waited, tensing her hand as she held the phone. Fiona felt if she gripped the phone as tightly as she could, Arturo would be in his room. He was connected to her. She knew it was a crazy thought, but she continued gripping the phone. She held her breath, counting the rings of the phone and gasped when she heard Arturo's voice. She caught her breath and said, "It's Fiona. I'm in terrible trouble. I'm at the hotel Il San Pietro in Positano and had a row with Sergio. I'm scared. He was brutal and I need to get away tomorrow morning. Can you give me a ride to Rome?"

"Yes. Of course. I have to get my car in the lot at the harbor in Naples. I'll drive up first thing. I'll probably arrive around noon. Will that be okay?"

"*Certo.* I'll be fine until then. I just needed to know I could get out of here. I'll see you at noon in the lobby. Don't worry about me. Really."

"Take care tonight." Arturo's voice sounded gruff.

"Ciao, ciao." Fiona kept her tone of voice light and high-pitched.

"Ciao. *Buona notte.*"

Fiona hung up the phone and re-examined her list of

things. Packing can wait, she said to herself. *Calma, calma,* Fiona chanted to herself. Fiona soothed her nerves, concentrating her energy on being in Rome by tomorrow. She felt the roller coaster of a day had taken its toll on her. Fiona felt physically and mentally spent. She stripped off her clothes, found a silk chemise and pulled it over her head. Drawing back the duvet, she slid into bed and cried herself to sleep.

She awoke in the morning to the sound of the sea beating against the cliff. She pulled back the heavy drapes and allowed the brilliant sunshine to sparkle across the floor. She checked to see the chair still in the same position leaning as last night, against the door, allowing no entrance. Fiona reassured herself that it had not been disturbed. She determined the bolt was secure in the lock, decided it was safe to remove the chair and picked it up. Fiona looked down as she moved the chair and she noticed a small envelope. It must have been shoved under the door sometime in the night, she said to herself and stooped to pick it up. With a glance, she recognized Sergio's handwriting and tore it open. Sergio's scrawled note contained no apology, only informing her that he would return promptly to the room after his morning jog. Fiona furiously stuffed the note into the pocket of her robe and ordered room service.

She had a long shower and took measure of herself in the mirror. Her face was unmarked. Fiona combed her hair and donned the terry cloth robe. She heard a soft knock at the door and a voice announcing room service. Fiona moved the chair aside, unlocked the door and saw a small woman in a white uniform holding a large silver tray of breakfast foods. After signing the chit, Fiona poured the coffee and strode over to the French doors leading to the balcony. Sipping the hot milk laced with espresso, she looked at the view without registering its beauty. She was lost in thought about Sergio and how the unraveling of their marriage led to last night's ugly scene.

Fiona cast her thoughts back to the early days when she first met Sergio. It was in Rome, the summer of 1983. She was bending down examining the shards of an antique mirror. The shapes and framing of the shattered relic were graceful and had tracings of gilt and Pompeii red paint. It had once been an important piece and now was simply lovely bits heaped in a box. She had been sizing up the contents for a while. Fiona hoped her low offer would seem reasonable to the shop's proprietor. This was not an important shop, and its location was distant from the popular neighborhoods of antique dealers. The shop's two rooms were dimly lit with dusty furniture and paintings poorly displayed. The horrid display of furnishings did not seem to attract dealers or serious collectors. It appealed to people willing to buy furniture and bric-a-brac. Musing over what price to offer, Fiona was startled out of her ruminations.

"Che bella. This is interesting, isn't it?"

Fiona looked over the assembled furniture display to see a handsome man gazing at her. He was of average height, well-built from time spent in the gym. He radiated a self-assured manner. His long, curly hair was artfully groomed, his clothes were tailored and of beautiful quality. He had perfected *spezzato*, the casual but tailored combination of jacket and trousers that's not a matching suit. When he smiled, there were crinkles around his eyes, suggesting he smiled often. Fiona could detect high mischief in his eyes. The next moment, he flashed his white teeth, giving her a rakish grin.

"I'm not sure what you mean," she retorted, glancing back at the attractive man.

"Let me help you get the mirror," and he turned to greet the shop owner by name. A short conversation ensued and, after much head-nodding by both, he turned to Fiona and said, "It's yours. Let's go for an espresso." He softly took her elbow and gently propelled her out of the shop into the sunshine.

"You did well. It will be a handsome mirror." He named a price that was ridiculously low and also offered to have it restored for another low price. She never could have been so successful negotiating on her own, she thought. Quickly, Fiona thanked him for his help and, at the same time, offered up her most beguiling smile.

"Sergio Celesti. I live in Rome and have a boutique on Via del Babuino." He clasped her hands and waited.

"Fiona Appleton. Also living in Rome. I'm an artist. A painter."

"Well then, we are *simpatico* and must have lunch!" They were holding hands and Fiona was laughing at his words, throwing her head back and enjoying the sunshine. He concentrated his attention on her, seeming to be aware of nothing but her beauty. He whispered into her ear as they strolled down the via toward a welcoming piazza. They were young, beautiful and happy.

The piazza was warm from the strong sun, but the trattoria was prepared with awnings and a flowing fountain. There were potted lemon trees and window baskets filled with mint and basil. The air smelled sweet from the fragrant lemons, and the smoky scent of grilled chicken and rosemary wafted from the busy kitchen. They were ushered into a quiet, shaded alcove with a sprawling banquette covered in yellow-and-white-striped cotton. The waiter smiled at them, plumped the pillow and presented a handwritten menu. He quickly was dispatched by Sergio to find a magnum of prosecco. Once the sparkling wine was poured into crystal flutes and a sumptuous lunch was ordered, Sergio turned all his magnetism on her. He insisted on knowing everything about her. She remembered laughing and smiling during the entire afternoon.

It was an intense, short courtship, and their marriage nuptials were celebrated in Rome with Sergio's immediate family. Fiona dressed in a short, white, fitted dress with a white lace mantilla given to her by Sergio's stepmother. The mantilla was a special gift as it had been worn by Sergio's mother. It was a civil ceremony, albeit in a surround of elaborate floral décor in a crimson and gilt room at the top of the steps beside the Vittorio Emmanuel monument. Sergio and Fiona exited the gaudy public rooms and ran down the steps laughing, barely taking time to catch their breath. At the bottom of the steps, they were greeted by dozens of tired-looking tourists sitting wherever there was a horizontal surface. The bedraggled group hastily stood, snapped pictures of Fiona and Sergio, nudging one another to focus the lens on the lace mantilla. Fiona smiled as she looked up at the gigantic building, dubbed the "wedding cake" as it seemed to hover, a gigantic sugary confection of glaring white marble over the surrounding cluster of antique buildings. This florid ornamentation, unveiled in 1911, was built as a tribute to Vittorio Emmanuel II without any sensitivity to its surroundings or its sizable cost to taxpayers. Although hideous, it was a popular landmark and Fiona always would look upon it kindly. Fiona took Sergio's arm as they made a mad dash across Piazza Venezia to join the wedding party for lunch.

Sergio's family was not close, which surprised and disappointed Fiona. She had lost her parents in a car accident when she was thirteen and after graduating from boarding school, Fiona enrolled in an art school in Boston. While she was attending graduate studies at Harvard, Fiona's work won accolades and she was nominated to spend a year at the American Academy of Rome. Her only connection to Boston was a trust fund managed by an old brahmin bank. She learned that Sergio's mother died young in Naples and his father immediately moved to Rome with baby Sergio. Antonio Celesti quickly remarried a titled Roman beauty and started a new family. Sergio's half-brother attended the ceremony with his parents while Fiona was represented by her favorite professor, Graham Hughes, from the American Academy of Rome.

A wedding luncheon was served al fresco at Il Posto Accanto, an elegant restaurant in the nearby neighborhood. Antonio presided over the luncheon and made several toasts to the young couple. When the luncheon and wine waned, there was a small cake. Before Fiona was able to rise from the table to cut the wedding cake, she heard the familiar ringing sound of a wine glass being tapped by a spoon. Fiona looked over to see Professor Hughes standing with a raised glass, a broad smile on his face. Professor Hughes' eyes glanced over the wedding group and returned to focus upon Fiona. He took a big breath, projected his voice as if he were on stage, and exclaimed in his most plummy Oxford accent, "To the most beautiful bride and the lucky groom. Fiona, my dear, I wish you much happiness with your new, adoring husband. May you have a long, wonderful life together."

Professor Hughes raised his glass higher and continued, "To the blissful couple!" Looking around the room, his eyes scanning the assembled wedding party, Professor Hughes' eyes widened, he gave a wolfish smile and downed his champagne.

Fiona and Sergio kissed deeply and hugged. Fiona cupped her hand near Sergio's ear to whisper, "Time to cut the cake." Sergio grinned, beckoned to the waiter to find a cake knife and, at the same time, smoothly tilted his head to summon the wedding photographer. Once Fiona and Sergio were properly posed, they entwined their hands on the large, decorative knife and waited patiently to slice the delicate frosting. The photographer said, "*Piano, piano*, slowly, slowly," and continued, "A presto!" his signal to cut the cake.

With mock drama, Fiona served the first piece to Sergio, and the cake was whisked away by an attending waiter. Fiona whispered into Sergio's ear and he nodded. She quickly ran up to give Professor Hughes a last hug and he, in turn, slipped a small, wrapped package into her hand. He summarily air-kissed Fiona, doffed his panama and again wished them happiness in a low voice. Professor Hughes gracefully pivoted away from the clustered family and sauntered away down the winding street.

Soon, the small wedding party became quiet. Antonio cleared his throat, signaling it was time to depart. Although Sergio's family was gracious, they were quick to leave after wishing the young couple *buona fortuna*. It seemed coldly punctual to Fiona. Perhaps there was a long-standing strain between Sergio and his stepmother? His father was aloof to Sergio, suggesting he was siding with his second wife and son. And compounding the problem, their son, Dario, worked with Antonio in the mother's family banking business. Did Sergio feel excluded? These troubled thoughts ran through her consciousness; Fiona decided at that moment she would be vital to him. She determined that he would consider her enough. Fiona would do everything to please him, to help him succeed in this business. Sergio wouldn't miss his family. They would belong to each other. Their life together would be an ample substitute. They were young, Fiona reasoned to herself, and they would build a happy, fulfilling life together in Rome.

There was no immediate honeymoon, which was fine as they felt they were living in a continuous one. They moved into Sergio's flat on Via Margutta, the famed artisan's street in Rome with Sergio's shop one street over on Via del Babuino. They usually shared lunch hour and a long siesta. The antique business flourished, and Sergio was busy supervising a team of conservators restoring paintings and furniture in his laboratory on another site on Via Margutta. He made frequent trips to Naples and Veneto to acquire interesting old pieces of furniture, sculpture and paintings. The decorators flocked to his boutique and also to his laboratory. *Women's Wear Daily* did a feature about his alliance with an important Beverly Hills decorator and business increased to another level. Sergio was suddenly a star to the Americans and he became the primary source in Rome for fine antique furniture and one-of-a-kind items.

During this time, Fiona painted in her studio above the Spanish Steps near the Villa Borghese gardens. She also continued to be tutored by Professor Hughes. His wedding gift was extravagant. When Fiona opened the box on her wedding night, she found a key and a note detailing the address of a new studio. The note explained that the studio was sublet to her on a long-term lease with the understanding she would continue her painting studies.

The next day, Sergio and Fiona hurried over to the studio. They ran up the steps of the antique building, turned the key and the heavy door swung open. It was a large room with antique wood flooring and huge windows overlooking the park. Unlike their flat, which was filled with the cacophony of Rome's street life, the studio was an oasis of silence and peace. The limbs of the trees almost brushed the windowpanes, and the sole noise came from birdsong.

Sergio hugged Fiona and exclaimed in a booming voice, "It's a beautiful space – a grand studio for a beautiful artist. Your old professor believes in your talent, cara, and I'm delighted for you. You'll be happy painting here."

Fiona looked up into Sergio's eyes and kissed him intensely on the mouth.

Upon their return to their apartment, Sergio gave Fiona an immense canvas as a wedding present and suggested she paint their matrimonial double portrait. It was duly fitted in a modern frame and displayed in the living room. Soon, the days were filled with work and the evenings were spent at a fast pace of social parties.

But one fateful day, their blissful cocoon was upended. In the middle of the night, the phone's jarring ring signaled an end to their happiness. Fiona did not know it at the time.

The phone seemed to have a life of its own – almost ringing off the table top. On the other end were the Roman polizia demanding Sergio's immediate presence at his furniture restoration studio. As Sergio listened into the receiver, his eyes tightened and he modulated his voice so low that Fiona could not hear his conversation. Slamming down the receiver, Sergio hurtled out of the room, barely pulling his clothes on as he left the apartment. Fiona stayed at home, frantic with worry. She did not know when he'd be back.

It was evening when Sergio returned to her. His face was gray with tension. Fiona was alarmed by the sorry state of his clothes – a gritty gray from soot and dirty water. Sergio hung his head and reported in a dull monotone about the fire. Disaster had struck. His studio had burned to the ground from an intense blaze. The heat was so severe that the building's steel beams had twisted out of shape. All the finished pieces and works being restored went up in smoke. It was a total loss. The workshop itself was ruined with the roof and supporting beams burned through. Even the basement was destroyed by the collapse of the upper floors into it. There never had been such a blaze in this quadrant of the city, according to the fire chief. Fortunately, the fire occurred late at night and no one was hurt, but being located in an industrial zone, the fire raged before anyone notified the authorities. Fiona was surprised to learn about the large size of Sergio's fabrication studio and, moreover, she never had heard of this particular building or its neighborhood. The shop on Via Margutta, however, was safe and sound.

Sergio sat down in their kitchen and poured cold water into his red wine. He sat with his elbows on the table, a figure of fatigue and abject worry. His voice was hoarse.

"There's insurance for everything lost. Don't worry. We have money coming in from the shop on Via Margutta. I have partners I never mentioned to you. I didn't bother telling you about them as I never intended to introduce them to you. I only see them at their office or at the studio. Now I'll have to go and meet with them. They're more like investors acting as a bank in my business. I'll have to explain the financial situation to them. I'll leave tonight."

Fiona looked into his eyes and did not argue.

The big apartment was strangely quiet after Sergio left. Fiona went to bed early but could not sleep. When she finally drifted off, nightmares haunted her. She dreamed she was modeling for another painter. She was standing in a costume of bright silks with a long tapestry shawl draped over her shoulders. The artist, unkempt and wearing tattered, stained clothing, stood at his easel as he painted her portrait. He was examining her face when, without warning, flames danced across on the studio floor. Billowing clouds of smoke obscured visibility and she no longer could see the painter. She heard the painter screaming in pain. Flames engulfed her and she cried vainly for Sergio, for his help. Fiona, still in her nightmare of vision, was filled with despair as she could not find Sergio. Shaking with emotion, Fiona moaned and awoke to hot sunshine on her face. She had overslept.

Fiona sprang out of bed and began her daily routine, preparing to go to her studio. Once more, her anxious thoughts could be controlled by the demands of painting, or so she thought. Fiona hurried to her studio hoping to find the red message light blinking on the phone. Her eyes lit up – finally a message – and she quickly retrieved it: It was from Professor Hughes, asking her to ring him back immediately. There was an edge to his tone of voice, suggesting tension or worry. However, Fiona felt her anxiety dissipate as soon as they spoke.

"Fiona, I read about the fire in the newspaper. It sounded like a dreadful explosion razed the entire building! Is Sergio unharmed?"

"Yes, thank God. He was home briefly last night but had to go back to work with the police and the insurance company."

"Well, at least he's okay. That's good news. Let's have a cappuccino in the Borghese gardens. Ten minutes? I'll meet you at the trellis bar."

"Sì. Grazie. I'll be there."

Fiona combed her hair, splashed water on her face and applied some lipstick. She hurriedly walked down the meandering stone path to the garden café, all the while searching to see if she recognized anyone, either one of Sergio's clients or a friend out for a stroll. For an odd reason, Fiona felt as if she were being watched. She became unsettled, her breathing quickened, and she began to feel anxious as her thoughts turned to Sergio.

Arriving at the entrance to the garden café, Fiona quickly scanned the terrace and promptly located Professor Hughes sitting in the shade at a small metal table. She felt markedly relieved to spot him. Professor Hughes was a tall, slim man, always nattily dressed in British clothes. His ever-present panama and walking stick completed his elegant attire. He smiled and stood ramrod straight – almost military in style — despite his advanced age. Today Professor Hughes was wearing a beautifully tailored linen suit with a crisp-white shirt striped in a strong navy blue. Professor Hughes had an attractive English face, longish with smile lines around his very bright blue eyes. He still had all his hair, Fiona observed, although more white than gray, and it was too long – wisps of hair dragged over his collar. Fiona, all too aware of her professor's demanding work habits, smiled to see a little bit of normalcy in her chaotic life. At least Graham Hughes, the quintessential absented-minded professor, remained a constant friend and mentor during this confused, unruly time, she thought to herself; with that sudden realization, Fiona felt the tension in her shoulders relax.

He held her chair and gestured to the waiter for coffee service. Professor Hughes squeezed Fiona's hand as he scrutinized her.

"How are you holding up, my dear?"

"I'm fine. I can't do much but wait. Sergio tells me very little of any substance but, then again, he's learning about the fire and how it started. The restoration business, as you know, uses highly flammable chemicals. Perhaps a workman didn't discard used materials in a timely or proper fashion? The police, according to Sergio, have been responsive and professional. There are several insurance company adjusters on the scene too."

"Well, these old buildings do go up fast and who knows what the electrical wiring was like? Combine the hazardous toxic chemicals into the mix and you can imagine a ripe opportunity for an explosion."

Professor Hughes searched Fiona's eyes, patted her hand and said, "There, there, I didn't mean to frighten you. Sergio will do fine with the police and the insurance adjusters. Chin up, old girl! All will work out for the best. Now, what are you working on? Ready for a show?"

Fiona hesitated for a moment as she felt the tension from her emotions well up inside her. Professor Hughes continued, "Fiona, now is the time to pour yourself into your art. I'm truly sorry about Sergio and his business problems but you have a choice: Follow your passion and paint or be a victim. Live your own life."

"You're absolutely right, Graham," Fiona expelled a sigh. She continued, "And it's good advice. At first, I felt very low and physically drained by Sergio's business crisis. I tried to get him to talk about the fire and the insurance claim but he shut me out. Now he's in Naples and doesn't call me. I decided to throw myself into work and continued with my newest series. All of a sudden, I'm working nonstop – only taking time to sleep. I'm working on stretched linen panels that fit together almost like a jigsaw puzzle. I'm using a high-key palette, and they're expressionistic landscapes and of the Tyrrhenian Sea. They're my distilled memories of the Maremma. You remember, I visited Ansedonia and the beach near Porto Ercole?" Fiona looked at Professor Hughes to acknowledge his nod and continued with a rush of words, "I think I made a breakthrough. It's a natural progression from realistic portrayals of Tuscan landscapes to an examination of the core of the spiritual awareness of the beauty and the mystery of this ancient land of the Etruscans. I'm excited but feel guilty about Sergio going through such a business disaster."

Fiona looked over to Professor Hughes to gauge his reaction. Fiona's eyes opened wide when she saw Professor Hughes' smile, highlighted by a ring of sugar from a pastry.

"I say, we finish the plate of *cornetti* and off we go to your studio!" Before Fiona could reply, she saw Professor Hughes' eyes flicker away and focus on a man walking towards them. Professor Hughes smiled and whispered, "I believe this is your lucky day, Fiona." Professor Hughes pushed off his chair to greet the visitor. He beamed a smile as he shook the extended hand and said, "Orazio, allow me to introduce a new talent, Fiona Appleton. Fiona," Professor Hughes looked at her, "it's my pleasure to introduce Count Giustinani."

Fiona looked up at Count Giustinani and saw a man of striking appearance, just a shade over average height; he nevertheless carried the impression of a big man. His face, clean-shaven to the point of high gloss, was fixed with the expression of power and force. His smile was barely discernible as his lips moved, saying in a clipped manner, "*Piacere*, my pleasure." The count hovered over Fiona's hand as he blew a kiss. Fiona's eyes widened with sudden realization: The count's face was immobile, almost waxen due to having an overly pulled facelift. She noticed his hair and eyebrows were expertly dyed a golden hue. His tailored dark suit fit him smoothly. The overall effect was highly stylized, glossy and exuded the power of wealth.

"How divine to meet you Count Giustinani," Fiona fluttered her eyes as she tried not to stare.

"The pleasure is all mine, Ms. Appleton. I've heard about your talent from Graham. I hold his opinion in high regard and this is the first time he's been assertive in proclaiming you a future master of contemporary art. I'd like to arrange a private view of your new work. Graham," Count Giustinani gestured to his friend, "please coordinate a studio visit." He gave a mimic of a smile, clicked his heels and again air-kissed Fiona's hand. "Until we meet again," the count turned and resumed his brisk walk.

Professor Hughes clapped Fiona on the back and gave a whoop of laughter, "Well, my dear, you are on your way!" He looked down into Fiona's eyes and in a more reflective tone said, "The count is an arbiter of art trends and collectors will take notice. Let's go view your new paintings, eh?"

"Okay!" Fiona flushed a bright pink, "I'm famished so give me a moment," and Fiona smiled for the first time of the day. They finished their cappuccinos and cornetti, a crusty pastry similar to a croissant, and walked at a measured pace all the while discussing the contemporary art scene.

Soon they arrived at the studio and Fiona pressed the

metal keypad alongside the door. There was a loud click and Fiona ushered Professor Hughes through the old stone entrance. She took her time putting her bag and scarf away in order to give Professor Hughes a few private moments to view the stacked row of paintings.

Professor Hughes stared closely at one large canvas and rapidly moved to the next canvas. He remained silent as he examined carefully all ten pieces. Professor Hughes slapped his panama on his thigh, beamed at Fiona with a huge grin and wheezed, "You're ready, my girl! Let's have a show. I'll ring Orazio for a private view and I'm certain his gallery, The Venosa, will host an opening reception and a twenty-one day exhibition. Are you familiar with his gallery?"

"Of course. The gallery is famous for its Old Master holdings and for showcasing emerging artists. The Venosa openings are prominently featured in the newspapers. I'd be honored to have him represent me. Overjoyed, quite frankly."

"Count Giustinani is a close friend of mine. I'll arrange everything for you. I've mentioned your name to him as a prospective artist for his gallery many times since you took up residence in Rome. I took the liberty of showing Orazio a few transparencies, the large colored slides you gave me, of your work. He was thrilled."

Fiona felt her face blushing and stammered, "I had no idea, but I'm pleased. It was very generous of you, Graham."

"Count Giustinani is organized and well-connected in the art world. The gallery is a well-oiled machine and will not overlook any detail in developing your career. His staff will contact the media and get some PR going for you," Professor Hughes paused to catch his breath and continued, "The paintings are truly magnificent. They show a serious eye, good articulation and vibrancy of color! Ah, the creativity of youth, what energy!"

Fiona huffed with surprise and gave a quavering smile. Her voice choked with emotion as she said, "Thank you. This is coming at a strange time in my life but I'm grateful."

"All right, my dear. I must dash to another appointment but you'll have your show and soon!"

Professor Hughes mashed his panama onto his head, tilted it to a slight angle and let himself out the door.

The studio resumed its quiet, peaceful isolation from the boisterous street. Fiona again checked the phone but there were no messages. *Niente*, nothing. Where was Sergio at this moment, she wondered. Fiona was worried but only could wait. Several days dragged into a week of waiting.

One night she awoke, gasping for air. She had been in a deep sleep. Dreaming again of fires engulfing her while Sergio gazed at her. Fiona screamed until she realized he was not an apparition. Sergio hugged her and whispered how sorry he was to have been so delayed. He covered her with little kisses and stroked her hair. Fiona shivered and got out of bed with every intention of confronting Sergio. She wanted to understand the seriousness of the loss and learn more about his partners.

They sat in the dimly lit kitchen and shared some wine. Sergio's eyes were red from lack of sleep. His face was lined from exhaustion and he'd lost too much weight. He toyed with a piece of fruit as a distraction. Finally, Sergio sighed and said, "There was an important picture being restored. It burned without a trace. It was too valuable, too complicated for me to insure. I took a chance as I thought I'd only have it for a short time in the studio." His voice trailed off.

He continued in a soft voice, "I owned it with several partners. They're upset, angry with me. The polizia are investigating and the insurance company was on the site with me going over everything. The insurance adjusters examined the wreckage and reviewed the inventory list. It's a substantial loss to them so they sent several people from their claims department. I barely slept as everyone wanted my attention. I had no time to eat. No sleep. Now I have to wait for the insurance settlement."

'What about your partners? Will you be able to continue in your business?"

"*Basta*! Let me sleep. I'll tell you the rest tomorrow," Sergio said with a strangled voice. He dragged himself to the bedroom and collapsed into sleep. Fiona sat up in the kitchen, looking at the shadows.

The next morning was uneventful. Sergio went back to work as usual. He no longer seemed worried about the insurance settlement. Again, he explained they had to wait to be reimbursed for the business loss. In the meantime, Fiona should continue to do the same – to paint and not worry. Sergio smiled in his most charming manner, urged her to relax and went out the door. Fiona pretended to believe him and went off to her studio. They planned to meet for lunch.

The daily routine of their married life resumed; they saw their friends, attended gallery openings and cultivated prospective clients. Time passed quickly. At times, Fiona almost managed to forget about the insurance investigation.

One day, Sergio arrived at her studio clutching a huge bouquet. The flowers were a riot of color, so much so she burst into smiles. Fiona fluttered her eyes and looked up at her husband. He was beautifully dressed in a new custom-tailored suit. He also was carrying a large Pucci shopping bag.

"This is for you, a little dress from Pucci and sandals from Ferragamo to wear for our special day. You'll be the best-dressed and the most beautiful woman." Sergio's eyes sparkled as he held the bag aloft for her to see. "We are going to lunch and taking the rest of the day off. I insist. Andiamo."

Fiona rushed into the powder room and changed quickly into the clinging dress. The hot pink sandals made her legs look toned and long-stemmed. She opened the door and swung her hair; Fiona stepped out with high, prancing steps, mimicking the runway models she'd seen at the fashion shows. She strutted over to the mirror to primp and to see how she looked. She giggled as she heard Sergio's wolf whistle. Turning away from the mirror, she ran to Sergio and hugged him.

With a chortle, Fiona said, "The flowers and clothes will go to my head. You're spoiling me."

Sergio kissed her and said, "Let's go before I muss your dress. We have a reservation. I've planned a special day." He smiled as he took her arm and they left the studio.

They strolled through the Borghese gardens and onto Via del Banco di Santo Spirito in the direction of Hotel Hassler. The way to the entrance was congested with tourists overflowing from the top of the Spanish Steps. The hotel's doorman elbowed his way to them and ushered them into the lobby. Sergio and Fiona kept a measured pace through the grand foyer as they were familiar with the hotel.

They were greeted by the bartender, and he smoothly led them to an alcove of the grotto-styled lounge. The walls of the grotto were covered in antique stone with artfully arranged wall plantings of flowering orchids mixed with climbing vines. Antique statues were scattered around the grotto, and Fiona could hear the soft fall of water from a bronze urn. The lounge was decorated in a soothing palette of muted colors and had luxurious cushioned seating. Sergio chose a deep banquette and the bartender served crystal flutes of prosecco, smoothed the linen tablecloth and quickly retreated into the shadows. Fiona, meanwhile, nibbled on an olive while she waited for Sergio to explain the reason for such an extravagant lunch.

"The insurance company settled to my advantage," Sergio eyes shifted as he told Fiona. "My partners were pleased and all is fine. I also sold an important suite of furniture and made more money than I ever expected," he crowed with high-pitched laughter. "We have everything to celebrate. I have even more exciting news: I leased a villa on Capri for the season, and you can paint to your heart's content." Sergio looked at Fiona with wide eyes, flashed his white teeth and preened with overwrought pride.

"This is extraordinary. What great news! Can you afford to take the summer off?"

Sergio grinned even more broadly and said, "Sì. Tutto bene. Business is good again. All is taken care of. I have a competent staff, and you know we always close for August. I can hunt for antiques in Campania, the province surrounding Naples. There's always a treasure to discover." He hugged her and called for more prosecco. He continued, whispering in her ear, "We're at the Hassler, so let's pretend we are the fabulous Medici. We should always live in such luxury. It would be easy to get used to and, Fiona, you look like you were born into it!"

"But I'm happy in Rome, painting and taking care of

our home. I'm content." Fiona patted Sergio's hand, trying to reassure him that their life was fine as it was.

"I want a bigger life. A permanent home on Capri someday. A villa, maybe. Don't be a drag, Fiona." Sergio took her hand, kissed it, urged her to have more prosecco and called for the luncheon menu. "We'll dine upstairs," he said to the waiter.

The grand dining room of the Hassler never failed to impress Fiona. The furnishings were ornate, the table covered with heavy damask linen and silver serving pieces. The walls were simply a backdrop for the dominating view of the Roman skyline with its multi-layered shades of terra-cotta rooftops.

"We are sitting on top of Rome. Look at the trees, the rooftop gardens. Oh, St. Peter's is always magnificent in its splendor. Rome is the most precious city in the world." Fiona gasped at the overwhelming beauty of the panoramic view and the history spread out in front of her.

"I accept your thanks," Sergio tittered, "and I have more gifts and news to share."

Fiona looked at him and waited. It all seemed like a fairy tale after the long months of tension and silence. She was afraid of them drifting apart. Now it was as if Sergio wanted to be everything to her.

"We're leaving tomorrow, very early. I booked us on the express train to Naples and then to Capri by ferry. Our Vespa is being trucked as we speak. I collected the medical papers for the dog, so now you only have to pack your clothes and art supplies. I'll help you." Sergio looked at her with mischievous eyes. He reminded her of the brash young man she had first met in the dusty antique shop.

They finished their lunch and strolled home. Via del Babuino was clogged with beetle-like Fiats and trucks belching diesel fumes. The noise no longer bothered her, but she never would get used to the air being almost colored grey by the petrol fumes. They took a right onto Via Margutta and walked down a narrow cobblestoned street. Their via ran parallel to busy Babuino, yet seemed centuries removed from modern life. The street was too narrow to accommodate traffic. Opaque windows of painters' studios overlooked the quiet street. Many of the studios had balconies with iron banisters. Fiona was pleased to see how most of the little balconies were crowded with young tomato, mint and basil plants. Artisans worked and lived on this street. They passed by the frame maker, a ceramic shop, a glass maker. Tiny antique shops lined the street on the ground floors. The antique dealers slowly were encroaching upon the ground-floor studios of the artisans. Many of the working studios had old courtyards decorated with sculpture. The only nod to modern life was the contemporary sculptures intermixed with antique.

There seemed to be a hush laid over the neighborhood. As they walked, the couple slowed down as if to gather some of their neighbors' simple joy in life before reaching their building. Sergio unlocked the tall iron gate and let them into the empty courtyard. Fiona admired the healthy plantings of rosemary and basil in the window boxes, and she breathed deeply to capture the scent from the plants. She smiled as the scent was strong and always announced summer weather to her. Fiona chuckled softly to herself as she imagined her summer vacation unfolding: An entire summer season spent on Capri surrounded by mint, basil and lemon trees with the azure water beckoning to her from every vantage point. A paradise to paint, Fiona thought to herself as she squeezed Sergio's arm and sighed with pleasure. The gravel crunched under their feet, and then they entered the vestibule of the private entrance. The next day passed swiftly. They arrived at their villa with their white spitz, Guido, straining on his leash. Fiona thought Anacapri was heaven-sent ...

Her mind shifted to remembering the violence of the previous night and she took a deep breath. Fiona shook her head, wiped tears away from her eyes and picked up the breakfast tray to carry it onto the balcony. How could she have been so fooled. What a complete idiot! Living in a fool's paradise, not heaven in Capri! Basta. Enough of this jaunt down memory lane, she scolded herself. Fiona's thoughts shifted to the present and all of its ugly future: separation and divorce. Fiona forced herself to look at the view: The sky and the sea were an infinite variety of blues. When she took the time to look at the sky and the sea, to truly observe seascape, she was able to banish her obsessive worrying.

Sitting down in the chaise, Fiona breakfasted and sipped the last of her coffee. She was about to call the front desk when she heard a knock at the door.

Fiona immediately thought of Sergio. Did he know the door was bolted and he'd been locked out last night? Did he knock as he was embarrassed by his behavior? Was he contrite? Wanting to make amends? She got to her feet and said, "Pronto. Yes? Who is it?"

"Carabinieri. Military police. Open up."

Fiona opened the door to see Piero, the owner of the hotel, standing there wringing his hands in worry. Piero was accompanied by two uniformed carabinieri officers, a man and a woman, who were wearing black uniforms with epaulettes. The woman had red insignia chevrons that designated her officer's rank as sergeant, vice brigadiere dei carabinieri. The man, however, wore more gold braid, which seemed to indicate he was the senior officer. Polished brass buttons, a large, brass-buckled belt and hats completed their uniforms. The colonel was a tall, slim man who held himself erect, thereby showing off his splendid uniform to maximum advantage. His peaked hat with an additional braid seemed to frame his brown eyes, which were very dark and fixed upon Fiona with intensity.

"Mrs. Sergio Celesti?" The inspector spoke in accented English.

"Sì."

"I am Colonel Beltrami and this is Sergeant Verde."

Fiona nodded and opened the door wide. The officers briskly marched past her and glanced around the lavishly appointed room. She noticed how Piero, usually so loquacious, was subdued with downcast eyes. He hung his head in embarrassment, not wanting to be there. Piero retreated into the background, so still that he blended into the furnishings.

The colonel looked her in the eyes and slowly ran them down, observing her robe. He cleared his throat and said, "Get dressed, Signora. Sergeant Verde will accompany you while you change."

"I don't understand."

"Get dressed now and we'll wait in the salotto. Piero order some more caffè and biscotti."

"Sì, Colonel Beltrami. A presto." Piero hastened to pick up the phone and called room service. Piero shifted his eyes onto Fiona and observed she had entered her room to change into clothes. He also noticed that Sergeant Verde seemed glued to her side as if afraid Fiona may hide something.

Fiona snatched at her clothes and managed to find a smart outfit to wear. She heard room service knock again on the door as she hurried to rejoin the colonel. Fiona, in turn, saw Piero take the tray and put the refreshments on a low table in front of the colonel.

Colonel Beltrami prepared his caffè latte and drank. By this time, Fiona was seated opposite him. She declined any caffè and waited to hear the purpose of their visit. She was painfully aware that Sergio was missing, long overdue from his morning jog.

"Mrs. Celesti, we have sad news. Very serious news. A tragedy. Your husband was killed when his motorcycle drove off the Amalfi Drive. We recovered his body and the Moto Guzzi by police launch. I am sorry for your loss." Colonel Beltrami watched Fiona's face as he delivered the sudden, shocking news to her. The colonel was intrigued by how Fiona reacted to the news: She was terrified.

Feelings of disbelief flittered across her face as she absorbed the information. Fiona stammered, "I don't understand. He'd gone for a jog, not for a ride." Her voice trailed off. She clung to the hope as she remembered Sergio's note saying he'd be jogging and right back.

"Signora, what time did your husband leave?"

"Why? I don't know. I was sleeping. He left a note sometime this morning. I ordered breakfast so that's about the time I got up. I read the note after opening the drapes."

"Where is this note?" The colonel asked.

"It's in the pocket of my robe. The one I was wearing when you arrived. May I retrieve it from the next room?"

"Sì. But Sergeant Verde will accompany you."

Fiona and her human watchdog returned to her changing area and she picked up the robe. Holding it over her arm, she retraced her steps to the salon and looked at the colonel.

"May I retrieve it from the pocket?"

She saw the colonel nod an assent, although his eyes never left her hands. She searched the robe for the pocket and held the note up for them to see. The carabinieri examined the note while holding it with a handkerchief and then the inspector deposited it in a plastic envelope.

"Your husband did not go for a jog. He was seen riding his motorcycle away from the hotel. We need to know if your husband was meeting someone in town or somewhere near the hotel. The road was dry without any obstructions – safe for an experienced driver. We are inspecting the motorcycle for mechanical problems as there were long skid marks as if he tried to prevent the crash. It's a suspicious accident. No witnesses have come forward, unfortunately." The sergeant's mouth was drawn into a thin line and her brown nugget-like eyes were judging Fiona.

"What do you mean? It wasn't an accident?" Fiona gasped and came to rigid attention.

"Mrs. Celesti, what are you doing here? Do you live in Rome, Capri or are you moving again? Your husband's business is closed. Did he plan to reopen after the August holiday?" The colonel leaned closer to Fiona. She wondered if he wanted her absolute attention or simply wanted to frighten her off a prepared excuse.

"We're on a special holiday," her words rushed on. "Staying at Il San Pietro was a treat, a surprise arranged by Sergio. We only just arrived." Fiona whispered the last remarks. She cleared her throat, her voice growing stronger as she said, "Sergio plans, I meant to say, Sergio planned to reopen his antique shop and work rooms as usual in September. He told me this the night before we left Capri for Positano."

The colonel persisted, "We know there was a fire at his

workshop in Forcella, Naples, and a large insurance settlement was paid. However, the insurance didn't cover the entire inventory. Was he in danger? Did he express fear?" He hammered his questions in a staccato tone of voice as if he were trying to drill the seriousness of the matter into Fiona's head. The colonel leaned into her face, making the gold trimming swim in front of her eyes. Fiona steeled herself not to shrink away from him.

"Sergio told me the insurance company settled to his satisfaction. I was led to believe he got the total amount he wanted. Over the summer in Capri, he seemed to have nervous energy, very excitable at times. But Sergio was enthusiastic about our trip to Positano." Fiona looked directly into the colonel's eyes.

Suddenly, Fiona felt a whirling in her head as she tried to catch her breath. She collapsed into a chair and sensed she was shrinking in size. She felt dazed and disoriented.

Piero watched Fiona fall into the chair, hesitated for a moment and, at last, sprang into the role of professional host. Piero raised his voice, "Franco, I mean Colonel Beltrami, Mrs. Celesti is in shock and exhausted. Let her lie down and compose her thoughts. She's had enough questions for today."

"No! Damn it, Piero! You know what happened. You saw the crash site with your own eyes. This was a planned, well-executed murder. This was not about a simple antique dealer on a romantic holiday with his wife. This was about the Celestine Market and the Camorra!" The colonel bellowed and flashed his eyes at the hotel manager. Piero shrugged and looked away from Fiona in embarrassment. He backed away from the tightly composed group.

"What is the Celestine Market?" asked Fiona.

Sergeant Verde walked closer to Fiona and sat down in

a facing club chair. "The Celestine Market is named after your husband in acknowledgment of his business prowess. This area is one of Europe's largest cocaine markets. The area imports, processes and distributes cocaine and heroin in open-air markets."

"I don't believe this. My husband was an antique dealer in Rome. He was an established businessman on Via del Babuino."

Sergeant Verde's harsh tone of voice overrode Fiona's and continued, "Your husband, Sergio Celesti, was the mastermind who created this hub of illicit drug dealing. Labor is cheap in Campania because of the lack of jobs. Campania has dozens of clans operating with high-profit levels. There are vendettas and drug wars on a regular basis. We've been building a file on your husband, trying to link him to the manufacturing and distribution of hard drugs. We needed hard evidence to arrest him."

Fiona's eyes grew wide with fright as she listened to the officer. She licked her dry lips and managed to say, "I don't know anything about this. I'm certain my husband is innocent of any wrongdoing." She shook her head and looked over at the colonel. She saw that he was examining her as if she were under a microscope. Abruptly, something shifted in his eyes and the colonel straightened to his full height. He nodded at Fiona, and she knew he'd made some sort of decision about her. Her heart skipped with hope.

"Yes, we'll let her rest for now, Piero. Please get some rest, Mrs. Celesti. Calm yourself. You will need to identify the body. And don't leave the area without informing us." The colonel said this coolly as he ignored his inspector's exhortations about having more questions for the Signora.

The carabinieri marched out of the room. The owner

of the hotel said in a low voice that he'd make sure no one disturbed her for a while. He retreated from the room in soft steps.

Fiona sank into the big bed. She wanted to cover her head with the bed linens to lock out the light. Images of their last days in Capri and Positano played over in her mind. Despite the darkened room, she kept seeing Sergio. She sat up, pulled the curtains back and searched Sergio's belongings. She looked for paperwork or any business journals. She found a folded piece of paper under his pillow. Unfolding it, Fiona saw a column of numbers. No words, just numbers.

While examining the paper, searching for a clue, she recalled snatches of the carabinieri's questions. Did we meet anyone, see anyone we knew? She remembered the Venetian count she met at dinner with Sergio. Count Volpe's face came looming into her mind. Was that a rendezvous planned by the old man? He seemed like a harmless, wealthy art collector. She knew several dealers who reminded her of Count Volpe. He was the sole person they spoke to last night.

A subtle knock at the door was so quiet Fiona almost missed it. She hurriedly folded the note and ran over to her pocketbook. She shoved the note into an interior side pocket. The knock came again with a small scratching noise. Fiona ran across the room to reach the door.

"Yes, what is it?" Fiona called through the thick door.

"Fiona, it is Count Volpe. Please open the door, my dear."

Fiona cautiously opened the door. Count Volpe's tanned face was drained of color and his eyes were red-rimmed. He quietly and slowly entered the room and sat down in one of the low-slung chairs.

"I'm sorry to disturb you, Fiona, but we need to talk."

"The carabinieri were here. You just missed them. It was a shock. Sergio went for a morning jog and was killed on the road. I was lying down trying to absorb it all."

"I want to help you. I was shocked and disturbed to hear of Sergio's accident. He was such a charming man. I always enjoyed doing business with him. Sergio had exquisite taste and always managed to find unusual, significant pieces."

Fiona was moved by this and settled herself in another chair. With all the strength she could muster, she asked, "Did you just happen to run into us last night in the lounge? Or was this an agreed-upon rendezvous?"

"It was planned as a surprise visit. Sergio did not expect me, nor did I want to embarrass Sergio. I assumed he did not explain his business activities to you?" The count raised his eyes and waited for acknowledgment. "I was correct. I only wanted to let Sergio know I was at the hotel."

"Did you know Sergio long?"

"Certo. Almost from the beginning of his career. Sergio aspired to buy and sell important antiques and fine art but did not have the capital to pursue his early ambition. We met through mutual friends. It became a profitable business for all of us. Sergio prospered and became seriously wealthy. Rich, in fact. I saw him less and less as I live in Venice and don't leave the Veneto often." The count's voice trailed off as he looked at her with hooded eyes. He remained still, silent. Count Volpe seemed accustomed to waiting a long time for answers.

"Did it remain profitable?"

"I believe for Sergio," the count said with a sly smile. "But, alas, not for his partners. They suffered a tremendous financial loss after the fire. You remember he went to Naples. To Forcella?" The count's eyes narrowed as he asked this question. He was staring at Fiona closely, taking measure of her. He quickly relaxed as he realized she was innocent of conspiring with her criminal husband.

"What does Naples have to do with you? You live in Venice. Are you a partner in the shop?" Fiona was bewildered by the carabinieri's story of Sergio's byzantine life of crime. She began to imagine a network of criminal activities and wondered about the sincerity of Count Volpe.

"Not a partner in the shop. Let's say I was an early investor in Sergio's antique business. I financially guaranteed the inventory, which was, in turn, insured against loss. There was one particular piece that was not insured. The painting was valuable. In fact, it was a Caravaggio. When I was young man, I found a long-lost Caravaggio in the attic of a drafty palazzo. The painting was dirty, very dark varnish clouded the surface. It needed restoration in some small area and a thorough cleaning. I bought it from the last member of an old Venetian family for a smallish sum. He didn't know what a treasure he had in that attic. Eventually I needed more operating money and I approached Sergio. He, in turn, brought in partners, a consortium of friends, shall we say? Not insuring the painting, however, was Sergio's decision." The count's voice trailed off as he drummed his fingers on the chair's arm.

Fiona waited, sensing his hesitation to say more. What information could be so dangerous to reveal? She sat quietly, willing him to divulge his secret.

"Oh, my dear, I'm miserable about Sergio's death. I never thought they'd go so far! I thought I could negotiate terms. I thought I had time to arbitrate." The count's thickened voice croaked with tension and hoarseness. His hands nervously moved up and down, trying to smooth imaginary errant strands of hair.

"Arbitrate about what? The insurance loss?" Fiona stared at Count Volpe.

"The Caravaggio was a painting of great significance in Sergio's inventory. It had a dubious provenance, never properly authenticated by the necessary experts and, therefore, could not be adequately insured. It was, however, used as valuable collateral for a business loan. Sergio promised his partners that he wouldn't leave it in the studio. He was supposed to move it quickly to fireproof storage at one of the banks he dealt with but he didn't. Apparently, the fire occurred during the week it was in his studio. It was either a twist of bad luck or deadly timing."

"Was Sergio planning to cover the loss with his savings?"

"No. Sergio didn't have the resources to cover this financial loss. He lied about the insurance settlement to all of us — even to you, his wife." The count hesitated as if he was struggling with his emotions. His face turned red, he raked his fingers through his hair and stammered, "Fiona, I'm concerned about your welfare. I'm afraid for you! These men are dangerous!" The count's voice choked and he coughed into his handkerchief.

The phone's abrupt ringing startled the count and he almost tipped over his chair. Fiona jumped to answer the phone.

"Yes, that's fine," she murmured into the receiver. Almost simultaneously with the phone's ringing, there was a loud knock at the door. Fiona hastened to open it.

Arturo greeted her with subdued tones and she clung to him.

"You got my message at the front desk. Thank God, you came so soon," Fiona whispered into his ear.

Arturo smiled at her and gave her a big hug. Looking over her shoulder, Arturo eyed Count Volpe. Releasing Fiona from his arms, Arturo strode into the room. He did not seem surprised to see her visitor and addressed the old man by name. The count, however, did not know Arturo and tightening his eyes, he viewed him warily.

Arturo introduced himself to the count and saw the old man recognized his name. Arturo's blue eyes glinted steel as he looked down upon the seated Count Volpe.

"What have you been telling Fiona? That you're some nice, old man who deals in antiques in a backwater palazzo in Venice?"

The count, trying to look bored, shrugged his shoulders using an old Neapolitan gesture, essentially dismissing Arturo. The younger man dragged a chair over to face him and withdrew a buff-colored folder from his briefcase. Slapping the folder onto his lap, Arturo looked up and glared at his adversary.

"Fiona, do you know what a factor or economic marketing means, for people like Count Volpe?"

Fiona felt the knot in her stomach tighten and she almost choked on her words, "Not really. I'm listening."

"Loan sharking. They loan dirty money to desperate people. They charge crazy rates. The whole of Italy is tainted by this money. Even some banks."

"And Sergio went to Count Volpe to start his business?"

"Count Volpe is indeed an antique dealer, Fiona, but one with an unsavory reputation. He's lived up to his family name as Count Volpe is truly a wolf of the underworld. He loans money to finance robberies and burglaries. The

Camorra refers to him as a factor or an economic advisor since the count gets his cut first off of every deal. I got confirmation about this before I left Capri. The count charges exorbitantly high interest on the loans, many times driving his clients to desperate acts.

"That's not true! I loan money, sometimes, to businesses in difficulty. I've never had any trouble with the law. I have competitors who are simply jealous of my success. They're always spreading rumors about me. I am an established antique dealer in Venice. It's a family business – one for generations." The count sniffed into a huge white handkerchief.

Arturo gave the count a withering look and said, "Stop your whining! I want answers and information. Fiona is in danger and I want to protect her."

Again, Arturo consulted his file of notes and drawled, "We can agree you finance illicit activities? Just nod unless you want to elaborate."

The count gave a small nod.

"You had a valuable painting your group moved as collateral to finance continuing operations. As the painting grew in value, Sergio's ventures – or yours and Sergio's – grew exponentially. But then the insurance inventory reporting form changed. You couldn't list the Caravaggio because of the gray area of its provenance. You couldn't list the owners either, now could you? The painting became very valuable but you only use it as chattel, a personal possession, moving it from one deal to the next. It was still valuable as a black-market painting."

Again a nod.

Arturo turned to the bewildered woman and said, "Fiona, they used the painting for the equivalent of cash as they could not use their old currency. Remember during the summer that Italy overhauled and reprinted the currency? It was a new color and design, even size?"

"Yes, of course I remember. It was in midsummer. It took me a while to get used to the larger denominations. In order to use our money, I had to take a lot of old currency to the bank for conversion to the new. American Express could not process the order; only banks were authorized by the government."

Arturo continued, "Everyone had to recycle their cash and declare it at the banks. There was a deadline for the exchange of old bills. A passport and a signature were required with the lire. The black market took a tumble for a while. People were not so eager to do any business at all. Our friend here took advantage of the timing to negotiate better terms for his deals by using the painting. The painting simply traveled as a financial instrument to guarantee any pending project. Eh, Count Volpe?"

The old man flicked some ash off a sleeve and nodded.

Arturo cleared his throat and said in a firm, low voice, "I think it's time for you to talk, Count Volpe. If you care at all about Sergio's widow, please come clean now. I'm certain you do not want any innocent blood shed. Fiona doesn't deserve this."

The only sound was the measured breathing of the count. The old man took a few deep breaths as if he were nervous and then composed his hands in his lap. He began in a strong voice, "Sergio became wildly successful with my help. I mentored him like he was a second son. I was proud he was so inventive and industrious. He made a lot of money at a very early age and more money each year. It was never enough for him. The risks, the danger of exposure, more complicated deals never sustained his attention or ambition. Sergio was always restless after closing a deal. He enjoyed taking a risk as much as making money. I don't know exactly when but Sergio decided on making the biggest deal of his life. Cheating his partners out of their money added to the attractiveness of the risk. That fire in his workshop was at first ruled suspicious, but eventually the police ruled against arson. Perhaps the police inspectors were paid off? I don't know." The count looked up at Arturo and shrugged.

"Okay, so Sergio got through one hurdle," the count proceeded. "Then, the insurance company combed through the inventory records for every listed item and even the rolling monthly figure for the paintings. At some point, he had changed the insurance from a monthly reporting form of the paintings to a huge amount. Unfortunately for Sergio, a new, ambitious insurance agent was assigned to the job. The agent denied the declared amount and forced Sergio to settle for a lesser amount. That's when Sergio found himself in serious trouble with his partners. He could not make up the difference – not in time. Sergio indeed had been clever to commit arson and not have it detected by the authorities. But we, I mean, the partners discovered the accelerant used to start the fire. Not only was it arson, but he also had planned the job months in advance. To make matters worse, we never were informed about the change in his insurance coverage – the type of reporting form. He lied to the partners about the settlement amount and the time needed to settle. He went to Capri for the summer pretending all was okay. Sergio actually was planning his next venture without us, and not in Italy. I think he was going to do a bunk to disappear."

Arturo snorted in derision and in a sarcastic tone said, "You and your partners were not notified of the insurance reporting-form change as you could not be listed on the policy! Your partners, shady businessmen at the least but all known criminals, could not be listed on the policy as additional named insureds as it would have sent red flags to the insurance company!"

Count Volpe replied in a steady voice, "We were lucky to get the amount we did. But we weren't happy." He looked at Fiona and said, "I'm sorry, my dear. I know you loved Sergio and believed in him. I hate to be the one to blacken his memory."

Fiona stared back with tears streaming down her face. She was shocked, shaken to her core. Her whole life with Sergio – her marriage, their home – was built on lies. She'd been living in a shadow world of cracked mirrors and unholy smoke. How had she never seen the truth? She started gasping for breath and her body shook.

Surprisingly, it was the count who touched her shoulder and said in a brisk, businesslike tone, "You must get a hold of yourself. Be strong. Quickly! Your friend is right. You are in terrible danger. You must act fast."

Withdrawing from his touch, Fiona stirred herself and, catching her breath, said, "Do what? Act fast about what?"

"Why you must find the painting!"

Arturo and Fiona both looked incredulous at the news, thinking the old count must be mad.

The count looked at their faces and did not like their reaction. "Sergio was going to sell it to a private collector. He moved it before the fire. I'm certain of it!" The count's voice rose to a rasping shriek. "I knew him so well. Like a son, he was to me. He learned everything and then played me, played every one of his partners and you, too, Fiona." His voice subsided to a snuffling tone as he blew his nose.

"You're only angry because he outplayed you. Sergio betrayed you, your training. He was your disciple and he deceived you. The fox outwitted the wolf." Although Arturo spoke in a soft tone of voice, his words penetrated the old man's mind like a knife, wounding the count's pride.

"Certo," grumbled the old man.

Fiona sat up straight, shook herself and interjected, "Count Volpe, you told me you found the painting in a dusty palazzo. Who owns the Caravaggio? That is, assuming it's found."

"As I said, it's a murky provenance. But it needs to be returned to the archive storage room of the Knights of Malta." The count shifted his eyes back and forth between Fiona and Arturo but never settled.

"That's an evasive answer," replied Fiona. "Then how would the Camorra be repaid?"

"I think the Order will have cash reserves by then, and I also think there will be other valuables stored with the missing Caravaggio." Count Volpe hung his head.

"What do you mean by other valuables? Portable items? Or do you mean heroin? It's the heroin they want, isn't it? The street value of that poison is higher than the Caravaggio." Arturo's voice became stronger as his anger rose.

"Sì. I only leveraged the appreciation of the painting, not its total value. I leveraged the spread to the Camorra for old lire. I'm not a drug dealer." The count wiped his hands nervously with a crumpled piece of linen.

For a moment, Arturo looked as if he would strike out at Count Volpe, but he restrained himself and said, "What a mentor. What an education. What an unholy mess." Arturo closed the file and sighed. "What do we do now?" Arturo gestured at Fiona, whose eyes were round with terror.

In a halting voice, the count said, "I think you go to Naples. After the funeral, you begin with the shops. Pretend you're wealthy tourists on a shopping spree. The polizia and the carabinieri will be watching. You can also pretend Fiona is thinking of selling Sergio's business. And then you meet with private art dealers. Ask your questions about a missing antique painting in absolute privacy, perhaps in their storage areas where no one watches. Find a thread. Find the buyer. You'll discover Sergio's plan, and then you'll find the painting." He lapsed into silence and shrugged.

Arturo exploded with rage and shouted, "And the partners?" His voice dripped with sarcasm, "How will Fiona survive for a day? This is not a plan but a suicide mission. You want to be rid of her so she cannot cooperate with the authorities."

"No one can protect her. You can take her away, but they'll hunt you both down." Turning to address Fiona, the count continued, "I'm sorry, my dear. I don't want to shock you. You must know the gravity of your situation. You will be murdered if you don't succeed in locating the painting. You're Sergio's widow and now his crime has become your death sentence. I can buy you time, tell them you will locate the missing painting. Speak to Sergio's partners. You already met one? You met Umberto? He tipped me off about Sergio cheating me. He tipped me off about your sudden trip to Positano."

"Oh, my God, yes. He's a horrid man and he's your informant? Are there more like him?" Fiona's voice cracked.

"More?" The count hissed, "They're like a gang within a gang. They're not Sicilians, although the root of their gang is the Sicilian mafia. They are Neapolitans. They're called the Camorra, separate from the Mafia, and they control all businesses in Naples. They own the politicians. At one time, many centuries ago, Campania and Naples were ruled by the noble families. The *guappi*, the senior Camorristi, replaced this aristocracy in power and entitlement. The Camorra is built on poverty and has its own class structure. The top mobsters dress elegantly, mix with the highest society and bank legitimately all over Europe. Their tentacles reach from Naples throughout Italy and then throughout the world. They're organized like a global corporation. The Camorra bought politicians, the judicial system and prey on every level of business. They started during World War II, smuggling tax-free contraband cigarettes by establishing a secret distribution network. Over time, this route expanded into illicit drugs, arms, even stolen counterfeit pharmaceuticals. They fixed soccer playoffs and tamper with the quality of our wine. The Camorra has beautiful offices in the city but it's only a front for their dirty enterprises. The Camorra will either strike soon or wait until you think you are finally free of them. No Italian government has successfully challenged the Camorra or the Mafia. The carabinieri have the authority to investigate all branches of the government but even they fear the Camorra. Some carabinieri have disappeared or been murdered while working on other investigations of the Camorra. The Camorra will toy with you, play a cat-and-mouse game and then kill you and your loved ones when they want. Sergio should never have tangled with them. He knew better. I told him never to get greedy. Ever! And now poor Fiona is answering for his avarice. You must find the painting!" The count slumped in his chair, sweating profusely from his loud outburst.

Arturo leveled his eyes at the count and did not mince

his words, "Basta. I'll look with Fiona for this painting. What is the subject and size?"

"It's a religious scene in Caravaggio's late style," the count said and continued, using his hands, "It's this high and this long, a small oil on canvas about 24 by 20 inches, easily portable. He could have carried it on his back. The painting was stretched on the original wooden bars." The count delivered this information in a hushed tone. When he finished, he avoided Arturo's eyes and lapsed into silence. The count shifted in his chair and calmly composed his hands by laying them flat on his legs.

Arturo sat up and exclaimed, "A lost Caravaggio painting? What a colossal mess you and Sergio put her in!"

Fiona interjected, "Is this the lost painting owed to the pope or the Vatican?"

"Yes. I even have copies of the Vatican's invoices and a signed contract dating back to 1610. There is also a detailed written description of the painting along with its measurements. You won't have any trouble identifying the painting. It's a St. John painted in the same time period as the St. John in the Galleria Borghese." The last was delivered in an officious tone as if the count, the antique dealer, was dealing with a recalcitrant client.

Arturo said, "I know Caravaggio is important and realize there are not many of his paintings. I can wait to learn his life story and career as an artist later, alone with Fiona. I also want to know how this painting ended up in the archival room of the Knights of Malta. Count Volpe claimed he found it in a dusty palazzo." He glared at the count.

"I wanted to protect the Order. They are not part of this. I only borrowed it from the storage room," Count Volpe grumbled.

"The riddle of ownership can be solved at a later time," Arturo retorted. "I don't want to debate the merits of ownership between the Knights of Malta and the Vatican."

Quickly, Fiona summarized to Arturo how two paintings had been commissioned and prepaid by the pope. "Caravaggio," Fiona recounted, "although considered the finest painter of his time, was also afflicted with an irrational temper – explosive, which led to a murder. He fled Rome and stayed on the run until the pope pardoned him. In the meantime, the Knights of Malta were pursuing him as he had gravely injured a fellow Knight. The Knights were ordered to return Caravaggio to the Order to stand trial. The poor artist was on his way to Rome when his boat was blown off course and he subsequently lost all his belongings, including paintings promised to collectors. He died while in Tuscany and all of the paintings were recovered except the two commissioned by the pope. The pope's two paintings have been missing since Caravaggio's tragic death."

Arturo listened and then interrupted her, afraid she would launch into a lecture about the important Baroque artist. "Fiona, you can tell me about Caravaggio in the car on the way to Naples. Please, can it wait?" Arturo looked into her eyes and Fiona nodded her head. Turning to Count Volpe, Arturo contracted his eyes in anger.

"How much time do we have?" Arturo snarled at the count, looking as if he'd like to throttle him.

"I can stall for a while. Keep me informed by telephone. I'll postpone returning to Venice and stay here at the hotel. You need to start in Naples. See who attends the funeral and then visit them. I'll be at the services and can point faces out to you."

Fiona gave a start. "How do you know the funeral will

be in Naples?" I haven't spoken to Sergio's father yet. He may not even know."

The count's voice shook when he said, "Antonio Celesti is a good man, an important banker in Rome. Naturally, he was deeply disappointed in Sergio's choice of business. By now, Antonio would have been contacted by the carabinieri. I'm certain he'll want his son buried in the mother's family plot in Naples. Antonio will return to Rome and his family immediately after the funeral. And then," his voice faltered, "Fiona, you will be on your own to find the painting. Antonio made it clear a long time ago he was finished with Sergio. He did not want to expose his second family to such viciousness. He detached himself from Sergio to protect his new family. You're on your own. The Camorra will not touch Antonio and his family. They'll go after you!"

With a loud gasp, Fiona shrunk inwardly into her chair. Arturo grimaced and said, "She's not alone. I'll help her find the Caravaggio. Just stay in touch with me so I know what the other side is doing. I believe you are sincere in wanting to help Fiona. I also know you want your investment back with interest. So we have the same goals, although they are slightly shaded in value."

"Va bene," said the count as he shook hands with Arturo and blew a kiss over Fiona's hand. "I'll get on the phone with Sergio's partners and discuss the deadline. Let me give you my contact information. I'll see you in Naples at the funeral."

"Be discreet," cautioned Arturo. "I don't want the authorities to know we are working in concert."

The count inclined his head in mock severity and turned on his heels, closing the door quietly behind him.

Arturo turned his attention to Fiona. He removed his

glasses and wiped them clean with his handkerchief. Clearing his throat, Arturo asked Fiona, "How did he treat you?"

"What do you mean, how did Sergio treat me? Arturo, what do you want to know?"

He shrugged, "There are things I need to know about your life with Sergio. I want to understand."

"What things?"

"How you could meet a member of the Camorra and marry him. And how, in all the years you slept with him, you never suspected a thing."

Arturo stood still waiting for her to slap him.

"How could I be happy with a drug dealer? Someone who preyed on the weak and destroyed what little dignity they had? Sergio traveled a lot on business. When he came home, it was like a holiday. Everyone around us was happy and entertained. I worked in solitude in my studio, and my only sense of friendship was dining at the Osteria Margutta, a family-run tavern, down the street from my home. Sergio gave me a glamorous life and the freedom to create. I entertained his clients and his vendors. He never brought any strange people or rough business around. He loved me. I know he did."

"Have you been happy?"

"Happy? For a while, yes. I think so. Everything was going smoothly. My life seemed to have a rhythm. But in the last year, no. I looked back at the last year or longer and realized I was unhappy. I just wouldn't admit it."

"What happened? Was he jealous?"

Fiona rolled her eyes and exclaimed, "Sergio was Italian. He was always a little jealous. But it was never a problem."

"What was it then?"

"He stayed away for longer periods of time and when he came home, he never shared any stories about his business trip. In the early stages of our marriage, Sergio delighted in telling me about the treasures he found in attics or in a barn. He would embellish the story to make me laugh. But later he returned silent, withdrawn, and sometimes he'd be irritable and provoke an argument. I thought the argument was an excuse so that he could leave for the day, return late, still in a foul mood. He never explained his mood, where he had been and the next morning he would act like nothing happened."

"Did you feel the strain, the tension? How could you paint?"

"Are you kidding? I painted like crazy. All the time. I had a caffè with my fellow artists and spent time with my best friend, Valentina, who owns a frame shop near the Trevi Fountain. It was a simple routine but separate from my married life."

"Did Sergio ever threaten you?"

"Only last night. It was horrible. I had had enough. I decided only last night to get a divorce."

"So now you feel guilty since he was killed?"

"Yes."

"He's a killer. Any drug dealer is a killer. And he would have killed you. Think what it was like. He'd kill someone or order them killed and then come home to you, take off his clothes and slip into bed beside you, give you a good night kiss, an embrace ..."

"Basta!" Fiona was sobbing.

"No. You have to listen to me, Fiona. I am trying to force you to see Sergio for what he was: a monster. Confront the truth and become strong. You cannot deal with any pain or loss until you recognize the truth. Sergio exposed you to a cesspool of criminal thugs. I am trying to save your life."

Fiona felt her whole body shake and knew she was close to hysterics. She forced herself to listen. She calmed down as Arturo's words swept over her, wiped her face and stood up straight. "Va bene. I'll take the first step of my freedom from his filth."

Without saying another word, Arturo swept his eyes around the room.

Catching his eye movement, Fiona said, "There's nothing more to search. I was thorough. I need to identify the body. The carabinieri told me."

"His father could. Has he been informed?"

At that exact moment, the phone rang and they both turned at the same time to locate the trilling of the phone in another room. Fiona ran into the bathroom and saw a blinking light on the phone. It was a second phone line she had not noticed previously.

"Pronto. Si, this is Signora Celesti." Fiona listened to the message from the front desk. She cupped her phone over the receiver and called to Arturo, "May I have some paper and a pen?"

Arturo arrived with the writing implements and closed the door when he left. She sat down on a small stool by the vanity table and started writing. It was a message from Sergio's father and contact information. "I understand the message. Do you know if the carabinieri have been informed of this call? No, you don't know. Va bene. Grazie." Fiona hung up the phone and reread the message. She took a big breath and walked out of the room.

"Arturo, it was message from Antonio, Sergio's father. The carabinieri called him in Rome and he's on his way to Positano. He'll stop by the hotel once he's arrived. I think

I'll let him identify Sergio. Antonio offered and said he would handle the carabinieri and the local police so they won't be intrusive. I just cannot do it." Her voice cracked, she sighed and drew in her breath. "I don't mean to be weak. It's just too much to absorb. Sergio's death, his life."

Fiona started crying and turned her face away to wipe the tears. Arturo got up and gently wrapped his arms around her as if comforting a wounded child. He rocked her back and forth and said, "You'll be all right. Soon. Everything will be all right. I promise. I'm here and will not leave you."

"I'll call down and leave a message with Piero to get in touch with the carabinieri. They can be notified of Antonio's imminent arrival. We can make decisions about everything else once he's arrived." And with that, he started dialing the phone.

They rested in Fiona's room, each lost in their own thoughts. Fiona waited for the phone to ring announcing Antonio Celesti's arrival. Finally, the phone rang.

"Pronto. Ciao, Antonio. No, I'm fine. It's terrible and my heart breaks for you. I'll be down in the lobby in a minute. I'll bring an old college friend with me who's been helping me. Give me a few minutes. Thanks."

Fiona sat quietly for a minute, collecting her composure. "I'll just dash some cold water on my face and then we can go down to meet him." She looked at Arturo for agreement, saw it and went into the bathroom to freshen up. "Let's go."

Arturo walked with Fiona into the lobby and waited to meet Antonio. He stood several paces away as Fiona went into her father-in-law's arms for a hug. It was an awkward meeting with not much being said. Fiona considered her father-in-law practically a stranger and felt herself stiffen under his examination. She looked back and saw an older man, well-kept and fit, immaculately dressed and groomed. He was a tall man and handsome.

Fiona whispered something to Antonio and he wheeled around to greet Arturo. "Antonio, may I present Arturo Monti, an old friend from Boston who happened to be visiting Capri this summer. Arturo, my father-in-law, Antonio Celesti." She looked back and forth at the two men, smiling during each introduction. Fiona realized that she was relieved to have gotten through the social necessities without stumbling over the words.

"Piacere, a pleasure. I'm sorry to meet you under such tragic circumstances. Please accept my condolences," Arturo said while shaking the older man's hand. He looked into yellow-green eyes, which quickly were assessing him. They were dry-eyed and clear.

"Thank you for your kind words. I appreciate your being here to help Fiona. It's important for Fiona to have friends at the moment. Let's go into the lounge so we can discuss how to deal with the police and other pressing matters. Va bene?"

Antonio took Fiona's arm and escorted her into the lounge. Arturo followed and thought about what he had just heard. Antonio did not waste words and acted as if he were conducting a business meeting. Perhaps this is how he treated grief, or maybe he wanted to get the arrangements dealt with in an efficient manner. He joined them at an alcove table. Arturo noticed the table had been preset with a carafe of water and coffee.

"I already contacted the carabinieri. Colonel Beltrani heads up a small investigatory unit focusing on Camorra activities. I got here a little while ago and made arrangements to have them drive me to the morgue. It's easier this way. I don't want to bother you. I'd also like to organize the funeral. It should be held in Naples at the family church. How does this sound to you, Fiona?"

"It's for the best. I don't know anyone here, and I can understand you would want the funeral and burial to be in Naples. Thank you for going with the carabinieri for the viewing," Fiona's voice cracked, "I don't think I could do it." Fiona gave a little shudder and reached for a glass of water. She almost spilled it getting it to her lips but recovered her poise.

"I'll call you from Naples once I've organized a schedule and stay there rather than return to Positano. I suggest you check into the Hotel Excelsior in Naples. This evening, in fact. I made reservations." He looked at Fiona for confirmation of his plan.

"Antonio, the carabinieri have made accusations about Sergio's criminal activities. I don't know anything about this."

"Fiona, I regret to admit I cannot shed any light on this. My life was with my second family and at the bank. Sergio lived a separate life as soon as he graduated from school. He didn't want to attend a university and refused a training program at the family bank. He chose to pursue a career in antique dealing. It must have seemed like easy money." Antonio's voice hardened as he spoke. "I don't want to be involved in this. I chose to stay away and keep my family safe," he muttered. "Now, let me attend to the carabinieri and the church arrangements. I'll leave word for you at the Excelsior. Va bene?"

Antonio quickly got to his feet, not waiting for a response. Fiona looked at him as if he had thrown a glass of water onto her face.

Arturo put a hand on her arm to calm her. Speaking

slowly, Arturo said, "We understand and will wait to hear from you. Thank you for helping." Arturo stood up to shake Antonio's hand.

"Very well. Ciao for now."

"That was worse than I expected," Fiona paused as her voice cracked and she continued in a whisper, "Antonio must have known all these years about his son's criminal activities. He must have hated Sergio." Fiona shuddered and looked at Arturo for agreement.

"You'll never know. We need to stay focused on today and how to get you out of this mess. What do you feel like doing?"

"I want to go look at the crash site. I want to see where Sergio spent the morning so I can understand it's real. I have to accept it."

"Okay. We'll take my car. Andiamo."

They walked to the valet and got into the car. Arturo drove carefully out of the car park and along the Amalfi Drive. Fiona stared at the countryside rather than over the cliff and the spectacular view of the Mediterranean. They slowed down as they came to uniformed polizia and the carabinieri. Arturo lowered his window and identified themselves to the policeman. They were flagged over to a parking spot. Fiona breathed in deeply, exhaled and got out of the car. She looked over the edge of the cliff to the bottom of the sea. Waves battered the jagged rocks. She saw a police boat with a few officers looking overboard.

A young policeman came up to her and said, "The motorcycle and the body were already removed. We are getting ready to leave." He hesitated and said, "I'm sorry for your loss, Signora."

"Prego. May I stay here and just look at the spot for a moment? I won't be long."

"Certo." The policeman went back to his motorcycle. The carabinieri already had left.

"Are you all right?" Arturo was by her side, looking at her with concern in his eyes.

"Yes. This is enough. I know where Sergio died. He's gone. And I needed to see this to absorb it. To visualize it. Just a few moments more and we'll leave. I know they want to resume normal traffic on such a busy road."

"I'll be in the car. Take your time."

Fiona looked out at the sea, at the horizon line and whispered a prayer. She thought to herself that she'd seen enough and it was time to go. She turned and waved to the policeman, shouting her thanks. Fiona jumped into the car and said, "Va bene. I'm ready to go to work." She hoped her voice sounded forceful.

They went back to Il San Pietro and went up to Fiona's room. Arturo was surprised to see her moving around briskly, organizing her pocketbook. Soon all the bags were packed, including a sleek black Gucci duffle, Sergio's bag. Impressed by her rapid pace, Arturo said, "Fill me in. Do you have a clue to the whereabouts of the Caravaggio?"

Fiona looked into her pocketbook and handed him a scrap of paper.

It was a page torn out of a book with columns of numbers written on it. Arturo studied it:

3 9 15 21

15 6 9 27

24 33 12 3

"Some sort of code, a cipher. It makes no sense without a key. It's a classic one-on-one cipher because it's only known between two people, the sender and the receiver. It's impossible to crack without the key. This page is torn from a book?"

"I found the folded page under Sergio's pillow. Sergio didn't leave a book behind in his belongings. It must be on the island. It has to be! I'll have to search the villa. Do you want to go to Capri with me? We'll take the Riva, the hotel's launch."

"Let's go now. I'll settle the bill and we'll go to the hotel's dock. Let's hope the count doesn't see us. Presto!"

Fiona gave him a grim smile.

"Va bene."

Capri

CAPRI

AUGUST 5, 1985

EARLY AFTERNOON

The gleaming Riva dropped Fiona and Arturo off at Marina Grande. The captain instructed his mate to tie up the launch and he settled down to wait for the couple's return.

Arturo followed Fiona. She obviously had a plan, he thought, as they walked purposely away from the docks to board the funicular, the oldest but fastest way to reach the center of town.

Fiona looked out over the harbor and, for a moment, there was only the wind and the sea. Their creaky climb up the cliff was never long enough to capture the intensity of the sapphire-blue water and sky. Arturo and Fiona landed at the platform and disembarked with the other tourists, blending quickly into the crowded streets of Capri.

"Let's pick up my Vespa in the town lot. But first, I need to collect my easel and art supply bag at the café in the piazzetta. Sergio may have slipped something into the bag before Umberto dropped by for a visit. Stefano, the bartender, must have it. At least, I hope so!"

Fiona quickly led the way to the café and entered the dimly lit bar. After greeting Stefano with a warm hug, Fiona quickly claimed her belongings. She tipped the bartender and said they'd be back soon.

They walked to the parking lot and Fiona knelt down, opened the bag to examine the contents. It was a jumble of paint tubes and brushes but hidden underneath was a small book.

"Ha!" Fiona exclaimed, "It's a copy of Dante's *Inferno*. She compared the folded page she'd found in the hotel room to the book, nodded to the match and said, "Look, the numbers correspond to line sections in the book." She passed the book to Arturo.

Arturo riffled through the pages, noticed the slight pencil markings on the pages and tapped the book in his hand. "There is something here, a clue, but we need more of the code. Let's go. We'll examine it in my car."

Fiona put the book in her purse and, after repacking the art supplies, hopped on the Vespa. Fiona revved the tiny engine and the bike sped out of the lot. They wound their way down the paved road and turned sharply onto a dirt path. There were no other people on these dusty hills of Capri, the deserted land of the Roman emperor, Tiberius. Arturo and Fiona parked the Vespa and walked to the ruined imperial palace.

Fiona felt the past lives of the ancient world. The remains of Villa Jovis were a maze of Roman brick. The walls and floors were all interspersed with grass and wildflowers. The emperor's living quarters, loggia and terrace extended to the edge of the cliff with a columned terrace overlooking the grandest scenery in the world. It was on this hillside that the emperor decided life or death for his subjects. The lingering effect was of something pressed between two opposing forces: ambition and obliteration.

"It was here one day during the summer," Fiona recounted, "that I found Sergio hiding something."

She led the way down the worn stones with Arturo following close behind. All the while, Arturo surveyed the area looking for any strangers watching them. He was relieved to see they were alone.

They walked down a clear path leading to the ruins, which were honeycombed into the eastern peak of the island. Fiona examined a particular stone, took a knife from her bag and began chiseling at the crumbling stone. She managed to poke a small hole. Slowly, still using her knife, Fiona edged a small, green, waterproofed-wrapped package out of the cavity. She opened the tiny bundle and found a key.

Fiona fingered both sides of the key and looked up with bewilderment showing in her eyes, "It's an unusual shape. I'm not familiar with it. Are you?"

She placed the key in the palm of his hand.

Rolling the key around in his hand, he said, "It's a key to a bank vault." Arturo cleared his throat, "My company has business with many banks. I've seen the shape of this key before. Look, there's a number imprinted on it."

Arturo held the key in one hand as he pointed to the printed numbers. Fiona noticed that the numbers were etched into the metal.

"I can contact my office and have someone locate the bank for you," Arturo said. "Do you know of any banks Sergio used for storage of valuables? This may be the key to a safety-deposit vault."

"No. It's another mystery to me. One day, I decided on the spur of the moment to knock off painting and, on a whim, I headed for Villa Jovis. It was a little overcast so I decided to go hiking in the area. I rounded a path and saw someone acting suspiciously by an old ruined wall. I suddenly recognized Sergio and ducked down behind some scraggly bushes. At first, I thought Sergio had found some Roman antique coin, but I quickly realized he was stuffing something into a crevice in the stone ruin. I was struck by how strange he was acting and became frightened. Sergio had such an odd look on his face and he kept scanning the area to make sure he was alone. I hung back, not making a sound. Sergio finally left and chose another path. Thank God. I waited a long time and crept away. I don't think I was seen by anyone."

"Was this fairly recent?"

"Yes. Within the last two weeks. I knew he was worried about business but didn't want to ask him about the hiding place. Frankly, I was frightened to ask him. I decided to bide my time and hoped he would eventually confide in me."

Despite the sunshine, Fiona shivered, took a deep breath and sharply steadied her nerves. She turned back to the ruin, wedged the stone back into the cranny and pocketed the key.

They returned to the Vespa and drove to the villa. She checked on Guido and saw he had been fed and exercised by the maid. Arturo sat on the terrace, playing with the dog as Fiona inspected the villa. She was grateful Arturo respected her need for privacy. Fiona decided that she would share her secret worries with him, but only when she was ready. She came out onto the terrace with glasses and a bottle of chilled Pellegrino. They drank in silence while Fiona petted the dog. She was lost in thought but not defeated. Fiona knew she relied on Arturo's strength of character and his business judgment. She was glad she was not alone in this terrible situation.

"Niente, nothing." Fiona shook her head and continued, "There's a note from the maid saying she'll continue to care for Guido. We'll leave the Vespa at the harbor. Let's go to Naples."

After Fiona hugged her dog farewell, she nodded to Arturo and they left the villa. Fiona started the Vespa and Arturo hopped on, steadying his ride by holding tightly onto Fiona. They motored the hills descending into the Marina Grande. The Riva was waiting for them at the harbor. Fiona and Arturo sat quietly in the bow and basked in the sunlight. Soon, they were back at San Pietro. Fiona took the captain's hand as she jumped onto the hotel's deck. Arturo followed and generously tipped the captain. They quickly assembled their luggage, paid their bills and Arturo ordered his car. Upon ascending in the ancient elevator, Fiona looked around the tiny windswept parking lot. She murmured to herself, "Bye-bye, Sergio. Sleep well." She looked with tears at the brilliant water and shimmering horizon and said, "I'm ready, Arturo."

"Va bene. Andiamo." Arturo smiled and revved the engine. They were off.

Naples

AUGUST 5, 1985

LATE AFTERNOON

Fiona sat upright in the car as Arturo tore through the dark streets. The city of Naples looked as if it were a war zone, not a major city of southern Italy. It had long ago conceded its political and economic power to Rome after the unification of the regional states. There were no lights in the squalid apartment buildings. Most street lamps were dark and the few shining were dim. What she managed to see was not appealing. Giant mounds of garbage bags littered the sidewalks and overflowed onto the streets. Rats prowled the putrid debris and scurried into the shadows as the car's lights beamed onto the mess. The flies must be having a feast, Fiona thought. Naples was living up to its reputation of firsts, such as having the most polluted waterfront and air in Italy. What a hellhole.

See Naples and die? The refrain echoed in her mind. The ancient city gate of Porta Capuana served as a picture frame for her first gaze of Naples. The once-proud gate was a remnant left over from the industrious building by an Aragonese king. Names such as "Hope" and "Victory" decorated the intermittent towers still visible along the road. The decrepit walls once fortified the bustling city. "Honor" and "Virtue" were the names incised onto the two round towers flanking the gate at Porta Capuana. The moat was dry; the celebrated outdoor theater was now the grimy Piazza San Francesco. In the morning, Piazza San Francesco would be overflowing with small, battered cars that were using it as a commercial parking lot. It was worn, dirty and dark.

The Lancia slid on the oily lava road and Arturo made a fast correction. He continued to grip the wheel and struggled to make small talk to lessen the feeling of gloom in the car.

"We're almost at the Hotel Excelsior. It's a grand old hotel, but slightly shabby as one would expect." Arturo quickly looked over at Fiona to see if she was still calm. He continued with his well-intentioned summary of their accommodations, "We'll be overlooking the harbor. At least the view will be pleasant and there should be a cooling breeze." Arturo's voice was pitched to high as if he were trying to gain Fiona's attention. He suddenly blurted, "We need to concentrate on the present so we can find the Caravaggio."

"Arturo, thank you for being so kind to me. I'll be stronger tomorrow," Fiona murmured.

"Did the book reveal any of Sergio's business secrets?"

"I only decoded a few words about drugs. Sergio may have used a ledger system of numbers and stored the code elsewhere. I'll study the book again once I'm in my room. Do you mind waiting?"

"We can't act on any information until after the funeral. I'm fine."

"I want you to keep the key. I trust you and you'll keep it safe. Maybe you'll recall the bank it belongs to?" Fiona was holding up the key and slid it into his hand.

"Okay."

"There's a Caravaggio painting at a museum in the city. Would you like to see it? We can go tomorrow and then you'll realize the quality of the picture we're hunting. I promise to give you an abbreviated art history lecture about the Baroque period of art." Fiona looked at Arturo and gave him a broad smile.

"That's a plan," Arturo smiled back all the while thinking that he was happy to see Fiona engaged in the future and absorbed in the world of art. They were back on familiar ground.

Fiona and Arturo reached the tree-shaded waterfront esplanade of Santa Lucia with a row of luxury hotels lining the magnificent harbor. Pleasure boats docked at the nearby marina were illuminated by spotlights. The outline of Vesuvius seemed to burst out of the water in the distance. White-linen-draped tables were set out in the hope of attracting strolling couples. It was late so the Excelsior's café was quiet and ready to close. Members of the orchestra quartet already had shut their instruments' cases. The Lancia practically squealed into the hotel's entranceway and they gave the keys of the car over to the doorman.

A brilliantly lit lobby with ornate crystal chandeliers greeted their bleary eyes. Heavy, overstuffed sofas covered in crimson-flocked velvet were scattered around the lobby; interspersed were gilded Empire-style tables sprinkled with modern Capodimonte figurines that seemed to dance along the marble tops.

The front desk was manned by an elderly man with a short brush cut. He clicked his heels and came to attention as he greeted them. Processing their passport information with efficiency, the old man looked both of them in the eyes and thanked them for waiting. Arturo and Fiona collected their passports and turned to a uniformed bellhop. The man collected their luggage and pressed a button for the elevator.

They were shown their rooms with efficiency and were left alone in Fiona's suite. The silence dragged and tension hovered in the main salon. Arturo gave Fiona a quick hug and said, "A *domani*, see you tomorrow."

Fiona looked at Arturo with steady eyes, nodded and said, "I'll be ready."

The door clicked behind him. Fiona looked at her luggage and rummaged around her large Louis Vuitton duffle bag. She quickly drew out the book and reattached the torn pages. Fiona scrutinized the text and the columns of numbers. She sat down on the big bed, stretched out and began to read. Sergio had used the copy of Dante's *Inferno* as his personal business journal: one composed of columns of numbers and the other a repetition of coded words. Fiona needed more columns of numbers to find the Caravaggio.

Beside her, the alarm clock was beating out the seconds and moving its illuminated hands. A click from the alarm clock signaled every passing hour. There were a few muted traffic sounds outside her window but the abutting rooms were quiet. At midnight, Fiona finished her examination of the book. Tomorrow she'd share the coded information with Arturo. Unfortunately, there was very little information gleaned from translating or decoding the columns by reading Dante's *Inferno*. She needed more columns, Fiona said to herself. There must be pages of numbers stored somewhere, she clucked her tongue. Fiona forced herself to imagine how Sergio thought, to think like Sergio and discover his secret hiding spot. The cipher would reveal the secrets of his illicit business. It would reveal dates of payments, shipments of drugs or stolen artwork.

She yanked the covers off and got up to sit at a carved wood vanity. There was a mirror in front of her. She looked directly into the old Venetian-styled glass. The mirror was dark with age and was an old flatterer. Fiona stared into her image, trying to assess her character in the reflection. She wondered how she could have been such a colossal dupe. Gradually, she became aware of someone quietly moving in the hallway. It seemed as if the person hesitated at her door. Fiona pressed her fingers onto the main light switch of her suite and watched the door. The handle never moved and suddenly she knew the mysterious presence had left. She looked out the window and up at the invisible sky. There was no movement below or in the hallway. A vast silence gradually took hold, but she could not sleep.

When she finally drifted off, nightmares haunted her. Flames engulfed her and she could not find Sergio. Fiona came gasping to life. She'd been in a deep sleep. Dreaming again of fires engulfing her while Sergio was gazing at her, or was it the long-dead Caravaggio?

Fiona got up for a drink of water and picked up the book. After pulling the covers back up over the bed, she put the copy of Dante's *Inferno* under her pillow and drifted into a fitful sleep. She awoke with a start and was relieved she was alone.

Fiona dressed quickly, slung her pocketbook over her shoulder and glided out the door. Arturo was waiting for her in the lobby.

"Shall we breakfast on the harbor?"

"Absolutely." Fiona took Arturo's arm and they sauntered out to a café overlooking the harbor. The sky was brilliantly clear and the salt air enlivened her senses. The waiter served a platter of biscotti and cappuccinos. Fiona and Arturo munched, drank their fill and were content in the sunshine. Fiona looked at Arturo and decided to broach the subject of going to the museum immediately after breakfast.

"There's an important Caravaggio, the *Flagellation of Christ*, at the Museo di Capodimonte. How about driving over to it? It's not an easy ride, however, as we need to take the Tangenziale, which usually has heavy traffic, but at least we've missed rush hour."

"Fine. It's the best time to go. Let's order the car and have one more caffè while we wait? Va bene?"

Fiona nodded her head and Arturo summoned the waiter, ordered more coffee and his car. They did not linger over the coffee and went over to the parking attendant.

Fiona and Arturo sped away and drove up the winding road to the grand Bourbon palazzo in the Capodimonte park. While Arturo drove, Fiona explained that Charles VII, king of Naples and Sicily, built the Capodimonte to house his art collection and his mother's art collection, the Farnese collection. The museum was a national treasure and the *Flagellation* was installed on the second floor.

After they parked the Lancia, they strolled through the extensive gardens of the surrounding park. The land overlooked a magnificent view of Naples and, for a few moments, Arturo and Fiona enjoyed the birdsong and the fresh, citrusy air – a powerful scent from the grove of lemon trees. The garden was awash with blooming roses, not yet wilted by the Neapolitan sizzling heat. Fiona stroked Arturo's arm and said, "Che bella."

"Yes, you can find peace here," Arturo responded. "But now, let's enter the world of the Baroque for a while. We don't have a lot of time as we must get back to the hotel soon. Antonio will be trying to reach you."

The museum guide directed them to the second floor and they stood in awe of Caravaggio's masterpiece. Fiona broke the silence by saying, "Caravaggio painted the *Flagellation* in 1607, toward the end of his life. Caravaggio was a gifted but tormented man, and I think this painting demonstrates the darkness of his art and character."

Fiona continued, "Caravaggio had a tumultuous life. He was born in Milan during the plague – the plague that killed his father and grandfather on the same day. His life became divided through his feudal loyalty to the great family that had protected him throughout his stormy, short life. He grew into a conflicted man as he led a life of a courtier, painting religious pictures and protected by the church. Away from the households of cardinals, however, Caravaggio was a man of the streets, gambling and consorting with criminals in brothels. Caravaggio could not control his temper and he murdered a man over a game of tennis. No doubt, a wager was involved," Fiona rolled her eyes.

"He fled Rome knowing the pope would excommunicate him and there would be a warrant for his arrest. His painter's vision portrayed the poor and suffering while capturing the richness of his belief in spirituality. I believe," Fiona's hand dramatically swept over the painting, "the *Flagellation,* one of his most important paintings, helped transform the Neapolitan art world. Caravaggio's new manner of using shadow and focused light on the subject conveyed a more natural depiction of his subject matter: figurative painting. Caravaggio fused his remarkable ability to capture the essence of a realistic scene while demonstrating his complete devotion to the spirituality of the Catholic faith. His technique was revolutionary. He used simple street people as models, never bothering to clean them up. He painted their dirty feet and hands, their shabby clothes."

Fiona inhaled deeply and continued, "Caravaggio developed naturalism, a true revolution in style, and altered the course of Neapolitan painting. He enjoyed immense success and all its attendant riches after finishing several altarpieces in Naples. Despite being on the run, he had a burst of creativity in the last years of his life spent in Naples. Caravaggio was at his height of fame in Naples, and suddenly he fled to Malta in 1607. The small fortress island offered none of the trappings of success Caravaggio so appreciated. Yet, the island fortress offered something very appealing to the scrappy artist: knighthood. Overnight, Caravaggio, the man from a humble background, was an equal to the leading nobility of his day. Social rank mattered to Caravaggio, and he happily painted portraits of his benefactors in the Knights of Malta."

"While in Malta," Fiona paused dramatically, waited a beat and resumed, "Caravaggio's fame increased in Rome and he was summoned by the pope. The pope demonstrated his compassion and support of the wayward artist by commissioning and paying for two new pictures. This benevolent act, a papal pardon, allowed the artist to return to Rome under safe passage. Caravaggio immediately started the pope's paintings and also painted portable pictures, a form of tribute to his many benefactors. Caravaggio yearned for his return to fame, fortune and a luxurious life in Rome. Along with the pope's pardon, that was once again within his reach. *The Flagellation of Christ* was a dark and tragic work as it showed Christ in an awkward pose, drooping at an odd angle from having been beaten by two workmen. Christ is painted in a dark, Neapolitan dungeon and is isolated, held by one thug as another brutally kicks his knee. Look how a shaft of light from the left sweeps over Christ's body, creating a picture of transcendent brightness." Fiona swept her arm along the arc of light in the painting and looked at Arturo.

Arturo nodded his comprehension and Fiona continued her critique of the artist and of his life. "The viewer is encouraged to meditate on the sorrows of the Flagellation, how Christ was treated as a common criminal, humbled himself and was condemned by man. Perhaps the painting addressed the concerns of the flagellant community. This community was present in Naples but hidden away from the general public as they practiced their self-torture alone with a single light shining on an image of Christ in the darkness."

Fiona looked over at Arturo and stopped to catch her breath. She continued, "A good docent knows when to quit," she rolled her eyes, "when her audience cannot absorb any more information." She winked and said, "And now for lunch out in the park?"

"Basta, enough!" exclaimed Arturo. "Thanks. That was just enough art history. You gauged your audience well!" Arturo gave Fiona a broad smile. "That was a splendid overview, and I have a true appreciation for the caliber of the painting we need to find. I can understand the importance of its beauty and place in history. I can also comprehend its monetary value." Arturo took Fiona's arm and they walked down the grand marble steps leading to the entrance.

"Do you notice how long and shallow the steps are?" Fiona pointed at the worn marble. "They were made to accommodate the horses so the courtiers would not have to walk up the stairs."

"Basta così." Arturo made a face as if in mock fury and said, "No more historical facts. I want a good lunch!"

They found a café nestled in the shade of a corner of the palazzo. Fiona savored an insalata Caprese, the heirloom-tomato-and-mozzarella-cheese salad she had enjoyed all summer long in Capri. Arturo enjoyed a plate of spaghetti alle vongole, angel hair pasta loaded with tiny clams, so much his chin dripped with olive oil. He wiped his face one last time and signaled for the bill.

"All good things must end. Let's get back to the Excelsior and our messages."

Upon entering her suite of rooms, Fiona found several sealed envelopes from the reception desk. Ripping them open, she read the messages: They all asked for her to call Antonio. She telephoned her father-in-law and learned that all the funeral arrangements were made. The funeral would be tomorrow, in the morning. Fiona agreed to Antonio's wishes and sat down to review all that happened. She then called Arturo to alert him to be ready in the early morning for Sergio's funeral.

She was ready for bed. As Fiona got under the covers, she took some time to reflect. Fiona felt as if she were adrift in the sway of Antonio. Once the burial arrangements were confirmed, it seemed like everything was moving at a rapid pace, and only Arturo managed to shape some of it to her advantage. He was the sole person thinking of her feelings and how much her life had changed overnight. Thank goodness for Arturo, she thought to herself. Not only could she rely on him, she also enjoyed his company. Fiona realized she had regained her strength, her confidence through his help. It was a nice feeling to have such a loving man by her side, Fiona mused. I hope I deserve it, she thought to herself.

The next morning, filtered shafts of daylight struck the lobby as Fiona strode purposely toward the entrance to greet Antonio Celesti. He was holding himself erect and his full silver mane was well-combed. His suit was dark with a sober tie. A typical funeral attire for a proper Roman banker, thought Fiona. She saw resignation and sadness in his gray eyes. Although he was well-tanned from his holiday, his face was drawn with fatigue lines. Arturo joined them.

Fiona reintroduced the two men. "May Arturo ride with us to the cathedral?"

"Certo. My car is out front. I have a driver who will take us to the service. Shall we go?"

Fiona wanted to perpetuate the fantasy of Sergio having a close, loving family, but Antonio's attitude quickly shattered this image. She realized he was resigned to honoring his family duty to his lost son. His behavior reflected cold, civil manners. Fiona sensed that there was a longstanding strain between Sergio and his stepmother. After all, Antonio was the sole representative of Sergio's family at the funeral. It was sad that Sergio's young mother died while giving birth to him at home in Naples, Fiona thought to herself. Despite the talk and gossip, Antonio moved to Rome with baby Sergio and never returned to Naples.

Fiona knew she'd never hear from Antonio again. He would turn his back on her, his son's widow.

With a quick step, Fiona walked to the limousine and climbed into the back. Arturo clambered in and sat beside her with Antonio across from them. There was a strained pause in the sleek, spotless compartment. She looked out the window and watched the stone clusters of terraced apartment buildings slide past. Fiona heard Arturo, once again, try to alleviate an awkward situation by promoting a discussion about Roman politics with her father-in-law. A smile glanced fleetingly over her face as she realized how fortunate she was to have Arturo helping her.

Fiona allowed her thoughts to drift while the two men were thus engaged. She knew they were going to the Cathedral of San Gennaro, and Fiona thought back to the last time she visited this area of Naples. She had been an art student and had read about the history of the city, along with its numerous art treasures. San Gennaro was a socially prominent cathedral located on the wide Via Duomo. The cathedral was placed on a stretch of road, providing a breath of fresh air in a woefully crowded district. The city fathers chose this strategic location when they demolished Old Naples after the cholera epidemic in 1884. The poor were kept at bay so that all church business could be conducted in an orderly, quiet fashion. Although the city fathers cleared many of its old slums, underlying conditions remained the same and a subsequent cholera outbreak occurred in the 1970s.

The limousine stopped at the cathedral's entrance on the paved stones, and they walked into the gloomy entrance. The cathedral's interior was embossed with sumptuous gold decorations and marble mosaics, all funded by the poor of Naples. It was the only beauty in their lives. San Gennaro still attracted the old noble families, perhaps due to the legend of its patron saint: Several vials of San Gennaro's blood miraculously would liquefy three times a year, thus protecting the Neapolitans. At least, this was the official story presented to the world and published regularly in the Italian papers. Superstition was rampant in Naples.

"Has your family been long-standing members of this parish?" Fiona asked Antonio.

"Sergio's beloved mother always attended Mass at San Gennaro," Antonio's voice faltered, and he cleared his throat with a violent cough. He made the sign of the cross and kissed his fingers. Antonio continued, "Her funeral was here. I thought this would be a symbolic link to the past for Sergio. He'll rest with her in the family plot. There are beautiful cypress trees surrounding the land, and there is a panoramic view of the city. It's truly removed from the cacophony of modern-day life …" Antonio broke off the sentence as he swiveled his eyes upon someone else. He called out, "Ah, Father Mannato, the representatives of the family have arrived. It's a small group, but we are all here!"

Fiona peered into the dusky gloom and saw a priest costumed in white vestments. The priest briefly glanced at them, clicked on the lights, dispelling the gloom. He walked towards them briskly, his frock swinging to and fro around his ankles and across his black patent leather shoes. Although the room's temperature was cool, the priest was perspiring profusely. Mopping his face with a handkerchief, he seemed flustered when he realized Fiona was staring at him. She quickly averted her gaze and sighed. She could see the chapel in the distance, set with elaborate chased silver pieces and decorated with white flowers and greenery. She knew the wooden outline must be her husband's casket and she gave an involuntary shudder. Fiona rearranged her lace mantilla and shook the offered hand of the priest. It was clammy and wet with perspiration.

"A sad day, my dear. I christened Sergio and now am here at the end. I celebrated his mother's funeral. Antonio, the others are already seated. I think we are complete as no one has wandered in for the last fifteen minutes. Shall we begin?" Father Mannato arched his bushy eyebrows, paused and silently disappeared. Antonio led Fiona and Arturo up the aisle to the private chapel. They sat down with no acknowledgment to the grieving witnesses.

Arturo squared his shoulders and glanced around the chapel. He spent no time on the flower-bedecked altar or near the casket as he surreptitiously examined the mourners. Beside Antonio and Fiona, no other family members seemed to be present as this was a certain type of crowd: Although they were well-dressed, their faces were shuttered. No visible signs of grief registered on their faces. There were no women mourners present. The men were of all ages. They were rough in appearance, despite their expensive clothes and highly groomed hair. Some smoked in the pews, not caring if they were being rude. They ground their cigarette butts into the marble floor, and some suffered from a hacking smoker's cough. On the whole, they sat quietly and detached from the three of them.

No one looked Arturo in the eye as he stared at them one by one. They simply looked straight ahead or stared at the casket. He felt, but did not see, a presence in the back. Someone was standing there acting as a sentinel. A bullet could ricochet endlessly off the marble wall, Arturo thought to himself. His mind raced with further images of siege: It was possible they could be attacked at any time.

Arturo wondered if Count Volpe would attend the service. He did not see him in the group.

There was a rustling of vestments and a smell of incense. Arturo looked behind him and saw two altar boys swinging antique metal buckets of incense. A swirl of smoke followed them down the aisle. The priest walked majestically behind them and reached the altar. Father Mannato proceeded with his blessings. The Mass was celebrated and the motley group of mourners shuffled up to be blessed.

Arturo stared at Antonio and noticed the older man had clamped down on his jaw and compressed his lips into a slim line of flesh. As the service droned on, Antonio sat more erect, rigid and tightly composed. Arturo was curious about Antonio's feelings for being at the burial. Arturo did not trust Antonio or his motivations after reading the detective's file on him. Arturo discovered that the file made for interesting reading as Antonio Celesti was more than just an average Italian banker. Yet, Arturo had held back this information from Fiona. He knew she had enough to deal with today and, after all, perhaps Antonio's emotions were raging about the death of his son. Arturo did not want a confrontation with Antonio at this time. Antonio looked furious, but Arturo didn't feel sorry for him.

All during the service, Fiona sat rigidly between the two men. Out of the corner of his eye, Arturo saw Count Volpe scoot into a pew. The count winked surreptitiously but said nothing. He sat quietly and studiously examined his nails as if he'd never seen them before.

At last, the ritual of the funeral mass ended and the priest retreated to the rear of the chapel. They filed out and joined the priest at the entrance. Arturo was impatient to talk with Count Volpe but stayed close to Fiona's side. He saw Antonio speak softly to Father Mannato and then loudly thank him for attending to the family's concerns. Antonio pressed a small envelope into Father Mannato's hand and backed away. The priest smiled at him and then turned abruptly, causing his frock to wrap around his legs. When it settled back in place, he stepped forward and invited them to follow.

Count Volpe nodded to Arturo and made gestures with one hand to join him. The other mourners huddled near the priest, who eventually announced that they would now adjourn to the cemetery. People could assemble their cars and would be given banners proclaiming they were in a funeral procession. The ragged caravan of mourners was led by the hearse and their black limousine. There were a few worn Fiats following them and one new Mercedes sedan. Count Volpe was being driven by a well-dressed chauffeur and a burly man sat in the passenger side. Arturo wondered if they were his bodyguards. Arturo found himself swept quickly outside and back into the limousine with Fiona by his side.

Arturo spoke gingerly, "Antonio, did you recognize anyone? Were there any friends or business associates of Sergio?"

With a grimace, Antonio sighed and said, "I wasn't familiar with Sergio's business or his associates. Sergio had lost track of his old school friends. I didn't recognize anyone." He replied while brushing away nonexistent lint from the sleeves of his dark suit. It was more a nervous tick to keep his hands and mind busy. Antonio slumped in his seat.

"We're almost there. You'll see a large white marble

mausoleum. It will not be a long ceremony." Antonio finished the last sentence and rubbed his temple.

The limousine slowed to a crawl and then stopped by an elaborately carved statue. Antonio helped Fiona out of the car and Arturo followed them as they walked toward the priest. Fiona saw the open grave with a handful of mourners standing near the priest. Fiona shivered when she saw the professional handlers carry the casket and, in turn, lower it into the gaping hole. Father Mannato said a brief prayer, but the words or message did not register with her. Fiona was brought up short when she realized the priest had finished speaking. The service was over too soon, Fiona moaned to herself. The finality of Sergio's leave-taking swept over her and Fiona gave a little sob. She shook her head and reined in her emotions. Fiona chose to look around the gravesite and observed the other mourners – how the people huddled nearby in clusters but made no attempt to approach her. Fiona saw the sprays of flowers cover the casket with additional arrangements of brightly colored flowers banking the perimeter of the open grave.

Fiona watched Father Mannato. The priest swayed back and forth as if meditating, his eyes lowered. Antonio approached the priest, shook hands and thanked him. Antonio was profuse with his praise of the beauty of the service. He turned to Fiona, motioning her to join them. Suddenly, Fiona heard a whirring noise and Antonio swiveled his head at the sound of a camera clicking away. He whirled away from the camera, started running and yelled over his shoulder, "Fiona, the limousine is at your disposal. Take it back to the hotel or wherever you want to go. I have my own personal car to use from here." He said the last in a louder voice, making it clear to the observers he was leaving Naples. Antonio got into a low-slung red Ferrari and bolted out of the cemetery.

Arturo stared at the back of the hastily departing Antonio. Like a rat scuttling away, he thought. Arturo recalled the detective's file and wondered to himself, why would a Roman banker react so violently to having his photograph taken at his son's funeral?

Looking back in the direction of the camera, Arturo was rewarded by having his picture taken. He saw one man with the camera and another man by his side smoking a cigarette. They were well-dressed in suits, wearing heavy shoes made for walking long distances. The one smoking a cigarette nodded to Arturo, briefly flashed his police badge and then said something to his camera-toting companion. The two policemen turned toward the rest of the crowd, staring. One of them shrugged and they left.

Sighing deeply, Arturo smiled tentatively at Fiona and whispered, "So much for Daddy. That was short and cold."

"Do you blame him? Antonio offered Sergio all the advantages of a socially prominent, refined home. Sergio did not come from the street. He had family connections and a first-class education. Why mix with these thugs and make such a sordid mess? It's a shameful end. What a wasted life!" Fiona spat the words out. Her eyes glittered. Arturo stared at her as if transfixed.

"It's better to be angry. We'll get more work done. I spoke to Count Volpe. He assured me that we have time to search for the painting. The count also took pictures of the mourners and promised to give them to me later today. I made an appointment to meet him in the *centro storica*."

"I'm going with you. I have my own questions for

Count Volpe," Fiona huffed. She folded her lace mantilla and shoved it into her large shoulder bag.

Arturo and Fiona decided to part with the limousine at the Excelsior. They made quick trips to their rooms to change into street clothes and sensible shoes, met in the lobby and started walking. They were to meet Count Volpe at Gran Caffè Gambrinus, a centrally located bar frequented by the local politicians and merchants. The richly paneled room was foggy with cigarette smoke. It was filled with well-dressed men and a few tourists. The café had a reputation for the best pastry in the area and was always crowded. With luck, no one would take notice of Fiona. They quickly located the count and sat down with their backs to the door.

Wasting no time, Count Volpe pulled out photographs from a manila envelope and said, "These are the pictures of the attending mourners. At least, the ones of interest. I've noted their names on the back of the photos. I've also written a short list of names and businesses Sergio used. Many of them are around the back streets near the Archaeological Museum. The merchants also have old storage areas within walking distance of their shops. Please, keep me informed by telephone. I'll be nearby as I'll stay at the Quisisana in Capri." Averting his eyes, Count Volpe carefully gave Fiona the small sealed envelope.

"Why are you so certain the Caravaggio painting survived the fire?" Fiona looked directly into the count's eyes. He did not flinch and gave a subtle shrug. No verbal response, just the Neapolitan gesture to indicate that it was too obvious to discuss.

The count stood more erect, clicked his heels and said, "Fiona, the Camorra is allowing you time to search for the Caravaggio. Start immediately as your time is precious.

Buona fortuna." On this ominous tone, the count was out the door, walking fast for his advanced age. He did not look back.

Fiona stared at the retreating back of Count Volpe. "I feel as if someone stepped on my grave. I wonder how long they will let me live?"

Arturo said brusquely, "I have a map. Let's go to a trattoria and pull out the count's list. I don't know if we are being watched. We'll pretend to want lunch and we'll also be able to relax for a few minutes away from the crowded sidewalks of Naples. Besides, anyone watching us would expect us to have lunch."

They strolled up the street and selected an out-of-the-way trattoria. They were seated in the rear where they could watch the entrance. Fiona suddenly realized she was hungry and looked forward to the brief respite from their grueling ordeal.

Thinking about the squalid living conditions surrounding the cathedral, Fiona burst out, "What a place Sergio picked to do business! His criminal drug operations no doubt contributed to the demise of Naples and ruined countless lives. He preyed on weak, poor people."

"So, you believe the carabinieri? Sergio was involved in drug dealing?"

"At first, I resisted their statements. I never suspected any wrongdoing while Sergio was alive. But after learning the truth revealed by the cipher and sitting through the funeral service with that tough-looking group of mourners, I do believe it. Sergio was involved in some elaborate criminal enterprise."

"Exactly my sentiments!"

Fiona looked up in surprise to see the photographer and his colleague from the funeral. The one who had not taken the photographs looked at her while he flicked away his cigarette and said, "We're with the Neapolitan police, the local police. You've already met the national police. I'm Inspector Abruzzo and this is Detective Giannaro. We're assigned to this investigation and we think it involves the Camorra. Detective Giannaro and I feel we have a vested interest in this city as we grew up here." Both men smiled broadly, abruptly pulled up two chairs and sat down.

Trying desperately to maintain her composure, Fiona acknowledged their introduction and said, "No doubt, you have our names along with our photographs. Have you been following us the whole time?"

"We know you're staying at the Hotel Excelsior and followed you to your meeting with Count Volpe. We'd like to talk to you and also Mr. Monti for a few minutes." The inspector lit another cigarette and glanced at Arturo.

"We can delay ordering our food for a few moments," Arturo cleared his throat and said to the hovering waiter, "Just pour the wine and leave the bread, please. We'll order in a few minutes as these people are not staying." He looked at the inspector, who nodded.

"We took some photographs of the mourners." Inspector Abruzzo spread out two dozen pictures of the attendees, including Antonio Celesti and Count Volpe. "Do you know any? We, of course, know your father-in-law. But what about him? How long have you known him?" Pointing out the count, the inspector waited for her reply.

"I met Count Volpe for the first time at Il San Pietro in Positano. It was the first night of our holiday on the Amalfi Coast and he introduced himself while my husband and I were having drinks in the hotel lounge. Of course, Sergio knew him through the antique business, but I had never met him or heard of him until that night. Count Volpe was staying at Il San Pietro. We had not planned to meet him. It was a coincidence that we were all there at the same time. He was kind enough to attend the funeral."

"Count Volpe is a well-known antique dealer and bon vivant from Venice. We suspect he's involved in other businesses, all illegal, but it's never been determined. I'm from Naples and love it here, even though it's fallen on hard times after the war. My city is afflicted with the same modern-day ills prevalent in industrialized societies," Inspector Abruzzo mused out loud, "hardcore unemployment, a high crime rate, environmental pollution, drug trafficking, rootless, uneducated young people roaming the streets and a useless public service sector. It's been one long slide."

"Poor Naples," he droned on. "The 1980 earthquake further weakened the aged, fragile infrastructure and exacerbated all of the social problems. This, in turn, allowed the Camorra to expand and strengthen their power. The Camorra spread from simple drug trafficking and prostitution to construction and industry."

Inspector Abruzzo continued, "The countryside, farmland and coastline were ruined by the unregulated sprawl of ugly housing developments and industrial factories. Politicians and magistrates were paid off and remained silent to the dreadful construction of unplanned suburbs, nightmarish traffic and pollution."

Inspector Abruzzo paused for a moment and then said, "The Camorra rebuilt the infrastructure and infiltrated all the major businesses, making Naples more lawless than our other cities. Now you know what we're confronting; so what about helping us?" Detective Giannaro placed more photographs on the table and stared at Fiona.

Fiona shook her head, jerking it back and forth, licking

her lips as though her mouth was so parched she couldn't speak. "I don't know any of them. I'm sorry, but I can't help." She trembled and grabbed for her glass of wine. She looked away while sipping her wine.

"You said you did not know Count Volpe when interviewed by the Positano police. You also said you had met the count on the first night of your stay at Il San Pietro. What about this?" Abruzzo pointed his finger at the photo of Count Volpe gesturing to Arturo at the funeral. The inspector's voice took on a grating edge and he leaned into her. She could smell the cigarette smoke on his breath, he was so close.

"I was in shock and couldn't collect my thoughts. I'd just been told my husband was dead and possibly by foul play." Fiona looked up at the inspector and saw his eyes harden. He had no sympathy for her or her loss.

"Signora, you would be wise to cooperate with the police. We can protect you." He waited for her reply.

Arturo pushed back his chair, stood up and said, "Inspector Abruzzo, you made your position clear. We'll think about what was discussed and appreciate your offer of protection. Detective Giannaro, thank you for the photographs. We'll look at them again and if we think we can help, we'll contact you."

He waited for the two men to get up. They grudgingly pushed back their chairs, making the legs squeal on the tiled floor. The inspector threw a card on the table, saying, "You need our help as much as we need yours. You'll see." He gave a last drag on the cigarette and threw it on the floor, grinding it with his heel. They turned and left the trattoria.

The waiter made his way across the room to their table. Arturo said, "We'll have what the cook recommends and a large insalata verde. Thank you." When the waiter retreated, Arturo held her hand gently and said, "The Neapolitan police are just acting as bullies. That was a lot of bravado to rattle you, Fiona. The inspector is frustrated by the rampant drug trafficking and the rise of the Camorra. He said he was one of the good guys, but who knows? I suggest we keep our plan simple. We know what we have to do, so let's decide which antique store to approach first. In an attempt to distract her, he said, "We'll adapt to these conditions as if we were typical Neapolitans and improvise!"

The pesce spada, a succulent piece of swordfish grilled to perfection, and pasta primavera, local vegetables with a light red sauce, came and they ate well.

Fiona dabbed at her lips once her plate was polished clean and said, "According to the count's list, the nearest shop is DiBiase on Via Morelli off Piazza dei Martiri. It seems as if many of the shops are clustered in a row." She made a short list as she consulted the count's handwritten note. Reviewing her notes, she put the pen down and looked up at Arturo with a slight smile.

"That's the spirit," Arturo said, looking at her with admiration.

She lifted up her chin, smiled and winked. "Andiamo. Let's go and shop!"

The shops were indeed near one another. It was a street known for serious antiques. Framed old paintings and lovely antique prints were displayed on the walls. The cobblestone street was narrow with a pronounced curve rounding a tight corner. Ancient soot discolored the buildings, which seemed to loom over Fiona's head. Salt lines on the buildings indicated a history of poor drainage and the cobblestones were slippery from seeping, aged garbage. Small cars and motor scooters came screeching around the corner of the antique district. The overall shopping area presented a sinister image more conducive to scavenger hunting than pleasure. They located a shop with the sign for DiBiase and observed that, although the lights were on and people were working at their desks, the shop's door was locked. A man wearing a blue duster ran to the door and stood at attention as he awaited orders from an elderly man seated behind a burled walnut desk. The old man stared at Fiona, frowned and then nodded to his attendant. The door clicked open.

Fiona and Arturo entered the shop and pretended to look at the displays. As they wended their way to the manager's desk, the help drifted away, disappearing into the rear of the shop. The man seated at the desk looked at them warily, not intending to initiate any conversation.

"Signore, I remember you from Sergio Celesti's funeral?" Arturo began.

"Sì. I was there."

"How did you know the deceased?"

"You're not the polizia. I don't have to tell you anything." Flicking his cigarette ashes with impatience, the old man looked away.

"May I introduce his widow?" Speaking in a firm, clear voice, Arturo continued, "Signora Celesti needs answers about her late husband, Sergio Celesti. You knew him. Any information about his past life in Naples would be helpful."

As she stood in front of the desk, the shopkeeper saw that her hands, holding her purse, were trembling. He stubbed his cigarette out in a dish and said, "Do you know why the door is locked even to clients?" Not waiting for a response, the man continued in a raspy tone, "All shopkeepers must pay a weekly tribute to local gangs, the Camorra, for protection. If we don't pay, our windows will be smashed. The second week, our faces are smashed. We never get a third week. In addition to protection money, we also must contribute to a separate fund to support the families of gang members who are in prison. It does not encourage trust or an open-door policy." By the end of his litany, he was almost shouting and glared at Arturo.

Fiona was silent for a moment, trying to keep track of the sordid information. Finally, she said, "I had no idea." Fiona blinked away tears.

"Signore, we are not part of this problem," Arturo began. "Don't blame us. We are trying to solve a mystery about her husband. We don't understand how his business worked."

"I cannot help you." Shaking his head with weariness, the shopkeeper squashed his cigarette into an already overflowing ashtray. "I have a family. I'm lucky to be able to pay my weekly expenses and have a little for pasta. I was about to close for the day. So, if that's all?"

A long silence settled in the shop. Minutes passed and finally Arturo shrugged his shoulders and replied, "We're staying at the Excelsior."

They turned slowly, walked out of the shop and the door clicked. Fiona looked back and saw no one. The shop was dark and empty. She looked at Arturo and he said, "Let's continue to the next shop. We'll go through the entire list."

Arturo lifted his head with determination and linked arms with her. They walked up the gloomy street. Again, they looked through a glass door into a well-lit shop. There was a lone person sitting at the desk in the rear of the shop. Antique bureaus lined the walls with paintings and wall sconces were strategically placed for optimum viewing. Arturo rang the bell and the shopkeeper came to the door. With an audible click, the door opened. The shopkeeper poked his head out, glanced at Fiona and then stared at Arturo.

"May we come in?" Arturo asked politely.

The shopkeeper's eyes grew sharp, "Sì."

The door opened a little wider and they were ushered in by the shopkeeper's sweeping hand. They began looking at small, primitive ceramic sculptures of animals. The shopkeeper returned to his desk and answered the phone.

"Pronto. Eh, sì." As he listened intently, he jammed the receiver against his ear. He seemed to have no interest in ending the conversation.

Arturo stood at the desk holding a file of notes and photographs. The man put his hand over the receiver and looked at him with narrowed eyes.

"I have some questions," Arturo started saying.

Interrupting him, the man removed the telephone receiver for a moment and muttered, "I know who you are. I cannot help you." The man swiveled his chair and turned his back to them.

"It's about something important," Arturo prodded.

Fiona touched Arturo's arm and said, "Let's go."

Calmly, with an easy smile, Arturo said, "We're at the Excelsior."

On his way out, Arturo looked back at the shopkeeper, who only dismissed them by waving his hand holding a cigarette. He kept his back to them.

Arturo closed the door softly behind them and crossed the street to yet another shop. A solidly built peasant woman answered the door. Fiona blinked as the woman was like one of Picasso's Hellenic women come to life. The peasant woman stared at them and explained, "Il padrone, the owner, is away. I only clean and dust. I'm not hired to sell or to tend the door."

Arturo again asked for help. The older woman hesitated and said shyly, "We were told to expect you. I don't know what you're looking for, but I do know the owner doesn't deal with religious items."

Arturo was puzzled and the expression on his face showed it. "What are you talking about?"

"There is much dealing of religious artwork. We are afraid they are stolen works from cathedrals or small churches. There is no legitimate overseas market for this. I only know this as the owner is clearly upset when anyone approaches him with old marble, large canvases of religious subjects or silver candlesticks." She whispered, barely moving her lips, as she continued dusting, never looking at them. Anyone observing them from the street would think she was ignoring the couple.

"Do the religious items support the families of the Camorra?" Fiona asked gently.

"Certo. We're fortunate we don't have to do business with them. It's an organized shop with frequent turnover of the inventory. There is demand for these items, maybe because the prices are so low. The shop is well-run. The owner has always been current with his expenses and his tribute to the Camorra, so we're not involved."

The phone rang and she said, "You should go. Stay away from those people." She never looked at them, and the phone continued to ring as they stepped onto the street. Fiona quickly glanced back over her shoulder and saw that the shop's lights were turned off and she could not see the peasant woman.

Arturo took her arm again, saying, "Let's go up the street to some of the workshops and storage areas."

The street wound upward, becoming increasingly dirty. Its lava stones were slippery and difficult to walk on. They walked into a pool of quiet amid the confused structure of stained walls, iron railings, homes and hovels. They passed by wine shops, a laundry, an old forge, a small electrical repair shop. There were the sounds of a saw and hammering. Arturo and Fiona rounded a corner and saw two carpenters doing their job on the street. The area was cluttered with their tools and they worked noisily on an inlaid wood bureau. The battered wooden bureau was either being restored or being fabricated as an antique. The carpenters stopped working to look at the handsome, young couple.

"We're looking for Sergio Celesti's workroom. I believe it's nearby?" Arturo looked at them and held some lire out. The two men exchanged a look; in it, Arturo read the struggle between the urge to remain silent out of an old allegiance to the neighborhood and the desire for *soldi*, cash. One reached out and pocketed the money that Arturo extended. The man pointed up the street and gave a street number. The sound of their hammering resumed.

Arturo and Fiona passed the cell-like, shuttered shops. Many only had garage doors as entrances. The road was almost blocked with parked cars and motorcycles. After a dark, narrow, long passage, they went up to another open space. They were in another courtyard. It was an old, sadly neglected courtyard looking onto an old building. Enameled nameplates identified the businesses. In front of one open garage door, two men wearing black aprons were working on metal work. They were smoking and chatting while their radio blared a local melody. Thinking the couple were prospective clients, the craftsmen smiled with encouragement. When asked, they simply pointed to another garage door.

Sergio's workshop once had been a stable and now apparently was a storage room. Arturo was struck by a yellow glow on the glistening pavement. He noticed that the barred windows on the second floor were illuminated. In the same instance, he caught a glimpse of someone moving in the window. Arturo nudged Fiona, quickly pushed the door and discovered it was ajar. The room was cavernous, dank and had a packed dirt floor. They went up the worn stairs and stepped into an office. The ceiling was bare except for a naked light bulb, which produced a yellowish light. Something crunched under Arturo's feet, making a loud sound. Out of the gloom, a slim man whirled around and glared at them. He was tall and slender with swarthy skin and a trimmed mustache and goatee. He had an air of self-absorption.

"This is private. No clients are allowed."

"I believe Signora Celesti is the owner," retorted Arturo as he indicated with his hand Fiona's presence. "Who are you? What are you doing here?"

The well-dressed young man blinked and wiped his hands free of any dust. He nervously patted his slicked-back hair.

"How did you find this place?"

Arturo answered in a stern voice, "That's our business. We're trying to settle Sergio Celesti's estate. Again, what is your name?"

"I'm an antique dealer. I supplied Sergio with bits and pieces to sell. Mostly collectibles, nothing precious. Here's my card."

"Luigi Frascatti of Naples?" Arturo asked while staring into his eyes.

The other man avoided eye contact, nodded slowly while studying Arturo as if he were trying to read his mind. His face revealed nothing but the prolonged practice of corruption and intrigue. Something in his eyes warned Arturo not to lower his guard.

"What are you doing here?" demanded Arturo while he stood with his legs apart, ready to defend himself.

"Sergio owed me money," the young man whined while clasping his hands together and wringing them nervously. "I was looking for some of my collectibles."

"You were looking through his desk and files."

"I left my valise downstairs with all my records. Shall I retrieve it to show you?" He quickly shifted to the left and brushed by them. "I'll be right back," he called over his shoulder. Frascatti bounded down the steps.

Before Arturo could overtake him, the man was out the door and running down the street. He had no hope of catching him.

"*Oddio*, my God," Arturo said under his breath. "I'm sorry, Fiona." Arturo banged his hand onto an old bureau.

"Frascatti was clearly looking for something so maybe we can find it. Let's get started," Fiona said while smiling at Arturo with encouragement.

Arturo pulled up a dusty chair and sat down at the big desk and began reviewing piles of paper. Fiona searched another file cabinet. It was old with deep, worn drawers. The top drawer was stuck and could not be pulled all the way out. Sticking her hand in, Fiona pulled a wad of paper from the jammed drawer. Unrolling the roll of paper, she looked at columns of numbers. Fiona gave a low whistle and waved to Arturo to join her.

"This is it!" Fiona passed the papers to him.

Arturo said quietly while looking at the dense list. "Va bene. It will make sense to us once we put all the pieces together. Let's go. We've been here awhile and there's only furniture downstairs. We need to rest and clear our heads. Andiamo!"

She swished her hair back behind her ears and gave him a broad smile. Putting her hand on the old railing, Fiona walked downstairs.

Arturo found an iron key attached to a fringed tassel and locked the old-fashioned gate. Fiona pocketed the key. They walked down the street, found a taxi idling on a side street and were soon back at the Excelsior.

There was a sea breeze off the harbor and the distant purple-hued Vesuvius shimmered in the rose-colored light. Attractively dressed people sat at the café tables with beautiful, exquisite drinks. The pleasure boats in the marina rocked on their moorings in the calm harbor. The hotel and its promenade was an oasis of gentility. The rotten business of the Camorra seemed to be left behind in the slums and side streets of Naples. Arturo and Fiona agreed to meet later for dinner.

Fiona entered her room and started to run a bath. She needed a good soak and would groom her hair. Things would look more normal once she resumed a little of her daily routine. Her overwhelming desire was to wash away the city grime as if soap and water could get rid of the stench of the Camorra. She would deal with the column of numbers only after getting herself clean.

Toweling off, she chose a Campari from the well-stocked minibar. Fiona sat down and unfurled the papers from the storage room and the copy of Dante's *Inferno*. Decoding the numbered sections was painstaking work.

She kept her mind on the job as the information slowly revealed itself. It became obvious that what was detailed in the code was the movement of large sums of money and goods from Italy to various countries. It began to make sense to her: The fragments of information were pieced together to form a mosaic puzzle.

She looked at the time and scooped up all her notes, the book and the reams of pages with columns of numbers into her shoulder bag. Slinging the bag firmly over her shoulder, she made her way to the lobby. She walked with a confident stride to meet Arturo.

Arturo smiled and looked at her with open admiration. "Your eyes are sparkling again!" He laughed gently and asked, "Is it me or are you rested from a nap?"

Fiona grabbed his arm and kissed him lightly on the cheek. "I think I've made some headway with the cipher." Her eyes flashed and her skin glowed pink. "Let's go to a quiet place so we can examine my notes."

They took the funicular to Vomero, an exclusive residential neighborhood. The wealthier citizens lived in this area of greenery and gracious old buildings. There was a restaurant built on the extreme edge of the hill with tables arranged on a terrace. Fiona could see the Bay of Naples curving round to Vesuvius with Capri in the distance. Immediately below them were the crowded roofs and domes of the teeming city. She began to relax a little. An image flashed through in her memory: Arturo in Boston, always patient with her and her early attempts at painting.

"You're looking at me that way again," Arturo said playfully.

"Which way is that?"

"The same way you used to look at the Renaissance

paintings at the Fogg Museum. You are assessing. You're looking for cracks and abrasions – wondering if the canvas is still intact, sturdy. What's the answer?"

"The canvas is fine. It's strong and durable."

There was, suspended in the space between them, so much more that needed to be said. But now was not the time. Shifting his feet, Arturo leaned forward and said, "So, have you found something?" Arturo looked at her steadily, now assessing her.

Fiona gave a start and then realized he'd only meant the code she'd found on the office papers. She drew her work out of her bag and handed it to him.

Arturo turned the pages and reviewed the detailed list of illicit activity. He took a breath, blew it out and said, "Your work is thorough, Fiona. You'd make a good corporate lawyer. Your review indicates Sergio had regular partners in his routine or cover business. He made consistent payments and transactions for furnishing and paintings. His restoration business is also indicated. This is pretty easy to decipher. There is an additional reference for his private or secret business?"

Fiona nodded, an unhappy nod, but affirmative. She looked over her notes and said, "The covert business had fewer partners, but I believe it dealt with larger sums of money. I'm also trying to unravel who owned the Caravaggio and how it was most recently leveraged. What was being purchased also needs to be determined. And finally, I think Sergio was immediately selling his new inventory, some sort of goods, to a third party." She rested and sipped some water.

"Do you suspect what was purchased?"

"Sergio was a drug dealer, but I don't know if he took possession or processed any of it."

"You seem to be okay."

"I guess I have to be."

They became aware of the waiter hovering over them with their food. He cleared his throat and set the platters down, offered grated cheese, poured more wine and then gave Fiona a small note sealed in wax.

Fiona looked at the sealed envelope and raised her eyebrows at the hapless waiter, "How was this delivered?"

The waiter slid his eyes away and stammered, "A *scugnizzo*, a street urchin, pointed to you and said you were expecting it. The kid handed it to me and ran off. I'm sorry to bother you, Signora." He looked into her eyes and gave a tight-lipped smile.

"Niente. It's nothing. Thank you."

Fiona waited for the waiter to leave their table. After a long silence, she quickly cracked the seal and scanned the contents.

"Frascatti wants to meet me tonight at the Sansevero Chapel in the old Spanish section. He promises important information." She gave Arturo the note. "He's been shadowing us! Do you think he saw us reading the notes?"

"These people are willing to do anything. But it's too dangerous, I'll go," Arturo said gruffly.

Fiona fought the panic rising up in her throat, choking her speech. She caught her breath and regained her speech. "No! I must see him to get answers. Frascatti's the only one willing to talk to us. Why don't you go, but stay on the periphery and observe? That way we can know if he's alone."

"Sansevero Chapel is an odd place for a meeting and downright creepy at night! The Neapolitans believe the grounds are haunted by a prince who murdered his wife and lover when he caught them together. The collector was a member of the royal family, some sort of dilettante mystic and mad as a hatter."

"I know, I know," Fiona moaned. "*The Veiled Christ* looks as if the effigy was sleeping and only lightly covered in marble. It's an homage to the artist's pursuit of alchemy, pyrotechnics and magic. Frascatti must have chosen carefully, hoping to frighten me away from my search. Basta! I'm still going." Fiona said the last with a grim voice.

"The chapel should be closed in the evening," mused Arturo. "Let's go a bit early and look around at the displays and chambers." He picked up his fork and knife and said, "But it's important to keep up our strength, so enjoy the food. The branzino is grilled to perfection and the pasta primavera is wonderful-looking with its tiny vegetables." He smiled at Fiona and encouraged her to eat.

They took a taxi to the Piazza del Duomo and had a quick caffè standing inside a bar. Arturo warned Fiona to be careful with her handbag and she immediately strapped it across her chest.

Arturo was suddenly busy on the phone at the corner of the bar and when he returned to her, he said, "Let's explore the area."

They walked up the thin street, the Spaccanapoli, or "split Naples," and noticed how frequently the names of the street changed. The narrow, straight road bisected the city, and it and the tall apartment buildings had not changed much since early Roman city planning days. The buildings were dull with dirt and no light was let in as the street was so narrow. This was also known as the Spanish Quarter and was the poorest slum in Naples. Its people lived much of their lives on the streets, working at their craft by the curb. It also was the most dangerous place for outsiders.

They passed by the famous Christmas market, where everyone shopped to buy their *presepe, a Nativity crèche of* carved figurines, and gaudy accessories for their manger scenes. Hundreds of stands clogged the narrow streets of the neighborhood. Fiona stopped and stared at an elaborate manger scene and glimpsed at her reflection in the pane of glass. She looked farther into the shop and saw walls of elaborately carved puppets with realistic faces. She had the bizarre thought that she saw her face carved onto one of the puppets and she started shaking. The narrow streets with the desperate poverty of the buildings and their cell-like rooms must have made her claustrophobic. She shook off her feelings of suffocation and turned away from the store. Holding onto Arturo's arm, she struggled up the hill and they reached Via Francesco de Sanctis and the Sansevero Chapel.

The dirt-encrusted building was small as it was once the private chapel of the Raimondo di Sangro family. The carved wooden doors, equally dirty and lined with dust, had been carved by special commission of the aristocratic family. The carvings were foreign to her sensibilities. The bas-relief was teeming with leering, grimacing faces wearing feathered costumes. The street was ill-kept and the chapel façade was worn. One had to know about the strange artifacts within the chapel or have a special interest in the carvings in order to bother with such an obscure location.

Around her, the street took on a malevolent tone with the waning light. Evening was approaching and the neighborhood began to take on a sinister air with its grim buildings. Fiona shook her head as if she felt wisps of cobwebs on her hair.

They stepped down into the chapel. The first room

was small and well-illuminated by overhead bars of light. Arturo pointed out a group of sculptures all executed in a showy rococo style. She studied the carved marble fishing net, the turning pages of a book and elaborate shroud. The work displayed a remarkable illusion of figures under transparent veils. She looked up and saw a crazy heavenly vortex in the ceiling fresco. Fiona craned her neck, trying to get a better view of the fresco and felt lightheaded. She felt herself spinning and sat down heavily onto something wooden. At the same time, the lights snapped off. Fiona felt bile rising in her throat. She called out to Arturo, who whispered he was near. She frantically looked around to get her bearings and realized she still could see a little in the gloom since there was ambient light in the adjacent room.

"I have to feed the light meter! The lights are controlled by this box over here." Arturo reassured her as he pushed coins into the machine. The lights hummed back on. Brushing the dust off his hands, Arturo urged her into the second room. Fiona moved shakily toward him. They stepped down into the crypt and saw two mummified bodies with complete cardiovascular systems on display. A posted sign informed them that the two bodies had been preserved by Prince Raimondo during his alchemical experiments.

"If this was meant to frighten me, it didn't work. It's similar to a display found in Boston's Museum of Science. Look at these display cases. They're an institutional design, old and dated but still well-designed for a scientific demonstration."

She heard Arturo suck in his breath as they listened to a dragging noise. Something was being pulled or dragged along the stone floor. She let out a shriek as she saw fingers curve around the stone lintel of the entrance to the crypt.

Then her face became hot as she recognized the blue coat of a church guide. Fiona was embarrassed to be so skittish. The chapel guard was a hunchback and was dragging his leg. Arturo said, "We understand the chapel is closing and we are leaving, a presto." The door slammed shut behind them and they were again on the gloomy street. The bolts of the old door slid shut behind them.

"How do we get back in for our meeting?" Fiona asked.

"Let's have a caffè and then look for a second door. These old buildings always had an escape route or at least a servant's entry."

They found a hole-in-the-wall bar and stood at the counter. It was a neighborhood tavern and they did not feel welcome. Arturo ordered rolls and indicated they would sit at a table. The proprietor signaled where to sit with a flick of a filthy bar towel. Arturo examined the locals and nodded at one as if he knew him. Fiona wondered if she was imagining things.

Arturo tossed some change onto the table. They returned to the dirty street and picked their way to the chapel. They decided to explore an alley and found an almost hidden door to the chapel. It was a small plain wooden door with a simple lock. Arturo tried the lock and pushed it open. Fiona slipped into the darkened room, not waiting for him. It took Arturo some time to secure the door as he had disturbed some debris on the floor. A glowing night light allowed her eyes to adjust to the dim passageway. Fiona squinted her eyes and walked slowly so she could avoid the towering boxes standing in the storage room.

Fiona continued on alone and found the steps going

down to the crypt. She crept forward, waiting for Arturo to catch up. He slid by her, hugging the wall and turned a corner. Fiona heard him stuff more coins into the light meter. Suddenly, the lights clicked on and she again stared at the displayed mummified corpses. She looked around and shrieked in horror.

Arturo grabbed her and hugged her close. He did not want her to keep looking at the butchered body of Frascatti. He was sprawled on the floor, a bloody mess, wearing the same clothes from earlier in the day. His briefcase was beside him and it, too, had been sliced with a knife.

Fiona gasped as she saw near the body a pink silk scarf. She felt goosebumps tingle over her body, her chest tightened and she inhaled deeply to quell her rising terror. With a shaking finger, Fiona pointed to the scarf and said, "I've seen that before! I recognize it! It was worn by that jogger I told you about. The one who accosted me in the parking lot in Capri. Maybe he's a member of the Camorra."

She started to bend down to touch the scarf but Arturo held her back. "Leave it! Don't touch it! Let the police do their job. We have to get out of here now!"

Suddenly, they became aware of someone moving around in the adjoining room. Someone was trying to move quietly, stealthily toward them. Fiona and Arturo only could sense the determination of their predator as the adjacent room was dark due to the light meter having expired.

"We must go!" Arturo whispered into her ear. "Now! We cannot be found here either by the Camorra or the polizia."

Arturo took her hand and they fled out the door not caring if they bumped into anything. They ran down the street past the neighborhood bar and into another alley. Arturo saw a lone motorcycle leaning on its kickstand and hopped onto it. He beckoned to Fiona and told her to sit behind him. They swung into the street and roared away from the Spanish Quarter.

Arturo only slowed down once they were near the Excelsior. He released the motorcycle to the doorman with instructions to give it to his friend and gave the name along with a hefty tip.

The hotel lobby was reassuringly illuminated by the crystal chandeliers. The staff looked at them with smiling faces. Their uniforms were spotless and well-pressed. In this corner of serenity, the seediness and strangeness of the chapel receded from Fiona's spinning mind.

"Let's have a brandy," she croaked, leading him into the lounge. Arturo and Fiona chose a large banquette and they both collapsed into the leather couch. They ordered large snifters and sat back.

Fiona wrinkled her forehead and looked at Arturo. As if he read her mind, he said, "I ordered a motorcycle to be delivered near the chapel. The driver was waiting for us at the local bar and that's who nodded to me. I wanted us to be able to escape fast in case things got dicey."

She drained her snifter in one gulp. The brandy warmed her and its strength seeped into her.

"Shall we order room service? How about in my suite? I don't want to be alone right now." She looked at Arturo and led the way to the bank of elevators.

Arturo took her keys and opened the door to her room. There was a small envelope lying on the floor. Fiona quickly bent down to pick up the note card. She saw that its flap was embossed with Count Volpe's family crest. Ripping it open, she read the short note and said, "We're to meet Count Volpe tomorrow morning at the Galleria." Looking up from the note, she asked, "Do you think he knows?"

"Of Frascatti's death? I'm sure we won't discover the time the note was delivered to the hotel. We'll just have to wait to hear Count Volpe's story." Arturo sighed and rubbed his forehead as if fatigued.

Fiona gave a shrug. She thought of the Christmas market and wondered if she was indeed a puppet. But who was pulling the strings?

The next morning, the sunshine sparkled, making Fiona feel better. She looked out her window and saw the waiters setting up their tables, boats speeding out of the harbor and Vesuvius looming over the city. She thought of all the previous generations of artists who had painted this same view.

Fiona finished dressing, found her shoulder bag and ran down to the lobby to meet Arturo. They were on their way to meet Count Volpe at the Galleria, a famous shopping mall.

Arturo heard her heels clicking on the marble floor and glanced up from his papers. He gave an appreciative look and said, "Que bella. We'll take a taxi."

They entered the huge glass-and-iron structure and strolled to their rendezvous, Café Pronto. Along the way, they looked into shop windows like idle tourists. The Galleria was a nineteenth-century example of a glass-enclosed shopping mall and it was a popular meeting place. Although the café was crowded, they soon spotted the count and joined him at his small table. Count Volpe quickly dispatched his bodyguard and swiveled in his seat to look at both of them. The count scrutinized them without saying a word, his expression never changing. After barking out an order of caffè to the hovering waiter, he lit a cigarette. Exhaling a plume of smoke, he quietly said, "This has to stop." He gave Arturo a stern look.

"Why? What's wrong?" Arturo countered.

"There is no more time. Searching any further in Naples is a waste of time. Go back to Rome and look there. You should leave immediately." He deeply inhaled his cigarette, sitting still as the cigarette smoke drifted out of his nose. Arturo marveled that with his tanned, wrinkled face and long nose, Count Volpe resembled a man wearing a carnival mask masquerading as a smoke-filled dragon. Arturo watched the count as he tapped his gold cigarette case with short, nervous strikes and waited. Count Volpe continued smoking.

Arturo began to remonstrate with him, but the count cut him off, not countenancing any speculation about Frascatti. Count Volpe raked his fingers through his white hair as his voice burst into a sharp tone, "Go to Rome. Look through all of Sergio's workshops, his boutiques, the home, even Fiona's studio. But get out of Naples immediately. This is a dead end. Don't take this advice lightly."

Scattered ashes from his cigarette dusted his shoulders and sleeves, but the count did not try to brush any off of his suit. He slowly ground the used cigarette into the glass ashtray. Nothing more was said. Count Volpe got up from the table and left.

Rome

AUGUST 8, 1985

THE AFTERNOON

In bright sunlight, Arturo, at the wheel of the white Lancia, sped across Rome, the boulevards and then the narrow streets, dodging pedestrians and swarms of motor scooters with their loud, menacing, killer-bee hum. Fiona tried to stay calm by braking her feet into the floor of the car and touched his arm, hoping he would slow down. On Via Margutta, Arturo spotted a parking space, darted for it and deftly slid into it.

Fiona looked at him, smiled slightly and said, "Well, I guess any landing is a good landing."

Arturo looked at her quickly and said in a soft tone of voice, "Sorry. Lost in thought. I wanted to get here quickly so we could start our search. I didn't mean to alarm you, Fiona."

He jumped out of the Lancia and opened her door with fanfare. Arturo looked at Fiona, his gaze steady as he offered his arm to her. Fiona slipped her arm into his and held on tightly.

Arturo wondered if they could ever become a couple again. He hoped with all his heart they would. He looked over at Fiona and a smile flitted across her worried face. Arturo liked to think there was trust in her eyes.

They walked down the street arm in arm at a slow pace and looked at the bedraggled greenery growing in small clumps between the granite stone and in the front terraces of the studios. The old stone buildings seemed whiter in the shimmering heat of the day, and the street was strangely quiet. No noisy artisans were working outside, no neighbors puttering on their balconies and even the traffic noise of nearby Via del Babuino was muted. All they noticed were potted basil plants and small tomatoes listlessly growing on the balconies of the upper stories.

They stopped at an imposing iron gate, and Fiona searched in her handbag for her house keys. She held them aloft in the air and said lightly, "The keys to my grand estate." With a smooth gesture, she turned the key in the large lock and a loud click sounded. She gave a ceremonial sweep, bending her body at the waist as she looked up at him saying, "*Avanti.*"

Such off-street parking in Rome was a luxury, and Arturo realized the value of this residential address. As they walked along the packed gravel in the car park, Arturo asked, "Is any one of these your car?"

"Sì. La."

Fiona pointed to a silver-gray Porsche parked in a protected corner of the lot. It was dusty due to a summer of disuse. At the same time, her mind flickered back to the early days of summer. She recalled the scent of basil and mint. She quickly looked at the plantings and noticed only the grubby remnants of her hard work. She clucked her tongue and cursed the property management. "I'll have the building manager wash it and check the battery for us," Fiona said.

"Va bene. We can use my car whenever you want. Whatever is most convenient," Arturo said.

"Let's go upstairs, I'll show you my apartment and we'll put our things away. I'll need to get some food for snacks and breakfast, but I'd prefer to have dinner out. How does that sound to you?"

"Eminently sensible," replied Arturo with a small smile on his face. "But I want to enter first so that I can make certain no one is in the flat. Va bene?

Fiona took a large iron key out of her bag and inserted it into the lock of a small door cut into the magnificent antique door. It clicked and she slowly pushed the door open. "Watch your step," she called to Arturo as she stepped over the wooden ledge. "At one time, this entrance must have been for horses."

They were inside the lobby, but it was an abrupt shift from the bright Roman daylight to almost none. Arturo did not move as he waited for his eyes to acclimate to the dim light. Fiona snapped on a light switch by the side of the door and low-wattage bulbs gleamed from a series of glass lanterns. The transparent glass lanterns were glazed with antique, wavy glass, giving off a few shadows in their glow. They were framed in old bronze, having a rich patina. Holding the lantern out from the wall was a bronze bracket carved in the shape of an arm. The lantern rested in the stretched fingers of a hand. As Arturo stood still, he could see that the ground-floor hall was vast with a long series of lanterns lighting down its long length. The floor was black-and-white marble; the walls were painted in Venetian plaster to resemble marble. Farther down, he could see a staircase on the right. It was wide and made of old, smooth stone, which showed wear.

At the first landing, there were a series of windows and Fiona pointed out the private garden hidden from the street. It was filled with a riot of flowers and a working fountain. Several pieces of sculpture were strategically placed on the crushed stone terrace. He also could see an artisan's workshop backing up to the garden. There were doors on the landing, but Fiona urged him on, heading up the next flight of stairs.

Upon reaching the landing, Arturo saw a row of painted, wooden doors perhaps fourteen feet high. When Arturo got closer, he realized they were decorated in a graceful, floral design so popular in the eighteenth century. Against a blue-gray background, animals were cavorting with courtiers.

"Do you like the entrance?" Fiona asked.

"It's superb. The painting is lyrical but not too serious. Wherever did you find it?"

"Sergio found the panels in an old stable in Naples. One of his dealers had stored a batch of antique frames there and also had these interesting wooden panels. Sergio thought it would enhance the hallway. I'm glad you like it."

The doors were the entrance to the *piano nobile*, the grandest apartment, in the building. It was also the biggest as it covered the entire floor of the gigantic building. Fiona gave Arturo the key to the door that, surprisingly, had a modern lock. He turned it and said over his shoulder, "Please wait to hear, "All clear.'"

Arturo ventured in cautiously. Fiona, endlessly fearless, tiptoed in after him and flicked on the lights. He signaled Fiona to stay behind him as he checked each room and closet. Looking around, she nodded with relief and murmured, "Everything's fine. It's exactly as I left it."

She sat down wearily at the kitchen table and reviewed the list she had prepared during the ride from Naples. They needed to search Sergio's two antique shops, three storage areas and the one surviving workshop. There was also a substantial list of private dealers, consultants and pickers who routinely supplied Sergio with new inventory.

"Let's look at the vendors who did business with Sergio on a regular basis – the ones who supplied collectibles and antiques. We should contact the framers, print dealers immediately. Maybe Sergio left something with them? We'll take turns calling them. We can visit the storage areas tomorrow. My studio also needs to be searched. Va bene?"

Arturo quickly nodded, saying, "Certo."

"I can walk to my studio now while you call the vendors. I'll help contact the vendors as soon as I'm back. The studio's just a ten-minute walk from here," Fiona paused as if anticipating his objections and continued, "I'll walk through the Borghese gardens, which is always filled with people. It's never deserted."

"I don't want you going there alone," Arturo replied in a gruff tone of voice.

"As long as I'm busy searching for clues, I'm safe from the Camorra. There's still time to find the painting. Count Volpe said to look in Rome. If we divide the work, we'll get through the list of vendors faster. It makes sense. Please understand." She gave him a winsome smile.

"I don't like it," he said sharply, "but I'll agree as long as you telephone me once you've arrived at the studio. Agreed?"

"Absolutely," Fiona said, "let's look at the list together and then I'll be on my way."

"Go ahead. I'll pretend I'm your financial adviser, sorting out receipts."

She passed him the list of names and contact information. Fiona bent down to hug him as she said, "I'll be as quick as I can."

Arturo watched her close the door and scanned the list of names. "I don't recognize any of these names or companies," he muttered to himself. He started dialing.

Fiona walked down the quiet street and turned onto Via del Babuino. A traffic light caused the automobiles to accumulate. A cluster of tourists was staring into the shop windows. She took a hard left before the Piazza di Spagna and took Rampa di San Sebastianello, the hilly road, up the embankment to the Borghese gardens. Fiona walked along the gravel paths, not noticing anyone following her. She quickly reached her studio and unlocked the wooden door. The handle squeaked horribly as she turned it. Fiona pushed inwards and entered the quiet studio. The air was musty from disuse, so she opened a window to air out the large room. Natural light filtered into the studio and she began searching each canvas in the stacks. Finding nothing out of order, no old stretcher bars, Fiona searched the cabinets holding art supplies. She clicked her tongue when she saw an unusually large order of rabbit skin glue but found no old canvas. Her small kitchen and bathroom yielded nothing. She rang Arturo, "There's nothing here. I'll leave in a few minutes. I have a suggestion, if you don't mind?"

"What is it? I'm all ears."

"Let's take a break and go to the Galleria Borghese. I'd like to show you their collection of the Caravaggios.

That way you can see another example of Caravaggio's late style. There's a particular picture I want to show you as it may be similar in theme as to what we're looking for."

"Va bene. Anything to get away from the telephone," Arturo sighed. "Seriously, I'd appreciate the tour of the museum with such an informed guide. Shall I meet you there?"

"Yes. Just enter the garden and follow the signs to the museum. I'll meet you in the lobby; I'll get the tickets in advance. Okay?"

"Sì. I'll leave now. Ciao."

"Ciao."

Fiona closed the door and scanned the immediate area. No one was lurking suspiciously and she walked confidently through the gardens. Fiona followed the direct route to the Galleria Borghese and walked down the steps to the biglietteria, the ticket counter. She purchased two tickets from the bored-looking civil servant sitting on a stool.

As she turned away from the ticket booth, the fine hairs on the back of her neck lifted, and Fiona tensed. Someone was behind her, stalking her, and she whirled around. Fiona noticed tourists standing in line. Suddenly, out of the corner of her eye, she saw a blur of hot pink, and a blond-haired man disappeared around the corner. With a flash of recognition, she knew it was the ruffian she had encountered in the dusty parking lot in Capri.

Fiona rushed over to confront the thug, but he was gone. Fiona saw the empty turnstile was still rotating. She gave an exasperated sigh and returned to the central area of the museum. Fiona took a deep breath, decided not to dwell on the incident and strode over to the gift shop. She searched the rows of books. There were several about Caravaggio, but she was looking for a general interest tour guide. Finding one that looked promising, she picked it up and leafed through it. It will do, she said to herself and paid the cashier.

Fiona looked around the small waiting area and decided to move closer to the entrance to wait for Arturo. He arrived in another five minutes, almost out of breath.

"You didn't need to hurry," Fiona said laughing out loud. "Really, there's plenty of time before closing."

"I didn't want to leave you alone right now, even if it's a public place." Arturo sounded sheepish but looked at her with a large smile on his face.

"I'm only teasing. I'm happy you care, but really, I'm not fragile. Andiamo. We need to go out and enter by the outside front stairs."

Arturo looked at her with raised eyebrows, searched her face for any additional lines of worry and then put up a show of his hands in mock defeat. "*Brava*. I stand corrected." Arturo beamed at her. "Please lead on, McDuff."

They laughed at the old joke they shared from college days and took the stairs to the museum's front doors. They handed their tickets to the attendant and walked over to a grand salon on the left side. The room was furnished as a private sitting room with furniture either once owned by the Borghese family or pieces that reflected their taste and time of collecting. All the flooring and wall treatments were intact. It was a room reflecting an unlimited budget.

Standing erect with the guidebook in her hand, Fiona asked him, "How much do you know about the museum and its collection?"

"I read about it in grade school but have never been for a tour. I'm interested, however, and hope you'll enlighten me." Arturo rolled his eyes, as if waiting for her to start a canned speech prepared for a guide.

"This is the room with the Caravaggios, but before we start looking at them, I'll briefly review the history of the Borghese's villa and their collecting habits. It will only be a quick overview."

Fiona looked up at Arturo and saw he was staring at all the objects d'art around the room. The room was beautifully decorated with the original antique furniture, porcelain and sculpture. The woodwork was elaborate and the walls were covered in damask silk. The room overwhelmed the viewer with opulence and wealth. The décor almost overpowered the oil paintings.

"The Galleria Borghese was originally named Villa Pinciana and it was never meant to be a home. The Villa Pinciana was built as a museum to house the finest examples of ancient and modern art, as a music center, and also as a place for the contemplation of nature since it's surrounded by an immense park. In fact, the Villa was a showcase or showplace for the artistic flowering of the Roman Baroque. Pope Paul V Borghese had an unusually long papacy. He was pope from 1605 to 1621 and his nephew, Cardinal Scipione Borghese, helped him launch the new exuberant spirit of the Roman Baroque. The Borghese family wanted to influence taste and recreation. The architecture, inspired by ancient Roman villas, also had to reflect the seriousness of being a diplomatic seat of the papal court. Much later, the Borghese family sold the villa, the land and its contents to Italy for a nominal amount, thus making their final philanthropic gesture to the people of Rome."

"But let's go see the Caravaggios." Fiona led Arturo to a small portrait. She continued, "One painting to examine is Caravaggio's satirical self-portrait, *Il Bacchino Malato*, painted early in his career, 1593. Caravaggio took a typical genre painting of a studio model with fruit and made it into a tribute to artists: their divine inspiration, their creative urge, which manifested itself at night with the help of wine and debauchery. The pale flesh and the sickly circles under the eyes demonstrate the painter's vision of how an artist can self-destruct."

Fiona drew her hand to another painting saying, "This is Cardinal Scipione Borghese's *St. John*. I believe the one we're looking for is similar in style and has the same model. Caravaggio used his favorite model, a rough Neapolitan street boy, for his late paintings. See how the boy turns a downhearted look towards the viewer as he droops on the red drape. The ram, a symbol of the Cross, is shown behind St. John with vine leaves, the symbol of eternal life, in his mouth. Look, Arturo how the background is almost abstract, left in almost a raw state, painted in glittering blackness. The red shawl with its fringe, however, is rendered with layers of paint, which was Caravaggio's traditional method. The figure of St. John is brought up close, so the audience senses the immediacy of the figure."

Fiona pointed to another painting, "Then look at *David with the Head of Goliath*, painted in 1609 or 1610. One of his last or, many believe, his final painting. A young boy looks, perhaps in judgment, at the severed head. Goliath is a self-portrait of the mature artist. But the boy could be a young Caravaggio looking at his misspent youth and talent. The viewer looks onto a subject of a life ending in horror."

Fiona stood back from the painting and contemplated the power of the imagery. She thought of her husband,

Sergio, and how he had wasted his life, how he had fled from his companions of crime and debt. The tragic similarity between Caravaggio and Sergio struck her like a lightning bolt. Both men started life with so many gifts but chose to live a life of crime. Fiona's fevered imagination shifted to an image of the Amalfi Drive. She wondered, what were Sergio's last thoughts as he went over the cliff? She shuddered and turned to Arturo. He was looking at her with his eyes wide but remained silent. Arturo slowly held out his hand to her.

Fiona attempted to lighten the atmosphere and in a joking tone asked, "How was this for an impromptu speech about the Borghese? Basta così?"

"Arturo smiled and said, "Sì. Basta così. It was just the right mix of history of the Borghese family and the beauty of Caravaggio's work. Let's go for a drink and some food. Shall we?"

"I agree. Let's walk the long way home and stop at my favorite neighborhood spot."

Arturo and Fiona linked arms and walked out of the room. The splendor of the decoration and the grandeur of the architecture provided a distraction, albeit a brief one. Both of them wanted to hold onto the moment as long as possible.

The weather, although glorious, had a hint of September. There was a slight shiver of coolness when they walked in the shade of the trees in the substantial garden. The paths were well-tended, and there were many people strolling in the gardens. Fiona suggested they take a slight detour to walk into the heart of the park to the Giardino del Lago and look at the temple on the island. Fiona and Arturo stopped briefly to look at the ornamental pond and gazed at all the people rowing the boats – a popular

Roman pastime. Small children were held up to look at the ducks while older children threw bread at the birds walking around the edge of the lake. Fiona marveled at the perfectly groomed and immaculately dressed Roman children. She would never get used to it: They played with one another, organized games, ran and screamed at one another but never returned mussed or dirty. Fiona smiled at the picture of domestic tranquility and then turned away. She took Arturo's arm again and led the way to the exit of the garden.

They walked by the French Academy of Art and by Ciampini, a restaurant famous for its truffle risotto and the best mango gelato in Rome. Fiona pointed to the gated property overlooking Ciampini and said, "It's a famous private girls' school. Did you date any of the girls in your youth?"

"Certo. The girls wore their staid uniforms and their little pleated skirts just so. But as soon as they left school for the day and Mama was not nearby, they hiked their skirts into micro-minis and met their boyfriends. It was a rite of passage for all of us – the boys to look and the girls to show off."

Fiona and Arturo walked until they reached Via Sistina at the top of the Spanish Steps and then stopped to look at the view. She noticed a *gatara*, an old woman who doted on cats, throwing food scraps to the scrawny Roman cats swarming around her. Fiona waved to the old woman as she walked past.

Looking down onto the Piazza di Spagna, Fiona saw gypsies walking down the Spanish Steps in small packs, looking for an easy victim. Some young people were sleeping in the corners of a step and some were drinking wine out of bottles. The fabled Spanish Steps were littered with paper wrappings and bottles. There was a *fioraia*, a small flower vendor, selling bouquets out of a cart at the foot of the steps.

They returned to Fiona's neighborhood and arrived at the neighborhood tavern, Osteria Margutta. Fiona and Arturo entered a dark-wood-paneled dining room with small tables crammed onto the floor. The tablecloths were a woven colorful check, and royal-blue curtains brightened the mullioned windows. The overall effect was casual yet elegant. Freddo, the owner, rushed over to greet Fiona and was introduced to Arturo. Showing them to a window table, Freddo looked at Fiona and said, "Vino rosso?"

"Sì. Grazie."

"*Benissimo.*"

He bustled off. Fiona smiled at Arturo and said, "Yes, he's the owner of his family's restaurant. His uncle, Federico Fellini, was famous, of course, and always had an apartment here. Did you know Fellini encouraged the first street art fairs after the war? The artists would hang their paintings and sketches right on the walls of the buildings on Via Margutta. It was a fantastic time. People sitting outside, eating and drinking. Others simply strolled by with their children. Great art was shown, and the studios were all open for viewing. Now the real estate is too valuable and the artists are being replaced by antique dealers and fashion boutiques."

"The price of success?" Arturo smiled at her as he took the bread basket from Freddo.

Fiona said, "Grazie, Freddo."

"Welcome back, Fiona. We've missed you." Freddo ducked his head as he uncorked the wine and poured some into each glass. "I'm so sorry to hear about Sergio,"

Freddo's eyes watered and he continued, "We all mourn his passing."

"Thank you. It's still hard to believe. Arturo is an old friend. He's helping me with all of the business matters, which seem to be over my head."

"Of course. If there's anything we can do to make your life easier, let me know. We're a small community here and look out for one another. Eh?"

"Grazie, Freddo," Fiona said softly.

"Enjoy the wine; it's on the house. And let me select some of your favorites for dinner. Va bene?"

"Oh, yes. Thanks for being so kind, Freddo."

Freddo returned with steaming plates of spaghetti alla carbonara, an essential Roman dish. As with all things Roman, this dish was the subject of a much-heated debate as to whose creation reigned supreme in the Eternal City. Freddo's recipe was one of the finest Arturo had sampled, and he kissed the tips of his fingers with appreciation. Upon hearing such praise, Luca, the chef, promenaded over to their table still wearing his yolk-stained apron to survey the delight on his patron's face as Arturo devoured the last remnants on the plate with a piece of bread. After accepting their compliments, he presented them with glasses of limoncello, homemade vodka flavored with Caprese lemons.

After paying their bill, Arturo and Fiona returned to her apartment to continue contacting the vendors. She quickly skimmed the list of vendors still needing to be contacted and was discouraged. Fiona was deep in thought when the beautiful aroma of coffee wafted around her. She followed the scent and the comfort of familiar smells enveloped her. Fiona dropped into a kitchen chair.

"So far, no one had any interesting news," Arturo explained, "I reached about ten people. Here's the rest."

Reviewing the end of the list, Fiona was tired and disappointed not to have any new information about missing items. Arturo, however, was pleased to have made appointments with a few of the vendors. He attempted to encourage her by saying, "We're chipping away at the list. We're making progress. *Piano, piano.* Slowly, slowly."

While having coffee, their peaceful companionship was upended by the unexpected shrill ring of the phone. Fiona jumped out of her chair to answer the caller. Listening intently, she confirmed plans for a meeting within an hour at a warehouse in the quarter called Trastevere.

Parts of the neighborhood resembled a slum; in fact, many years ago, Trastevere had been a notorious quarter for thieves. The warehouse was on Vicolo del Cinque, Little Street of the Five – named for a thief's biggest tool, his five fingers. The thieves had moved out and many of the buildings were restored and had modern conveniences. Fiona knew Mimo as a dealer who supplied Sergio with exquisite pieces of furniture. Mimo had been to her house many times for parties and also small dinners with special clients. His warehouse was also a showroom for special high-end decorators or VIP clients. She'd never been in the neighborhood at night and knew she was taking a risk, but Fiona felt the man must have precious information to warrant a late-night meeting.

Arturo sat in the kitchen chair staring at Fiona, listening to what she was telling him about the importance of the hurriedly scheduled meeting. His face was a taut mask of silent fury. "You know who Mimo is, I assume." Arturo's silence showed that he certainly did.

"Mimo lives in Trastevere near his warehouse. He has

an important wholesale interior furnishings business," Fiona retorted.

"No!' Arturo shouted, interrupting her. He acted as if he had not heard Fiona. "We've been naïve. I realized just how naïve when I heard the name. This is a major tactical error! We should have anticipated the stakes would be raised. Mimo is not a simple antique designer. He's a valuable player in the Camorra and serves as a frontman for some of their legitimate businesses. He's only laundering their illicit money and also trading in stolen antiques." Arturo exclaimed in exasperation, "I don't like it. I don't think this is a good idea. It's too dangerous for you! Going alone into a deserted warehouse? And at night, too! No way! I'll go with you."

Fiona shook her head and sighed in resignation. She quietly said, "All right, I agree with you, but I'll enter the warehouse pretending to be alone. After all, I know the dealer, Mimo, and agreed to his proposal. He seemed tired more than guilty or suspicious," Fiona groused.

Arturo found the Ponte Sisto and drove over the slow-moving Tiber. He looked down at Rome's gigantic sewer snaking through the city on its way to the sea. The Tiber is a clean stream sparkling through the hills of central Italy, and in Rome it becomes turbid from untreated sewage and industrial waste. Arturo found a street near Mimo's shop and parked neatly along a wall, almost scraping the side of the Lancia.

"Are you certain this is for the best? To be here at night?" Arturo asked.

"Sì."

Arturo grabbed a large flashlight and muttering over his shoulder said, "Andiamo." Arturo switched off the engine and turned to Fiona. He cleared his voice, "I'm only concerned about your safety. I know you're not afraid, but this is serious and too dangerous. I've never mentioned this before since you were married, but now I must let you know how I care for you. I want to protect you tonight and always. I want ..."

"Shh, I know, Arturo. I think you're wonderful and kind. I know you want to protect me. I don't know what I'd do without you. But I have to do this tonight, and I have to go in alone as planned. I'll be strong by knowing you are nearby, waiting for me." With that, she leaned over and gave him a loving kiss and opened the car door.

They walked under a full moon that bathed the city in golden light. The moon's rays dealt kindly with the old, shuttered buildings they passed in the narrow streets. Trastevere, the workingman's neighborhood, had resisted modernization as shown by the chariot-width streets. Still, the neighborhood was a slum. They gingerly walked down the grim back street avoiding the debris that had accumulated during the day. The street was impressively dirty as the city street cleaners with their long twig brooms would not descend on the artisan neighborhood until the next morning at dawn.

The buildings looked equally forbidding with no light shining in any of the upper-story windows. Fiona found the number she was looking for on a corner building and knocked on the heavy door. Hearing no response, she pushed hard on the door using her shoulder, and it creaked open. She turned quickly and signaled Arturo to stay behind and watch the street.

It was pitch-black. Sweeping the flashlight back and forth, Fiona entered into the gloom of the warehouse. There was a little light in the space, and she edged slowly toward the source. Fiona entered a large anteroom with cement floors and rough walls. Every foot of space was crammed thick with used furniture in various states of repair. She stepped softly toward a door on the right; it swung back with a creak, letting out a gust of moldy air. Nothing, evidently, had been moved or dusted in the room since it was too overwhelmed with furniture stacked high to the ceiling. It was even more of a nightmare of clutter than the other room with chandeliers hanging uselessly from the beams.

Fiona stepped softly into the room. Instinct made her move as cautiously as a cat. An overhead spotlight clicked loudly, highlighting a desk in an interior room and a man standing behind it. Fiona barely recognized Mimo, the dealer, as the room was dark. Mimo was dressed in his usual garb of a white shirt, pressed blue jeans and lizard cowboy boots. Knowing the vanity of this man, Fiona imagined the boots added much-needed height to his diminutive frame. Mimo, moreover, was so slight that Fiona was not intimidated by him, despite the ominous surroundings.

"Shut the door," he said. "Move over here." Mimo gestured to her with his smoking cigarette and Fiona obeyed. She walked closer to him. All the while, he kept pointing his glowing cigarette tip at the pile of paperwork on his desk, leaving whorls of smoke spiraling up to the ceiling. Upon reaching the dusty desk, Fiona looked down onto the mass of strewn papers and saw he actually was pointing with a nicotine-stained finger to an open ledger.

"These numbers don't make any sense," Mimo started stabbing the ledger with his pointer finger. He continued to jab at the ledger, making it shift on the pile of papers.

"I'll try to make sense of them, Mimo," Fiona said in a soothing tone. She examined the pages of the ledger, but they did not match the code of Sergio's cipher. She shook her head and said, "I'm sorry. Perhaps we need more information or another file?"

Mimo narrowed his eyes as he looked at her. She felt a terrible foreboding now: Were his eyes stinging from the cigarette smoke or was he assessing her with suspicion? She never knew. He flicked his eyes away from her for an instant and looked into the cavernous darkness of the warehouse. Fiona's mind was racing, but her reflexes were slower as she stood still thinking. Suddenly, without any warning sound, she felt an iron grip around her neck; her body was pulled violently backward and collided with a massive wall of muscular flesh. Fiona felt her spine arch to an impossible angle as she started choking. The man heaved her higher in the air as her feet dangled off the floor. She could not breathe. As her head started to spin, the large man snarled in her ear, "Gimme me the list of names and locations, or I'll snap your neck." His accent was heavy, southern Italian. Fiona recognized the man's accent as being from the Spanish section of Naples. His dialect was hard to understand as he pronounced his words in a sloppy manner, not crisply like the Florentine Italian she had learned as a student.

Fiona managed to choke out the words, "I don't know what you're looking for!"

The man smacked her on the head and said, "Don't play games, lady. You'll die. Slow. I'll make you feel it but good."

She was not able to see him but felt his hot, putrid breath on her neck and felt his saliva drip down her back as he spit the words out. She felt the nausea roll in her stomach and fought back the bile rising into her throat.

Outside on the street, there was a loud noise, a crashing of metal. She heard the steady running of boots and saw Arturo carrying a slim, long iron bar, waving it over his head. Fiona squirmed and made what she thought was a good move away from the grasp of her assailant, but the brute cracked her solidly on the head, and Fiona felt herself falling onto the floor. She lay stunned on the floor and only managed to raise her head off the floor in time to watch Arturo burst into the room. He grabbed her assailant by the balls and squeezed hard.

"Listen, you piece of shit," Arturo yelled. The big man paled and fell back against the wall. "If you don't leave her alone," Arturo bellowed, "I'll make you see your own dick without looking in the mirror." Arturo squeezed the man's testicles harder and the thug howled in pain. Arturo continued in the same hissing tone, "If I had the time, I'd be glad to hand you over to a garbage incinerator, you asshole. Don't bother her again or you'll find trouble."

Arturo let the man go and watched the thug's face slowly regain some color. He saw there were tears in Fiona's assailant's eyes. In a rapid movement, Arturo slapped the man's head with the metal staff and the big man collapsed in a heap.

Arturo ran over to Fiona and gently cradled her in his arms. She looked into his panicked eyes and whispered, "I'm okay. I'm not hurt."

"I should not have let you enter alone. It's my fault. My fault! You were hurt because I left you alone," exclaimed Arturo.

"No, I'll be okay. Who made the noise?" Fiona croaked out the question while massaging her head.

"I heard a crash near the building and didn't look. I only thought of you and ran in. You were alone, lying on the floor." He drew her even closer to him and was beginning to shake.

"Let's go home before the polizia arrive. We don't want their attention," Fiona moaned when Arturo helped her to her feet.

They looked out the door and stared down the black, sinister street. Arturo whispered to Fiona, "Stay in the shadows. I want to see what the commotion is about."

Arturo crept up the street and heard angry epithets of "Cretino" and "Stupido" exchanged. The loud crush of metal had been a collision between a small sedan and an even smaller Fiat. The owners of the two crashed cars were absorbed in a fierce argument. Arturo looked over and saw a large object, the sedan's bumper, had been torn off in the crash and had landed on a three-wheeled truck. The truck's alarm system had triggered and no doubt would summon its owner. He ran silently to Fiona and they left the shadows. Arturo practically carried Fiona down the street to their waiting car. The wail of the police car could be heard in the distance.

Fiona's shoulders slumped at an angle as she and Arturo dragged themselves up the steps to the apartment. She snapped on the lights, trying to breathe in some calm from the familiar surroundings of her home. "I'll take a shower and then let's have some very large brandies in the living room." She looked over her shoulder at Arturo and gave him a cheery smile.

Arturo muttered, "Splendid." He went into the living room to make himself comfortable. It was an expansive room with a corner lined with bookshelves serving as a study. Each shelf bulged with fine art books and reference books on antique furniture. There were some old and modern pictures on the walls, a Persian carpet, a large sofa covered with a linen slipcover and a number of cozy and deep club chairs, upholstered in taupe leather. The drapes were drawn; a large Venetian mirror hung over the mantle and before it stood a table set as a bar. Over the drinks table hung a portrait of Sergio and Fiona. The double portrait was a wedding gift painted by Fiona for Sergio. Shaking his head, Arturo looked around the room slowly to regain his inner balance. The crystal decanter filled with an old brandy appealed to Arturo's present state of mind. He poured a generous amount and lifted his glass in an ironic salute to the matrimonial portrait of Sergio and Fiona.

The scent of jasmine and rose wafted into the room. Fiona appeared wearing a lovely silk caftan with her hair hanging loosely in damp tendrils. Arturo handed her a brandy and they clinked glasses. He began to relax and played host.

"You did very well tonight. I don't like to say that you rescued me as I don't fancy being a damsel in distress. But I thank you with all my heart."

"Yes, well ..." Arturo said coloring slightly. "You look very beautiful."

Fiona stood close to him, her face tilted up to him. Arturo reached for her and kissed her. It was a deep, satisfying kiss. As they broke apart, she lifted her face and murmured, "That was nice, but let's wait for more."

Fiona stretched out on the sofa. She rubbed her aching neck and grimaced in pain.

"Things will look more normal in the morning," Arturo whispered as he massaged her feet. The phone squawked in the kitchen and he jumped to his feet to answer it. Fiona stayed on the sofa and let him deal with the late-night caller, somehow knowing it would be unwelcome news. Arturo came trailing back into the room with a scowl mapped onto his forehead.

"That was Count Volpe. What timing! He's such a foul-smelling rat! He wants to meet us at Via Condotti tomorrow morning. At least it will be in the morning so we'll be able to see," groused Arturo in a beleaguered tone of voice.

"Our lives won't be normal until I find the Caravaggio. Let's get some sleep." Fiona was close to tears, hugged Arturo, turned and tottered off into her bedroom. Arturo sighed with frustration, shook his head while looking at her departing back and slowly walked to the guest room.

Arturo went into his bathroom trying to make as little noise as possible, washed up and went to bed. He was in a dreamy space, just falling asleep, when he felt a gentle movement of the duvet and a beautiful scent of jasmine and rose envelope him. He felt his hair stroked by her hands and she paused on his lips, her tongue tracing their shape. Arturo felt his mouth covered in a familiar kiss. He felt the caress of her tongue on his nipples and groaned from the magical hands stroking his body. Arturo gave a moan of long-held passion and was swept away with the movement of their bodies. As he held her tight and kissed her upon entering her, he sensed he was receiving her soul, her love and moved more quickly until, with a shudder, he gave into his desire. Somehow they finished together, he with a low moan and she with a series of piercing, wild cries. Afterward, Fiona gently wrapped herself along his body and quickly they went to sleep. Not much later, Fiona awakened him and whispered, "We must never take us for granted."

Arturo kissed Fiona on the mouth and whispered, "I will love you until the last breath leaves my body."

He awoke later than planned, the scent of her skin making him want to stay in bed awhile longer. Then he got up and went to look out the window. It was another cloudless day with the heat rising. He went into the bathroom, got dressed and sauntered into the kitchen. When he entered, Fiona turned from the kitchen table. She wore a tight-fitting, short-sleeved suit paired with sensible flats for walking the stone-paved Roman streets.

"*Buongiorno.* Good morning. We have to leave in a few minutes. If you want, we can have a caffè in the square." She continued to look at him with an open smile on her face but was holding her bag on her arm.

For the first time, Arturo felt a little awkward with her. Had he overstepped some boundary with her? Had he taken advantage of her vulnerability and ruined their future as a couple?

Fiona, however, didn't bring last night up. It was clear she sensed Arturo's uneasiness. She blinked at him. Finally, staring into her eyes, Arturo said, "Were you sure?"

"Absolutely certain."

With that, Fiona gave him a big hug, which Arturo returned with relief and abandon. Fiona found that she was in the air, Arturo standing very close to her, hugging her and spinning her around. Fiona was not quite sure how she came to be there – she hadn't meant to let him carry her away with emotion. She studied the pattern of his shirt and said in a small, gruff voice: "You're a hard man not to love, Arturo. Thank God for that!"

The moment of unease, the first curious glance of their eyes in the kitchen, had passed. Fiona looked at him and she glimpsed, deep in his blue eyes, the glimmer that she hoped would be there. It lasted only for an instant, and then his eyes were cloaked with the eyes he offered to the world. Yet that star-like glimmer was a revelation to Fiona. She knew she could trust Arturo and Fiona felt revived. The morning appointment beckoned and they started out immediately.

They walked down Via del Babuino, Street of the Baboon, where all the most expensive antique shops and upscale art galleries were and past Babington's Tea Rooms into the Piazza di Spagna, a square of dusty-orange buildings that stood in the shade of a few palms at the foot of the Spanish Steps. The square was central Rome's luxury shopping area.

They decided against Babington's Tea Rooms as it was a meeting place for many of Fiona's friends, expats living in Rome. It fronted on the Piazza di Spagna in a Renaissance building, standing on one side of the Spanish Steps with the other housing the Keats-Shelley Memorial and a quaint B&B. The tearoom served traditional or old-fashioned English foods with a Roman twist. It was a natural forum for rumors and gossip, and Fiona wanted to avoid it for a while.

In the middle was the Spanish Steps, a gift from France and namesake of Spain, made famous by numerous picture postcards and quick oil sketches produced for the tourist trade. The worn marble steps always were teeming with people. The tourist legend said you had to meet someone you knew on the steps or you'd never return to Rome. Nice for the tearoom's trade, thought Fiona.

Glancing at the crowded steps, Fiona shuddered and hoped she knew no one in such a scruffy, rough-looking crowd. People were squatting on the steps, cooking their food; small children dressed in garish clothes roamed the steps in packs pretending to beg while they pickpocketed naïve tourists. A few optimists catering to the tourist trade had set up umbrellas ready to draw a passerby's charcoal portrait.

While Arturo went in search of two espressos, Fiona found a seat on the low marble curb surrounding the Barcaccia, Pietro Bernini's boat-shaped fountain, and stared into the water spouting from the two fountains. She turned sharply when she felt a hand touch her shoulder. Fiona opened her eyes wide as she looked at the man seated beside her. Gone were the tattered clothes and old straw hat. Don Carlo Petacci was highly groomed and nattily attired in a beautifully tailored suit. She hardly recognized her farmer neighbor from Anacapri. The transformation was startling to Fiona.

"Don Carlo, what are you doing in Rome?"

"Fiona, I'm sorry to be here. You really need to find the painting soon. People will start to get hurt. I don't want anything to happen to such a beautiful, young lady." In one smooth movement, he sat closer to her, his thighs touching hers. Fiona felt her skin tingling, not with pleasure but fright. Signore Petacci very gently cupped her face in his strong hands and said, "Che bellissima, you have the face of a Madonna, Signora Celesti. Take care of your face. Guard your beauty well." And with that, he removed his hands, shifted over on the marble seat and sat beside her with a ramrod-straight back.

Fiona narrowed her eyes as she stared at Signore Petacci. She observed he wore a gold-and-diamond Rolex watch and an expensive silk tie. His eyes were steel-grey, cold as chrome and he was not smiling. Fiona's attention shifted as she saw Arturo coming towards her. As if he sensed Arturo, Signore Petacci stood up, brushing off the seat of the slacks. "You've been warned, Signora Celesti."

Signore Petacci turned to face Arturo, "Hello, young man. I saved a seat for you. Nice to see you, Fiona." He walked away with two young men following him from a discreet distance.

Arturo sat down with the two espressos and looked at Fiona with questioning eyes. "What did I miss?"

"If I'm not mistaken, I was just visited by the Camorra, maybe the boss. Signore Petacci was my neighbor in Anacapri and always seemed like a nice, old man – a peasant who worked all his life at an olive grove. I was shocked to see him here and dressed in a suit. Signore Petacci, I called him Don Carlo, said we had to hurry and find the Caravaggio." Fiona gave Arturo a haunted look. "The Camorra, they're everywhere," she whispered.

"We've known all along that the Camorra played rough and they are bullies. They can't kill us or they won't get the painting." Arturo stopped talking as he saw the desperate look in Fiona's eyes.

"They threatened to disfigure me." Fiona's eyes were ready to overflow.

"They are bullies; I said that earlier. Here, take my handkerchief and you'll feel better with some coffee. I won't leave your side. They'll have to contend with me first. Let's concentrate on solving the mystery and finding the Caravaggio." Arturo put his arm around her shoulder and hugged her.

Fiona wiped her eyes and took a deep breath. She smiled tremulously at Arturo and picked up the espresso. They sipped the coffee while sitting side by side, thinking their own thoughts while looking at the cool, green water.

After leaving Piazza di Spagna, Fiona and Arturo headed westward along Via Condotti, Rome's most fashionable shopping street. Although both knew Rome well, neither ever had visited this private address. Arturo found No. 68 and glanced into the shadowy courtyard, which also boasted a fountain, albeit one with a mossy basin. The wall behind the fountain bore a Maltese cross – white, eight-pointed, on a red background.

Fiona took a closer look to read a sign inside the gate and was startled to learn they had stepped across a frontier and were no longer in Italy. Palazzo Malta, a building on Via Condotti, was the seat of the Knights of Malta, Christendom's oldest surviving order of chivalry. A nervous giggle flooded her lungs and she let out a high-pitched peal of laughter as she considered the absurdity of meeting the sinister Count Volpe here of all places.

The territory of the Knights of Malta totaled only three acres, making it a tiny sovereign state, much smaller than the territory of the Vatican City, which has 109 acres. Fiona realized that the Knights governed this little land area and that she entered only by their permission and had to abide by their rules. Fiona wondered how powerful Count Volpe was in the ancient Sovereign Military Order of Malta. Were they in even more danger? She looked over at Arturo and saw he had squared his shoulders, looking thoughtful but not worried.

At the palazzo's gate, they asked for Count Volpe while presenting their credentials to the guard. They were escorted up the stairs to the second floor. The floor was carpeted in Persian runners that deadened the sound of their footsteps and along the walls were showpieces of antique furniture, very different from the modern office furniture on the ground floor. Pictures in heavy gilt frames hung on the pale walls. They were seated on one of the ornately carved benches and instructed to wait for Count Volpe. Two uniformed attendants stood nearby insuring that Fiona and Arturo stayed seated. The hallway was quiet with no sounds of nearby office work.

Count Volpe pulled distractedly at the strands of his hair as he read through some of his personal papers stacked neatly in the center of his desk. A wall clock chimed as he continued concentrating on his business affairs. The office was large with oversized Persian carpets. The carpets and the thick hanging tapestries deadened all outdoor sound. Count Volpe had no excuse to neglect his work. He fingered one line on the page of numbers and, suddenly, he felt the back of his neck prickle as he sensed a presence in his office. Count Volpe hurriedly looked up, startled to see two men standing at the entrance of his office. His eyes grew wide with alarm when he recognized them: Bruno and Tito Tozzi, members of the Camorra. One of them, wearing a short leather jacket, stood holding a small knife in his hand. Both men were wearing leather gloves despite the hot weather.

Count Volpe tried to maintain calm as he blinked and stared at the approaching thugs. He shivered and they were standing on either side of his chair. Bruno had a face like a punch-drunk old boxer with cauliflower ears. He loomed over Count Volpe and his beady, little eyes looked down with dull indifference. "Count Volpe, you really shouldn't be taking so long getting the picture. It's insulting to the boss. He's getting mad, which is never good. I'm afraid, Count Volpe, the next time we'll meet will be on top of a rooftop. You won't like the view," the big man smirked and the count heard the other snickering behind his back. Abruptly, the count felt his shoulders seized from behind, and he suddenly was lifted from his chair. Tito kicked the chair over and Bruno came in close to the count's face. Count Volpe shrieked as his knees buckled from fear. "We're not here for a chat and a glass of grappa. You get the picture or we'll cut the girl's face. She works with her hands, doesn't she? We'll crush her knuckles first and then we'll break her wrists. How's that? Next we'll go after your family. Let's see," he leered at the count as his eyes glimmered, "you have a little blonde granddaughter. Flora is about five now? She won't be so cute if we burn off all her blonde locks, will she?"

Count Volpe tried to arch his back, to wriggle out of the vise-like grip, but it was useless. He whimpered, "A presto. I understand. I'll get it."

"We're on a short leash from the boss. Don't keep him waiting." Bruno nodded to Tito and Count Volpe was released from his iron grip. He fell to the floor, breathing heavily.

In what seemed like an eternity but was actually mere seconds, time passed and the count sensed he was alone again. He slowly got up and righted the chair. Count Volpe sat down and gave himself a moment to collect his thoughts. "I must convince Fiona how desperate the situation is," muttered Count Volpe to himself. He slowly resumed his normal breathing and got on his speakerphone.

"I'm ready for my appointment. Send them in, please."

Soon Fiona and Arturo were ushered through a series of interlocking rooms, all richly furnished, to the spacious office of the grand chancellor, the second-ranking Knight of Malta. The beautiful, old paneled room that served as an office was quiet. It had a vaulted ceiling and fireplace. Sunlight was kept at bay by the heavily draped windows, no doubt protecting the antique furniture and Baroque paintings.

Count Volpe, seated at the rococo desk, looked up,

gave them a wolfish grin and said, "I borrowed the office from my good friend, the grand chancellor. I hope you've made progress, my dear girl?"

"We're trying to untangle Sergio's bills and statements. We've only begun reaching suppliers and we'll need to check the inventory," Fiona smiled back.

"I'm trying to keep the partners calm. It's tough going. Any news at all?" The count said waspishly as he raised his eyebrows and watched Fiona and Arturo.

"Nothing," replied Fiona while standing at the desk. "Are you a Knight of Malta?"

"Yes," the count drawled in an affected tone. "My family's from a distinguished line of knights."

In a soft voice, Fiona asked, "Assuming the Camorra is paid the monies they feel they are owed, I'm wondering, who is the rightful owner of the Caravaggio?" Fiona rushed on with her burning question, "Is the painting owned by the Knights? Not the Vatican? At the time of his death, there was a rumor Caravaggio didn't die of malaria or disease but was murdered by the Knights of Malta. They did indeed seize several paintings from the boat and claimed rightful ownership as Caravaggio was also a knight. The Knights of Malta only later returned them when threatened by the royal court — by the pope. It's on record that they kept one, so maybe they held an additional one or two back? Perhaps this one?"

"Bah. The prior of Capua did not know Caravaggio was a defrocked knight and mistakenly seized some paintings. He returned two St. Johns and a Magdalene upon the crown's request. One of them, *St. John the Baptist*, was returned to Cardinal Scipione Borghese and now hangs in the Galleria Borghese. You know this, Fiona. It's documented," Count Volpe said this while noisily lining his piles of paper in a row.

Fiona persisted, "There could be another St. John and rumors say ..."

Smashing his fist on the desk, the count interrupted her, "Forget this crazy thought about a conspiracy involving the Knights of Malta! I'm simply a guest at the palazzo, invited by my host, the grand master. I have business that brings me frequently to Rome, and I appreciate the privacy the grand master allows me. This palazzo also houses the superior officer and his family. The grand chancellor, Orazio, is a wonderful man and I've known him for years." Suddenly drawing a deep breath, Count Volpe stopped speaking and remaining still, he looked into Fiona's eyes. Without saying another word, the emotions running across his face betrayed his embarrassment. There was a long silence. The chair squeaked as the count shifted his weight and he emitted a long sigh.

"I misspoke." Count Volpe shook his head and continued, "I should not have mentioned the grand chancellor's name." The count hesitated and again locked eyes with Fiona.

Flushed with anger, Fiona snapped, "Do you mean Count Orazio Giustinani, the art dealer, is also a Knight of Malta?"

"Sì. It's a matter of public record. As the grand chancellor, Orazio supervises the Order's humanitarian work along with some of the ceremonial roles." Count Volpe drummed his fingers on the desk while waiting for Fiona's reaction.

"I think I missed something – what's so important about Count Giustinani? " Arturo looked from Count Volpe to Fiona.

Fiona gave a tight smile to Arturo and continued, "The esteemed Count Giustinani represents me. His gallery will launch my new series of paintings later in the year. This was arranged by my professor, Graham Hughes."

Fiona gripped the arms of her chair and looked at Arturo, then to Count Volpe. "There's no such thing as a coincidence," she snapped.

Count Volpe massaged his temple and spoke in a soothing tone, "Rome, in fact all of Italy, conducts business within small circles of old families. It's not so unusual to have a prominent art dealer who is socially connected also be a member of the Knights of Malta. After all, the Order was early populated by the flower of the European aristocracy. In its early days, the Knights of Malta were courted by the noblest families as the Order had wealth and power. Now, alas, we are greatly reduced in numbers and riches. We are no longer warrior knights but humanitarians." Count Volpe smiled sheepishly as he looked up from his desk. "But enough of this, let's consider our options. I was informed about last night's incident only after the fact. I'm sorry about the rough handling. Some of my partners are losing their patience and used this as a warning to me."

"A warning to you? I think that gorilla would have snapped my neck if Mimo ordered it!" Fiona realized she was shouting and forced herself to regain some of her composure. She saw out of the corner of her eye Arturo was straining to hold back from striking the old man.

"They're desperate men and want their property. Time is running out," the count paused. He examined his nails while he asked, "What about the stretcher bars? Sergio could have rolled the painting and hidden the stretchers somewhere. Have you thought of that?"

"Yes. But we haven't looked everywhere. Do you know something about any wooden stretcher bars?" Arturo drawled out the question while he looked around the room for eavesdroppers. His shoulders relaxed once he determined they were alone with the old count.

"Don't be churlish, young man. I only know you're running out of time," Count Volpe hissed. "The Camorra has warned me that they are willing to strike out even more seriously next time. Fiona, they've threatened to harm my five-year-old granddaughter. In fact, they're willing to harm your face or break your hands." Count Volpe voice petered out. He felt ashamed and didn't want to look at Fiona as she gasped in horror.

"What are you talking about? Has the Camorra visited you? Here at your office?" Arturo raised his voice threateningly.

"Sì. They were here all right. And they are dogs ready to rip us apart, including my family. I had to tell you the full truth. They will harm us, probably enjoy butchering our loved ones. They'll continue to torment us until they get their damned picture back."

Fiona sat still, absorbing the chilling information. She clicked her tongue and looked back at Count Volpe. The old man, while seated on his throne-like chair, appeared crumpled with a hunched back. Exhaustion lined his face and the count nervously combed his hand through his sparse, silver hair.

Count Volpe wearily waved a hand and shifted his gaze to Fiona. In a raspy voice, almost choking the words out, he said, "The two beasts of prey that the Camorra sent to my office crept into my office without anyone seeing them enter the building. They pounced on me and, after roughing me up, they threatened to harm you first, Fiona. Not to kill you but to disfigure you. Then these despicable thugs would go after my little Flora, my granddaughter. They ... they would torture her. Please, my dear, I'm in over my head. Things are getting out of control. Please hurry and find the painting!"

"Oddio! My God!" exclaimed Fiona. "Tell them we are making progress. We'll get the painting soon. Just buy us more time, Count." Fiona shuddered as she continued to stare at the old count and then she looked over at Arturo. He was alert, his eyes shifting back and forth between the count and Fiona. He kept silent as if waiting for the next one to speak.

Count Volpe looked Fiona over carefully almost like a prized piece of porcelain to see whether there were any telltale cracks. He was relieved to see Fiona unruffled and well-groomed despite last evening's harrowing activities. The nervous strain had not affected her demeanor. There was a sheen to her skin? Well, I wonder. Count Volpe chuckled to himself.

Fiona, recovered from her outburst, moved closer to Arturo. She looked askance at the count, saw him chuckling silently and wondered if the old man was demented. Arturo took Fiona's hand and clasped it. Count Volpe nodded to them with a knowing smile. He pursed his lips and remained silent, wary.

"Va bene. Let's get back to work. Addio," Arturo gave the count a warning look and, holding onto Fiona's arm, he escorted her out the door.

"Buona fortuna," they heard as they drifted down the hall.

In the courtyard, a chauffeur was standing by a car that flew a Maltese cross flag. Fiona and Arturo left the shaded courtyard and walked down the narrow, tangled streets to the 200-year-old Caffè Greco. The front of today's Greco, with Gucci and Hermès nearby, attracted a more fashion-conscious mob than the average tourist and was always busy with people standing by the chrome-and-marble bar, ordering un caffè and a voluptuous pastry. The bar resounded with the clatter of glasses and Arturo beckoned to the uniformed host. The man, dressed in black tie, solemnly ushered them into an interior room.

They chose a table in the back of the long, narrow room in a plush maroon alcove and sat down on a ruby-red velvet banquette. One of the ever-smiling waiters swanned over to their marble table ready to take their order. Arturo dispatched him speedily with an order of Campari e limone. He turned to Fiona and, trying to summon words to reassure her, looked into her tired but alert eyes and decided not to attempt it. Instead, Arturo gently took her hand and tenderly kissed it.

For once, they suspended any discussion about Sergio and his squalid business dealings and remained quiet, alone in their thoughts. Their bodies touched surreptitiously and they reveled in the brief interlude the quiet alcove provided them. They moved apart when the waiter returned with their drinks and a few tea sandwiches. Fiona blew a kiss as she gave Arturo a tea sandwich. They later rounded out their lunch with sfogliatelle, a shell-shaped, layered pastry with ricotta, and espresso. Refreshed, they went back onto the teeming street filled with shoppers.

"Don't we have an appointment with one of the vendors?" Fiona reminded Arturo.

"Sì. We're to meet another antique dealer on Via del Babuino. He specializes in decorative arts. Shall we go meet Signore Infanti?

"Va bene. We're almost there now."

Once again, they walked through the Piazza di Spagna, but this time Fiona did not look at the fountain. They arrived at the antique shop. It was brilliantly lit to better show off the crystal chandeliers and estate jewelry. Fiona stopped to look at a few paintings from the school of Caravaggio. An older man greeted them, "Signora Celesti and Signore Monti?"

"Yes. Thanks for seeing us," Arturo replied. He saw a slight man wearing a neat, linen suit with a tie and a pocket scarf.

"Please, let's go to my desk as I've written a list of consigned items."

They walked to the rear of the shop and sat down at the leather embossed desk. Signore Infanti picked up a one-page, typed list. He gave it to Fiona. "I'm sorry for your loss, Signora. Sergio and I did some business over the years. I'm prepared to return all of the items to you today."

"Thank you. That's very kind of you," Fiona said as she perused the list. It was ten pieces of estate jewelry.

Signore Infanti used a key to open the middle draw and withdrew a box. Inside were individual velvet packets. It was an assortment of brooches, bracelets and a ring, all set in semi-precious stones. After comparing the list prepared by Arturo, Fiona signed the release and dropped the packets of jewelry in her handbag. "It's all in order, so thank you for your time, Signore Infanti."

Fiona and Arturo stood, shook hands with the man and left the shop. "Well, that was disappointing, but at least we did one more thing. Are there many more today?"

Arturo looked at Fiona's white face and said, "No appointments. Let's go back to the apartment and look at the remaining names. Maybe some will look more promising than others and we can narrow the list down.

"Sounds good. Let's go. They walked more slowly down the street and Fiona seemed even more listless. She finally said, "Arturo, I have a bad headache. Would you mind getting some aspirin at the farmacia at the end of the street?"

"Certo, if you promise to go directly home." He smiled at her. She nodded thanks and took a right onto a side street to go to Via Margutta.

Arturo walked with a single-mindedness down Via del Babuino. He followed the sign of the farmacia, which was down a short alley off of the main piazza. The narrow alley was deserted, and then it wasn't. There was a man standing by a shuttered doorway. He caught sight of Arturo and whistled to another man further down the alley. The man started across the alley to Arturo but was not in any hurry. Arturo stopped and looked behind him, there were two men coming up fast behind him. The four men cornered Arturo and two pushed him up against the wall. Arturo only had enough time to get a foot pressed up against the wall behind him. He quickly pushed back hard and launched himself at the men on his right. He felt something tear at his arm, but by then Arturo managed to get his hands on one of the men and butted him hard in the face. Arturo was about to swing the man around to use him to block further blows when he felt another man grab the front of his jacket. Arturo stopped struggling and looked at them. They looked at him and one suddenly punched him in the face, striking his right cheek. He fell back against the wall, no longer balancing on the balls of his feet. The same man hammered him in the stomach, forcing him to double over. Arturo's head was ringing. He heard a voice threaten, "Your artist girlfriend is next. Find the painting. The boss is getting tired of waiting." The men suddenly disappeared and Arturo slowly stood up, took a breath to regain his balance and shakily walked to the farmacia.

The woman at the counter looked at him with concern, "Signore, did you trip and fall?"

Arturo looked into a mirror on the nearby counter and saw his nose was bleeding and his cheek was swollen. "Sì. A stupid fall. Let me have some gauze and tape and also some aspirin." He quickly paid the bill and retreated from the store. Arturo walked to Via Margutta, not bothering to look over his shoulder. He sensed the Camorra would leave him alone for now. He had gotten their message.

Fiona buzzed him into the apartment and he slowly walked up the stairs. She greeted him on the landing and then cried out when she saw his face. "What happened? Were you attacked?"

"I had a run-in with the Camorra. I'm all right. They wanted to warn me that the boss wanted the Caravaggio. Let me sit down for a moment."

Fiona led Arturo into the living room and then ran into the kitchen to get a bowl of warm, soapy water. She came into the living room with fresh towels and the bowl. "Let me clean your face."

"No, Fiona. I'll do it. Please take the aspirin and lie down. I'll do the same once I've cleaned up."

Fiona sighed and reluctantly agreed. "Ok, we'll take a siesta and regroup later. I'm sorry about all of this." She hung her head and left the room.

Fiona stretched out for a nap on her bed but quickly grew restless and got up. She tiptoed over to check on Arturo, saw he was sleeping and quietly closed his door. She tiptoed into the kitchen, grabbed her purse and a shopping bag and quietly slipped out the door. Fiona went to a neighborhood market for dinner provisions and then stopped by the Osteria Margutta for extra-special cheese and bread. She hummed to herself as she left the restaurant and walked down the now-deserted street. She sensed something from behind and shot a backward glance over her shoulder. Two men were closing in on her. She hurried to her front gate and fumbled for her keys. She almost did not get the key into the front lock and grunted as it struck home in the old lock. She panted as she looked down the street. She jumped inside, kicking the groceries into the courtyard. The gate clanged shut but a hand gripped her arm with iron strength. The man held fast as he said, "I can pull you closer, so close I can cut you. Or he can break your arm. He beckoned to the man standing beside him. She looked and saw he had a vicious-looking iron club. The two men smirked as if she was a dirty joke.

"The polizia patrol this street and the apartment building is full of people. With one yell, all hell will break out. You'll be caught and I'll go after you. Now, what do you creeps want?"

"We want the painting."

"*Caffonista*, lousy peasant, you're slowing me down! I'll tell your bosses directly that you're impeding my recovery efforts. Get lost, or I'll have your legs broken. Now let go of my arm, stupido." Fiona managed to snarl the last words.

The men were startled by her attitude and abruptly let go of her arm and stood still. The one who held the club said, "Remember, we know where you live. We can get inside whenever we want."

Fiona straightened up and said in a loud voice, "I can take care of myself. Now get out of here so I can get on with my work."

She turned her back, picked up the groceries and

walked toward the front door. As she unlocked the smaller, fitted door, she looked back toward the street. It was absent of any people and quiet. She sighed with relief. All of sudden, she felt pressure on the door and looked up into the entrance.

"Signora Celesti, is everything all right? May I help you with your groceries?"

Fiona recognized her downstairs neighbor and caught her breath and said, "I'm fine. I didn't hear you in the foyer. I'm sorry, I overreacted. Thank you for your kind offer, but I can manage. Have a good evening."

"*Buona sera.*"

Fiona walked upstairs and put the provisions in the kitchen. She found a bottle of sparkling water in the refrigerator and sat down with a glass at the table. She began to shake with unspent tension. She shook herself and silently cursed. Fiona determined she would not bend to the Camorra's insidious pressure. She'd find the painting and do what they wanted, and then they'd be out of her life. She'd be fine.

Finishing the cold water, she decided not to tell Arturo about the ugly confrontation. After all, she reasoned, it was another example of thuggish bullying. She had stood up to them and bargained for more time to find the painting.

Much later, Arturo joined Fiona in the kitchen. She had prepared a light-red sauce from fresh tomatoes and basil from her building's garden. "Freddo gave me fresh pasta, bread and grilled vegetables. He also found a great chianti and a hunk of Parmesan cheese. We'll feel better with food. Let's have a glass of wine and eat in the kitchen." She gave a tentative smile as she waited for his reaction.

"I'm fine now, Fiona. Don't worry. I don't fold at the first sign of a bully. Let me open the wine."

They finished all the food and took the remainder of the bottle of wine to the library. They sat in silence and listened to music. They decided on an early evening in order to start fresh the next day.

The next morning, Arturo said, "The cornetti were wonderful and the strawberry jam was perfect. Thanks for the breakfast, Fiona." Arturo smiled at her and extended his hand to hold hers. "What shall we do first?"

Fiona hesitated and then said, "I should have suspected something. The art studio is simply too valuable for an art student or a young artist," she looked up at Arturo. He saw all her refined mannerisms had melted away. Stress and exhaustion were etched on Fiona's face but behind that, Arturo saw something else, something he had not seen before – a spark of burning determination in her eyes. He admired her unbending will, her willingness to fight and an inner strength of resolve. Arturo squeezed Fiona's hand and waited.

"I need to see Professor Hughes. I want to clarify his role in this complicated plan. Shall we walk over to his office? It's off of Via Veneto, not far from here. I'd rather surprise him. I don't want an easy explanation." Fiona still couldn't believe she had been blindsided by her mentor.

"Certo," Arturo agreed. "Let's get ready to go out."

They reached a quiet, tree-shaded side street off of Via Veneto and Fiona found the tiny bell and pressed it. Upon hearing the buzzer, she pushed the small door, which was cut into the grand antique entrance door. She stepped over the wooden threshold and beckoned to Arturo. They stepped into a dim hall foyer and Fiona clicked on a light switch. She quickly indicated the stairs with a flutter of a wave and they nipped up the stone steps to the *piano nobile*. The door promptly was opened by Graham Hughes.

"I was expecting you."

"Oh? So, Count Volpe telephoned ahead?" Fiona continued, "I suppose you know about Arturo? How he's helping me?"

Professor Hughes gave Fiona a piercing glance and extended his hand to Arturo, "I'm pleased to make your acquaintance, Mr. Monti. I only regret it's under the present circumstances."

"It won't be long before we solve this puzzle. Perhaps, you can share any information you may have?" Arturo looked back into Professor Hughes' eyes with a shrewd glance.

Professor Hughes stared back with gimlet eyes and nodded as though he had answered. Pinching his lips together, Professor Hughes looked over to Fiona, giving her a kindly glance. "Shall we go to my study?" he asked.

He ushered them down a long corridor into a light-filled room furnished as a library. Arturo looked around the room and noticed that the collection of books was magnificent. Arturo further detected that one wall was devoted to reference works of Old Masters, many of the Baroque period of art. There were several leather armchairs and an old, dark-wood trestle table serving as a desk. The room, although well-appointed, also served as an office as there were mounds of papers and files on the desk. By the window was a comfortable reading chair with a table beside it. Arturo decided in a flash to sit there and walked determinedly to the window. He noted that the apartment had a sweeping view of the Borghese gardens. After sitting down, Arturo scanned the large pile of books stacked precariously on the table beside him and was not surprised to see all were about Caravaggio. Looking over toward the desk, Arturo smiled slightly when he realized Fiona had observed his Sherlock-like examination of the library. She shook her head at him and gave him a sign with her hand to stop his detective work. She then collapsed with a sigh of contentment onto a deep-padded leather sofa.

"What a fantastic plan," Fiona groaned, not without a trace of wonder in her voice. "The worldly professor promotes his young protégé and manages to find a subsidized studio ideally located in the Borghese gardens. Who is the true landlord? The Knights of Malta?"

Humbly, Professor Hughes closed his eyes. "I ask your forgiveness," he flushed. "I am the landlord and I was a fool. I bought the studio many years ago, more than a decade, when the Knights of Malta were re-energizing their outreach programs of humanitarian aid. Orazio and I knew each other from school days in Cambridge so it was natural for him to approach me to consider a quiet real estate transaction. I thought I was helping an old friend and an honorable, respected organization, which, in fact, was true for many, many years. In turn, I gained a valuable piece of property. It seemed a sensible bargain between friends."

There was silence. Professor Hughes, with a heavy sigh, continued, "Then the warehouse fire happened. I was shocked to see it involved Sergio Celesti, the painting conservator to all the stellar galleries. Of course, I thought it was due to the chemicals igniting one night. I never suspected arson. After reading about the disastrous fire to Sergio's business, I called you, Fiona. You remember, we had coffee and I had a private view of your new work in the studio. You met Orazio for the first time that very morning." Professor Hughes' tanned face set into worried lines as he stared unflinchingly at Fiona.

"How did Orazio know just when we'd be at the garden café that morning?" Fiona coolly asked.

"It was a coincidence! A happy coincidence at the time, you may recall. I was delighted with the serendipity of the introduction of a famous art dealer to my star pupil. Please believe me, Fiona." Professor Hughes' face was beet-red, his eyes almost overflowing with emotion.

Fiona closed her eyes for an anguished moment as she reflected on his narration of events and smiled to herself as she knew in her heart that Professor Hughes, her stalwart mentor, was being forthright. "All right," said Fiona, "I believe you. But what about Count Volpe? How does he fit in?" She looked back at Professor Hughes, hoping the rest of his story rang true.

Professor Hughes cleared his throat with a hacking cough and growled, "He's an old fool who thinks the noble families are above the law. Count Volpe was at one time the chief curator of the entire art collection of the Knights of Malta. He was in charge of everything: paintings, sculpture, antique furniture and furnishings. At some point, Count Volpe decided to leverage the overstock of the minor works of arts. His plan was to raise funds for the Order and at the same time strengthen his position within the ranks of the Knights of Malta."

Professor Hughes shook his head and continued, "Count Volpe hoped to become the grand master if he rebuilt the coffers. Indeed, he had already sold off many items with the approval of the board. Count Volpe, furthermore, always sold to your husband, Fiona, as the Order was very secretive about selling from their archives. The Knights of Malta didn't want any adverse publicity and they were afraid of the fiscal authority. The plan ran smoothly for years until Count Volpe became reckless. At the time of change in the currency, Sergio approached Count Volpe with an interesting business scheme: leverage the Caravaggio as collateral in a bank loan. Count Volpe never planned to sell the Caravaggio, only to borrow against its increasing value. After all, the painting had greatly appreciated over the years and would only increase in value. The most respected galleries were borrowing against the present value of their paintings and used the borrowed funds to purchase additional inventory. Knowing the Knights of Malta did not want to be active in the marketplace, Sergio reasoned he could pose as the owner of the Caravaggio. He would approach his banker to borrow against the appreciating value of the Caravaggio, use cash to buy and sell inventory. Count Volpe, representing the Knights of Malta, would share in the profits and could at a later date reclaim the Caravaggio. Well, we all know what happened," Professor Hughes drawled. "Count Volpe was hoodwinked by Sergio and his unsavory business associates. Count Volpe never knowingly participated in any illicit business; he was trying to avoid taxes while buying and trading art."

"Did Count Volpe ever suspect Sergio was dealing with the Camorra?" Fiona looked at Professor Hughes with horror in her eyes.

"No," Professor Hughes looked directly into her eyes. "Bear in mind, Count Volpe thought Sergio was dealing with a bank. The old codger did not know about the drug labs or about Sergio's partnership with the Camorra. He never knew the painting was being used in the Camorra's money-laundering business."

"*Un momento*, just a moment," interrupted Fiona. "What do you mean by a money laundry?"

"He means," Arturo jumped in, "Sergio didn't go to any friendly banker but took old lire as collateral. That way, the Camorra could 'wash' or use their old and ill-gotten lire. I'm sure they actually had to pay Sergio even more in old lire in order to orchestrate the currency exchange." Arturo clucked his tongue in annoyance and looked at Professor Hughes for confirmation.

"Most certainly this happened," Professor Hughes nodded. "Count Volpe only learned about the drug labs and distribution network after the fire and, of course, it was too late. Even after the disastrous warehouse fire, Count Volpe hid all of these underhanded business dealings from Count Orazio Giustinani as long as he could. When he'd exhausted all other options, Count Volpe confessed his transgressions to Orazio. By that time, Orazio represented you and was planning your solo show at his gallery. Old Count Volpe was a fool in the end. He skated around the limits of the law but was never a member of the Camorra."

Professor Hughes' voice rose as he said, "I also, by the way, called Orazio and asked him to walk over from the gallery. He should be here any time. I think it's important for him to clarify his position. I want everything out in the open, Fiona." Again, he looked steadily into Fiona's eyes, waiting for her reaction.

Fiona paused as she absorbed the details of Professor Hughes' recitation of events and then nodded earnestly. "I believe you."

She smiled and straightened up in the down-filled sofa. Fiona's posture was firm as she glanced at Arturo and observed his countenance to be inscrutable. Arturo continued to stare at Professor Hughes and then broke his stare abruptly, quickly shifting his gaze onto Fiona as if he sensed her silent examination. He gave her a discreet wink and looked away, out the window, as if he suddenly had found something of interest.

Fiona settled herself into the cushions and remarked, "Yes, you did the right thing by inviting Orazio, Graham. I'll be relieved to talk with Count Giustinani." Fiona hesitated, "Your thinking is very logical, Graham." With a sidelong glance, Fiona gave her old professor a broad smile.

Arturo cleared his throat and said, "I'm ready for that drink if it's still offered."

Professor Hughes jumped up and said, "How about a Campari and soda?" He smiled as he looked at Arturo. At that moment, the front door buzzed. "What timing! I'll just go and greet Orazio. Be back in a tick."

Fiona traced an imaginary pattern on the cushion of the chair as she waited silently. Arturo stood up and scanned the view over the Borghese gardens. In a low voice, he murmured, "Can Graham see your studio from this vantage point?"

"He can with binoculars. I've joked that he can spy on me so he knows when I'm in my studio working. I always thought it was funny until now." Fiona locked eyes with Arturo and grimaced. "I can't believe there was a long-term plan behind my renting of the studio."

"I agree. After all, what would Graham gain?"

"What would I gain about what?" Professor Hughes reentered the room accompanied by Count Orazio Giustinani. Professor Hughes' eyes crackled with anger as he looked at Arturo. Professor Hughes raised himself as if he were standing on the balls of his feet and was about to lash out when Count Giustinani pulled him back. The count gently nudged Professor Hughes aside and moved forward into the library. He stood gracefully by the desk, waiting for Arturo to continue.

"I remarked to Fiona about the curious proximity of the gardens to your apartment and how one could observe her studio from a particular vantage point – this window, in fact. Of course, one would need a telescope to spot the front door," Arturo replied in a cool, measured tone.

"Allow me to introduce myself," Count Giustinani interjected. "I know you were not expecting me, and I apologize for interrupting, but I don't want my friend maligned or misunderstood for a moment. You see, it was Graham's generosity of spirit when he agreed to help me. I was in a bind caused by Count Volpe."

"As the grand chancellor," Count Giustinani inflected his speech with a note of pride, "I'm responsible for the integrity of the mission of the Knights of Malta. It is my sworn responsibility to maintain the treasury and honor the Order's mandate to deliver aid to the poor. I harbor no illusions of resuming our past glories or world power. I'm at peace with the Order's present-day mission to deliver worldwide humanitarian aid." Spreading his arms wide, he said in a stage whisper, "Count Volpe, on the other hand, was overzealous and overstepped his bounds."

Arturo looked askance at Count Giustinani. He admired the count's dramatic speech but did not applaud his performance. "That's a massive understatement," grumbled Arturo.

"I respect your judgment, Signore Monti," the count continued smoothly, "and I appreciate the severity of the situation. I also know how deeply you're involved with helping the beautiful artist." Count Giustinani gave a sly smile to Arturo.

"Ahem," Arturo flushed and momentarily lost his momentum. "No doubt, you know about Fiona's college days and how we became good friends. I'm here to stay. I'm here to help her as a friend, but I won't hesitate to use my business and political influence to assist in the conclusion of this foul matter." Arturo looked levelly at the count.

"Va bene. Graham Hughes is an old friend and a much-respected expert in the field of contemporary art. He's directed gifted art students over the years to me. My gallery, the Venosa, has prospered from some of Graham's bright young painters, and I recognized Fiona as a major talent. I did not," Count Giustinani drawled, "realize Fiona was married to Sergio Celesti as she uses her maiden name, Appleton. It's become awkward, certainly." The count had the good grace to show his embarrassment as he gave a tight smile to Fiona.

"Hubris on the part of Count Volpe led to this scandal," murmured Count Giustinani. The library became silent as he continued, "Count Volpe's grand ambition dwarfed his good sense and ethics. Over the years, Count Volpe, with the approval of the directors of the Knights of Malta, sold assorted minor paintings and continental-styled furniture to Sergio Celesti. Whenever the Order needed any furniture or paintings restored, Count Volpe also went to Sergio and his workshop in Naples. The items were easily insured under a standard reporting form to Sergio's insurance company. When the newspapers first reported the warehouse fire, Count Volpe rang Sergio about the inventory the Order had on file with him. At first, Count Volpe did not suspect the Caravaggio was stored at the warehouse and, of course," Count Giustinani looked up at Fiona with a sad smile on his face, "Sergio didn't enlighten him. After all, it was not listed on the insurance reporting form."

Count Giustinani glanced up to see if Fiona was following his narrative, nodded to her and resumed, "Sergio delayed recounting any details of the uninsured loss to his shady partners and never told Count Volpe. The count began to hear rumors about an Old Master having been destroyed in the warehouse fire. The rumors spread throughout Campania, the entire region of Naples. Count Volpe smelled a rat: The destroyed painting was most likely the Caravaggio. The count put his ear to the ground and heard more rumors about a forgery being used as a substitute. That, in fact, a fake was burned and the genuine Caravaggio was once again hidden."

Pausing for breath, Count Giustinani looked around the room and his eyes lighted on Fiona, "By this time, Sergio had moved to Capri for the summer. His cavalier attitude convinced the Camorra, at least for a while, that he had no worries about collecting the insurance money on everything, including the Caravaggio. They eventually sent Umberto to collect the money. Sergio stalled him and fled with you, Fiona, to Positano.

"Count Volpe had followed Umberto to Capri and then jumped on a helicopter to fly to Positano and await your arrival at the hotel. He speculated that Sergio had the painting and also a lot of cash. By this time, Count Volpe knew about the partnership with the dreaded Camorra. That's when he decided to confront Sergio in Positano."

"I know," Fiona said with a stifled sob. "Count Volpe warned me that I was in danger. Sergio and I fought that night and," she rummaged in her handbag for a handkerchief, "the next morning he was dead."

Count Giustinani continued in a soft voice, "The Camorra may have murdered Sergio. I don't know. I recently learned that the carabinieri's investigation is stalled."

"How did you learn that?" Arturo asked.

"My personal banking is with Banca di Roma and I deal with Antonio Celesti," explained Count Giustinani. "I know he's the president and chief executive officer of the entire holding company, but Antonio's also an old friend. In fact, he's my original loan officer in the early days of the Venosa Gallery."

"Well, Antonio would certainly know about the status of the investigation," groused Arturo.

"As I was saying, Count Volpe hid the loss of the Caravaggio until Sergio's tragic death," Count Giustinani's eyes flickered onto Fiona and he quickly picked up the pace, "and he realized the Camorra had also been double-crossed by Sergio. Count Volpe wanted to protect Fiona from the Camorra's retribution and pleaded with me for help. I was stunned to learn the extent of his folly but recognized the extreme danger you were in, Fiona. I immediately turned to Graham for his advice."

Graham emitted a loud breath and hurriedly continued for Count Giustinani, "We won't allow anyone to hurt you, Fiona. Not physically, or your reputation. We want to assist your sleuthing endeavors."

"How?" snapped Arturo.

Count Giustinani jumped back in, "We can follow you and trail anyone shadowing you. We can't involve the police or the newspapers will seize upon the scandal, putting Fiona at greater risk. I know you don't need funds, Signore Monti." Count Giustinani coldly assessed Arturo and sat down tentatively on a high-backed chair by the desk.

"Will you hire private detectives?" Arturo returned an equal look to Count Giustinani.

"Sì. Graham and I are too old to maintain any pace of shadowing anyone spying on you. I'll give the detectives an assignment with limited information. They can act as security backup and if anything looks suspicious, they can contact either one of us through our direct lines. We'll also be watching Count Volpe and his activities. I'll keep him in the dark about this. Maybe we'll learn more by working together?" Count Giustinani gave an appraising eye to Arturo and waited for his response.

"Fiona," Arturo looked at her, "I think this is the best we can expect from them. Are you okay with this?"

"Yes, but I just don't want the private detectives to be obvious or we'll spook the Camorra."

"I understand, my dear. Your safety comes first." Count Giustinani spoke in crisp tones. He wiped his hands on his trousers as if the conversation was concluded.

"I'm glad that's understood," Professor Hughes rejoined and continued in a lilting voice, "Drink?"

Professor Hughes quickly made a tray of Campari and sodas and served them.

As they munched on crisp chips and olives, Fiona said in an offhand manner, "Thank you for clearing up this misunderstanding, Graham. Your friendship bolstered my career and smoothed my early years in Rome."

Fiona's eyes glittered as she said to Count Giustinani, "I believe you've been candid and that you're sincere in trying to assist our search for the Caravaggio. After all," Fiona narrowed her eyes, "you have much to gain."

Fiona grabbed her bag, stood, smoothed the wrinkles out of her skirt and stated, "We should get back to our work."

Arturo moved quickly from his chair to join her. He acknowledged the older man's concern, shook the count's hand and turned to Professor Hughes.

"I expect you to protect Fiona's interests." Arturo gave him a stern look and Professor Hughes returned his stare with equal intensity in his eyes. Arturo, assured of Professor Hughes' loyalty to Fiona, shook his hand. "Andiamo, let's go, Fiona."

Back on the cobblestoned street, Fiona admitted nervously to Arturo, "That was a lot to take in. At least it was neatly summarized by both of them. I'm overwhelmed by the extent of Sergio's betrayal. I married a thief, a drug dealer, the worst of parasites. I don't think he held anything sacred."

Arturo grabbed Fiona's hand and turned to look her in the eyes. He saw her eyes were clear and resolute. Relieved, he said, "Sergio had no values. Something was missing in him. You were never safe. But you've built up a family of friends who will help you. Even Count Giustinani admires you and is on your side."

Fiona tightened her fingers in Arturo's hands and quietly said, "In a strange way, I feel safe. I know we'll find the missing painting and put an end to this rotten nightmare."

With a flick of her hair, she looked up into Arturo's eyes and suggested, "We need to move forward in our investigation. Let's walk over to Valentina's frame shop. Do you know it? It's by the Trevi Fountain and she sells souvenirs in the front of her frame shop. Valentina told me Sergio dropped off a bundle and a few old prints to be framed. She said there's nothing of value in the bag and the prints are ordinary. I'll pay the bill and bring them home. It's a short walk and there's nothing heavy to carry. Shall we?"

"Oh, the famous Trevi Fountain, such a delightful tourist attraction, and such a bore. It'll be swarming with pensioners wearing white sneakers and toting cameras," Arturo groused. "Oh, okay." Arturo nodded as he offered his arm for her. They welcomed the walk and the sunshine, their arms linked together.

They decided to take the locals' shortcut, a more direct way to the Piazza de Spagna than the Spanish Steps. As they reached Via San Sebastianello at the end of the winding road, the late summer set the tone for moodiness. Fiona was wilted and melancholy under the hot sun and parched air. By mid-afternoon, Rome withered and suddenly the sky clouded over, the air sizzled with electricity and there was a sharp crack of booming thunder. The wind began to pick up and small gusts swirled particles of dust from the street. The sky darkened and then a downpour of rain hit the cobblestone street, making it slimy. Fiona and Arturo were forced into the nearest café, La Strega, to seek shelter.

They ran into the tiny foyer, which led abruptly to an improvised hostess area. Fiona ran her fingers through her dripping hair, trying to air-dry it. A woman took pity on her and handed her a small bar towel. She surveyed Arturo head to toe, gave him a saucy smile and swiveled her attention back to Fiona.

"Grazie," Fiona smiled at the tall, curvy, dark-haired woman. Fiona's quick glance assessed the woman to be older but still beautiful in her tightly fitted dress.

"Prego." The woman waited patiently for Fiona to finish mopping up her wet clothes. "Please choose a table and

I'll bring you some wine. Bianco or rosso?" The woman looked at Fiona with a slight smile.

"Bianco, per favore." Fiona chose a table and they sat down with relief. Fiona was exhausted. It had been a long day. She could hear heavy rain pelting the roof and murmured to Arturo, "This summer storm could last a couple of hours. Shall we sit it out and have a light dinner?"

"Va bene. Perhaps the food will be good?"

She casually looked around the lounge area and noticed it had walnut paneling and red leather banquettes interspersed with armchairs covered in a zebra print. It was old-fashioned in design but well maintained. The subdued lighting cast a warm glow in the room. Fiona was pleasantly surprised by the retro feel of the place and remarked, "How strange I've never noticed La Strega before, even though it's so close to Via Margutta and my home."

"That doesn't surprise me," Arturo muttered with an ironical look on his face. "It has a certain reputation."

"Okay. Once more I know I'm in the dark about something that seems so obvious, as you're practically looking smug. Please enlighten me." Fiona looked at Arturo in mock chagrin.

"Our hostess once worked at Il Baretto, the little bar, a popular bar on the corner of Via del Babuino, in the 1950s. The people who lived or worked on Via Margutta all frequented Il Baretto as a social center to drink or exchange the latest news of a local celebrity. During the day, students would hang out with the workers having coffee or wine. After dark, however, the scene changed to an artists' bar and a hub to spread news or outright scandalous gossip about the neighborhood personalities of the fine arts or movie industry. Don't forget how important RAI Cinema was at this time. Hollywood actors would hang out at the artists' studios and then go out social slumming at Il Baretto – it quickly became known as a pickup bar. Your neighborhood was unconventional compared to the more upscale Via Veneto. Via Margutta had rough, informal cabarets; polished cafés were evident on the more prosperous Via Veneto. After all, the very wealthy maintained suites at the Excelsior Hotel and, if one had less money, a simple room would be kept. Via Veneto had their upscale café society and Via Margutta had street walkers and brothels. Unfortunately, Fiona, your neighborhood bar attracted rebels and outcasts of society, street walkers and druggies. Drug dealers operated freely at night and, over time, they openly conducted their business during the day. Eventually, an eager, young investigative reporter, wanting to make a name for himself, exposed the drug trafficking. The cry of the newspapers forced a police crackdown. Il Baretto and other raffish cabarets were closed. I'm sorry to shock you, but it's in the past. Your neighborhood is more upscale today than Via Veneto."

Arturo fell silent as the hostess returned with a carafe of the house white wine and glasses. Arturo sipped a taste, pronounced it "buono" and examined the menu. After taking their order, the hostess bustled away to welcome more customers.

Fiona sipped her wine and looked with a fresh eye at the bar area. She watched customers greet each other with familiarity, helping each other dry off or store their wet umbrellas. There was much laughing and shouting. It was a chaotic, confusing scene – almost a stage set for a Fellini movie, she mused. Fiona contemplated her gloomy thoughts and rolled her eyes when she saw a man pinch a woman drinking a martini beside him. Fiona quickly looked sideways at Arturo and noticed he had witnessed the same scene. Arturo shrugged his shoulders and said, "What do you expect in a crowded neighborhood bar? It's like a club."

"Don't mind them," said the hostess as she presented small bowls of potato chips and olives. "They're regulars, married and trying to have a good time despite the torrential downpour." She looked at them and took their food order. A waiter delivered the food and waited discreetly to see if it met with their approval. It was surprisingly good and Fiona thanked him with genuine pleasure. He bobbed his head and left them in peace. When the espresso was delivered, the hostess glided up to their table and asked, "*Permesso?*" She was holding another espresso and indicated she would like to join them. Fiona gave a sideways glance at Arturo and gave a slight nod of assent. Arturo stood and helped the woman with her chair.

The older woman sat down, delicately crossing her long legs. "I'm Gina Martinelli, the owner of La Strega. I've seen you in the neighborhood, Signora," Gina continued, "but you've never been in before. Not that I blame you as it's such an unusual mix of characters. It must be confusing to determine who went with whom or if at all?" She gave an arch look.

"No, That's not it. I'm married and work over by the Borghese gardens. I don't have much free time."

"You're married to Sergio Celesti?"

"Sì," Fiona focused on the bar owner and continued, "at least I was. Sergio died." She waited for the rest of Gina's conversation as the woman obviously had something she wanted to discuss.

"I already heard the news. I'm sorry for your loss," Gina's eyes swiftly looked over at Arturo and she resumed, "but I wanted to tell you something." She again looked appraisingly at Arturo.

Arturo remained still and stared back at the woman. She finally broke her gaze and said in a harsh tone, "If you were an ordinary tourist, I wouldn't be talking to you like this, but you're a member of the neighborhood and I think you're in trouble," Gina barely paused for breath. "You're being followed by a real creep! A man known to be from Naples has suddenly been spending time at La Strega and other hangouts on Via Margutta. He's been asking questions about you, Signora Celesti."

"What type of questions?" Arturo broke into her conversation, not disguising his concern. Arturo watched the woman as she collected her thoughts.

"Oh, so you're the protective type?" Gina snapped. She turned and directed her tirade at Fiona, "Well, you'll need more muscle than him," Gina hooked her thumb toward Arturo. Her voice gathered steam and she said, "The creep asking about you is a known criminal, a thug of the lowest order. He's not welcome here."

"Can you describe him?" Fiona drummed her fingers on the table as she leaned toward the woman.

"He's a bottle blond, long hair, wearing tight-fitting shirts. He has a bad mouth and treats the other customers in a rough way. He's too rowdy for this bar. Oh, and one thing that stands out, he wears a pink scarf tied around his neck. He always wears that damn silk scarf," Gina muttered. Turning her head in Arturo's direction, Gina raised her voice and barked, "Well?" The woman glared at Arturo as if he might challenge her.

"How do you know he's a criminal?" Arturo dared Gina.

"He's done time. He's a drug dealer." Gina faced Arturo, giving him a stony look.

Fiona gasped and Arturo gave her hand a gentle squeeze. He looked over at Gina and saw she was enjoying herself. Arturo sat more erect in his chair as he said, "Thank you for your information, Signora Martinelli. When was this cretino most recently here?"

"That's easy," she rumbled. "He poked his head in during the storm, saw you two and he hightailed it out of here. That's when I decided to tell you about that snake."

Fiona could not help her voice cracking with nervous tension as she abruptly interrupted and said, "Thank you, Signora Martinelli. It was kind of you to take your time to tell us. I appreciate it."

"You can thank me by calling me Gina and you can visit La Strega sometime. After all, we serve good food and we need some classy customers," she hesitated for a beat of a moment and grumbled, "The hero can come too if you want him." Gina winked and got up from the table. "See you around and take care of yourself, Fiona." She gave Arturo another saucy smile, turned and swished her generous hips as she walked back to the hostess station.

"What do you think?" Fiona looked at Arturo.

"I think she's a broad, but an honest broad. I think she knew about Sergio's bad reputation and wanted to warn you about a dangerous thug who has taken an interest in you. Let's get out of here."

They left the darkened lounge and walked out onto the busy street. The dirty cobblestone street was refreshed from the rainstorm and the puddles were drying up fast. The narrow street was once again bathed in sunlight.

"We still need to go to Valentina's frame shop. Shall we?" Fiona looked up at Arturo and grabbed his arm.

"Sì. Andiamo." Arturo quickly looked over his shoulder but could not spot any pink scarf standing out in the crowd. He propelled them forward, saying in a joking tone, "Tell me about the Trevi Fountain, Fiona."

"Very funny. For that tired question, I'll bore you with standard tourist information." Fiona squeezed his arm and continued, "Actually, I was blown away when I first came upon the Trevi. I wasn't prepared for the mammoth scale of the sculpture or the white marble. It was a brilliant white in the sunshine and the sheer magnitude of its scale was startling. Although the water was gushing azure blue against the white marble, it wasn't a noble sight, despite the beauty of the monumental figures. The Trevi Fountain was crawling with tourists and, to make matters worse, there were seedy souvenir stalls bracketing the sides of the piazza." Fiona shook her head and said with a sigh, "Not beautiful."

"No Anita Ekberg in sight?" Arturo looked at her with an impish smile.

"Sadly, I take the fountain for granted and try to avoid the crowds. Ah, here we are." Fiona opened the door to the frame shop, causing an old bell to make a clinking sound as the door opened wider.

Arturo saw a tall, statuesque, middle-aged woman with a tanned, pleasant face. She swung her long, brown hair off her face as she finished rolling up a poster at the front desk. The woman appraised Arturo, winked slyly and gave him a brilliant smile.

"Ah, my beautiful Fiona. And who is this charming man? Come in, come in." She spoke to Fiona with her eyes sparkling. Valentina was overjoyed to see her friend and looked with open curiosity at Arturo.

"Valentina, I'd like you to meet Arturo Monti, an old friend, who recently returned to Rome."

"A pleasure to meet you, Arturo. Please, make yourself at home. There are comfortable chairs over there. Do you want a caffè? I can have it brought in. No? Okay, I've been busy fitting frames all day so it's good to have company. The shop's been slow. Let me get the prints. Do you want to take that old satchel too?"

Valentina's voice faltered as she saw Fiona's suit was light-colored linen. "I know it's too dirty for your clothes. You don't have to carry it today, although Arturo may be able to manage?" She grinned at them.

"I'll be glad to carry the satchel and the prints," Arturo quickly said.

Valentina smiled at Arturo, turned to Fiona and, in a singsong voice, declared, "I knew he was a gentleman. So gallant and so strong." Valentina smiled and disappeared into the back room. Valentina immediately poked her head back through the draped doorway and said, "Psst! Fiona, come here for a moment."

Fiona dipped her head and said, "I won't be long." Fiona followed her into the back room and suddenly felt Valentina's arm.

"I'm sorry about your loss, Fiona. I know you loved your husband." Valentina gave Fiona a warm hug. "I never liked Sergio, however. He was difficult to deal with, always paying cash but never the full amount. A really tough man. I also didn't like some of the dealers he used. I was suspicious of them. I always wondered if everything was on the up-and-up. Some of those dealers were from the deep-south of Naples and you know what that lot is like." Valentina took one of her fingers and pushed her nose to one side. It was the classic signal for a crook. Valentina raised her eyebrows and opened her eyes wide. "You understand me?" She scrutinized Fiona's face and said, "I see you're not shocked. Well, hold onto Arturo. He looks like a real man and he'll protect you. I'm your friend, too. I'm sorry if I spoke ill of the dead," Valentina said in a crusty voice, "but I had to knock some sense into you. No allusions, kiddo. Va bene?"

"Sì, va bene. I've learned a lot in a very short time, most of it was unpleasant, but I'm glad I know the truth and where I stand. Thanks for being my friend, Valentina." Fiona looked at Valentina with tears in her eyes and hugged her. She straightened up, smoothed the tears away and returned to the front of the shop. Fiona saw Arturo was examining a pile of old maps of Rome and joined him.

"I always relax around Valentina. She's so full of energy and bustles around her shop all day, selling to tourists and working on frames in her spare time. She's always happy to see me," Fiona said quietly to Arturo.

Valentina clicked noisily into the shop room on her jewel-encrusted high-heeled sandals carrying two small framed prints of an erupting Mount Vesuvius and a burlap bag wrapped in twine. Fiona admired the framing job and paid the bill.

Valentina and Fiona chattered and gossiped about the latest political scandals as Valentina wrapped the prints in tissue paper and ribbon. She put them in a bag embossed with the store logo and accepted Fiona's check.

With the old bell sounding, a few tourists wandered into the shop and Arturo grabbed the burlap sack. Turning to Valentina, Fiona air-kissed her on both cheeks, made promises to have a morning caffè soon and picked up the prints. Fiona and Arturo quickly left the store.

"Let's go home and unpack the bag. I don't want to

look at it in public. Va bene?" Fiona looked anxiously at Arturo.

"Certo," Arturo replied, "but let's take a taxi." He looked up the street, saw a group of cabs and waved to the one in the front row. The driver jumped into his car and squealed over to the frame shop. Fiona and Arturo quickly loaded the taxi with their packages and settled into the back seat. Arturo craned his neck to see if they were being followed and smiled at Fiona to signal they were safe. He then turned away and silently considered the contents in the satchel. Arturo knew Fiona hoped to find old wood. Old wooden stretcher bars. Perhaps the exact age and fit for the missing canvas? Had the missing Caravaggio been rolled and put away separate from its stretcher bars? He decided the best time to raise these questions were in the privacy of Fiona's apartment and over a glass of wine.

The taxi driver struggled to clear the mass of tourists snapping pictures of the Trevi Fountain. He pointed out a young woman who was urging her friend to toss a coin in the fountain to assure their return to Rome. The two girls found some coins in their bags and tossed them cheerfully into the bubbling water. Arturo looked at them with envy, wishing Fiona's life was as simple.

Arturo shifted the bags in his hands while Fiona balanced the lightweight but awkward satchel on her lap. The taxi moved swiftly once they cleared the knot of tourists by the fountain and reentered the Piazza di Spagna. They continued down the busy Via del Babuino and reached Fiona's home without noticing any car following them. Fiona dropped the satchel onto the kitchen table and immediately looked for a paring knife to cut the twine. She unrolled the folds of the burlap and looked into the bag. She gave a hoot of laughter and smiled broadly at Arturo.

"They're stretcher bars! And they're antique but still in good shape. No worm rot." Fiona was overcome with emotion she could barely get the words out.

"I'm not really surprised," she looked at Arturo and waited for his reaction.

"Were you looking for them all along? Or did you start looking for them once Count Volpe asked you?" Arturo spoke slowly and deliberately. He stared at her with no light reflecting in his eyes.

Fiona hesitated as she sensed Arturo's growing anger and hoped it was not directed at her. "I wasn't certain about the missing stretcher bars until Count Volpe suggested their existence," she said in a low voice.

"Why are the stretcher bars so important?"

"Stretcher bars support the canvas. They are made to the exact measurements of a painting. The original invoice indicated the size of the commissioned painting so it's relatively simple to know the lengths of the four stretcher bars," Fiona took a breath and continued, "Sergio made business decisions at a dizzying pace. He was secretive and developed a cipher I still haven't cracked." Fiona mused out loud while tapping her fingers on the old wood.

Arturo could not follow her line of reasoning. "What do you mean? Did you make more sense from the cipher than you told me?"

"I wasn't trying to deceive you, Arturo," Fiona said sheepishly. "I simply wasn't sure. I need to study the code and Dante's *Inferno* again. I know I'm missing something. I want to imagine a picture, the Caravaggio, in the mosaic of the cipher. The painting's value is an important variable. It was moved around as it was leveraged from deal to deal. Let me do this today and then we'll talk later. I won't keep anything from you, I promise." Fiona tried to give him an encouraging smile, but her face became a grimace of pain.

"I've trusted you this long. I believe in you. I'll go into the study and read a book about Caravaggio." Arturo gave her a hug and left the room.

Fiona examined the ledgers and papers late into the night, all the while making notes along the heavily marked margins of Dante's *Inferno*. She compared her notes to the ledger and saw a trail of transfers of money for goods and a growing profit for Sergio as she was able to decode more of his cipher. After reviewing the columns of information several times, she came to a conclusion – a logical conclusion and the only one making any sense of the data. Rubbing her eyes, she stood up and paced around the room. The large Venetian mirror over the fireplace showed her staring back with her mocking self-portrait behind her with Sergio by her side. The matrimonial portrait reflected her smiling, blonde self, once looking so content and now looking foolish. Fiona's eyes misted as she murmured, "Ah ha." She wanted to smash the antique mirror and also destroy the painted faces. Futile! Fiona pulled herself together and walked back to her little work table covered with her notes. Slapping the ledgers shut, she put them in a drawer and looked at the light shining from the study.

Striding over to the study, Fiona knocked on the door. Poking her head in, she said, "I've solved the cipher," as she waved the copy of Dante's *Inferno* at Arturo.

Arturo looked up from his book and shouted, "Fantastic!" as he practically flew out of the room to join her. He gave Fiona a bear hug, twirling her around. Then he gently put her down and looked into her eyes. Arturo asked, "Was it in the *Inferno*?"

"Actually, it was what was missing. I looked for any

reference to Dante's beloved Beatrice who plays a limited role in the *Inferno*. Then I was intrigued by the souls in the Second Circle of Hell, the Lustful. These souls committed sins of the flesh, such as Helen, for whose sake the Trojan War was fought, and Cleopatra. They were damned by love. A young couple, Francesca and Paolo, also tell how love was their undoing. I thought about my double portrait, a wedding gift to Sergio, and suddenly everything fell into place. Sergio was playing a perverse game with me from the very beginning. According to my notes, the painting was indeed used as leverage in lieu of cash to buy, process and distribute hard drugs. I think the painting is hidden within another. I need your help removing it from the wall."

"Where? Let me."

Arturo followed Fiona's eyes to her matrimonial portrait. "But it's not the right size. It's too big for the stretcher bars!" Arturo shook his head at her.

"I have a hunch. Let's be careful and take it down."

Fiona moved toward the painting and they carefully slipped it off the wall hooks. Walking over to the kitchen table, they gingerly placed the painted side on the table top. Fiona quickly went to find some tools to remove the modern frame. Almost holding her breath, Fiona freed the painting from its frame.

Arturo carried the frame over to a far corner in the living room. By the time he returned to the kitchen, Fiona was examining the sizing on the back of the canvas with a jeweler's loop. She saw that it indeed had been relined. She was scrutinizing the work and admiring the superb workmanship.

"Just as I suspected. There's a smaller painting here. What a clever job. I'm sure this was done by Sergio's own hands. Expert conservators should finish the restoration. I won't go any further on my experiment. Tomorrow, we'll need to take this to my studio for another test."

With an abrupt motion, Fiona turned her head, looked downward and brushed the sudden tears from her eyes. Shaking her head, she murmured, "I'm being silly, I know. I just can't believe he deceived me to the extent of using me and my love for him to cover up one of his frauds." Arturo held her gently, comforting her as he would a small child and remained by her side as she sobbed.

The morning light swept through the rooms and she awoke refreshed. Fiona welcomed the aroma of fresh coffee and toast. Arturo greeted her in the kitchen with a steaming mug.

"Ah, thank you, just what I need on such a momentous morning." Fiona smiled and looked into Arturo's clear blue eyes. "I want to take the painting over to my studio. Do you think we can get a small truck to help us? One of the artisans will help or one of the gardeners from the Borghese. I'll call Graham and alert him."

Quickly, Fiona dialed Professor Hughes and said, "Arturo and I are going over to my studio to examine an interesting painting. Do you have a truck we could borrow? Oh, please alert Count Giustinani in case we need additional protection at the studio," she waited and replied, "Va bene. A presto." Fiona hung up the phone and turned to Arturo, "He'll be right over with one of those three-wheeled trucks the laborers use. We can all sit in the front."

Rolling his eyes to the heavens, Arturo exclaimed, "We're not being very secretive with your discovery."

"We're being watched, anyway. Better to involve Graham and Count Giustinani. After all, the Knights of Malta have a lot to lose, too. They can watch our backs."

"Okay, okay. I'm overreacting," mumbled Arturo. "Let me help you with the painting."

Together, Arturo and Fiona wrapped the large canvas in thick padding. Fiona quickly stood the painting by the door and gathered the satchel holding the precious stretcher bars.

Arturo said, "I'm taking the extra packing outside so when Graham arrives we can line the truck with it. I'll be in to help you carry the painting."

"I can handle it. Just go out and help him get the truck ready," Fiona said as she was collecting her things. She heard the door close and she was alone with the painting and her thoughts. Fiona reminded herself that she had confronted her demons last night when she went to bed. Sergio was gone and so were her wonderful memories of their life together. He was a criminal and had led a double life, endangering her own. Fiona now had to deal with the loose ends in order to resume a normal life. She had dealt with the sordid truth and came out stronger. Fiona picked up the precious painting, opened the door and blinked at the sunlight. She slammed the door behind her.

Professor Hughes and Arturo were waiting at the rear of a dark-blue van stamped with a white Maltese cross. Professor Hughes quickly doffed his panama as his eyes alighted on the wrapped painting and gave an appreciative whistle, "Well done, my dear." He continued humming as he bustled to help carry it to the back of the cab. Arturo clambered inside the van and adroitly secured the painting with additional strapping. They slid onto the front seat and the truck spirited them to her studio. No one spoke.

Arturo was the first one out the door and he ran to the

rear of the van, grabbed the satchel and picked up one end of the canvas to help Fiona. Arturo shouted to Professor Hughes, "Thanks for the help. Will you stow the van out of sight?"

"Okay. I'll be back soon," Professor Hughes looked at Fiona, waved cheerily and then ground the gears into first. The van shot out of its space with the gravel squirting out from under the tires. Fiona chuckled and said, "I don't recall ever seeing Graham drive in all the time I've known him."

"Just as well," Arturo joked.

Once safely inside the studio, they placed the painting flat on the worktable. After glancing at the double portrait, Arturo looked quizzically at Fiona and cleared his throat to say, "I don't understand. How will we recover the original?"

"Oh ye of little faith!" Fiona chortled and continued, "Wait right here." Pulling a piece of paper out of her pocket, Fiona examined it quickly, dropped it on the table and went about collecting solvents and a mixing container.

Arturo studied the piece of paper and was surprised to see what looked like a recipe. Carefully mixing the formula, Fiona scrutinized her notes. Satisfied, she took a clean, soft cloth and with featherlight strokes began dabbing the paint of the double portrait.

Her concentration never wavered, and then she stopped her rubbing of the paint and varnish. She looked up from the portrait and, with a dramatic accent, exclaimed, "As I suspected. Would you like to see a masterpiece?"

The shock of the painting coming to life through Fiona's meticulous swabbing caused Arturo to run around the worktable in order to gain a better vantage point. He gazed upon the now-blemished portrait watching as another picture glimmered through the cleaned area. "Is it?"

"We found it! Under my nose all the time." She threw the dirty rags into a bin and, with a snapping sound, stripped her rubber gloves off. "This should go to museum services at the Borghese. Sergio protected the Caravaggio with a coating of varnish and then painted an overcoat. She got a magnifying glass to examine the brushstrokes. He was one of the best at conservation and this glorious beauty deserves the best. Either the Vatican or the Borghese. Of course, this will have to be authenticated and there will be a fight over ownership. It will take years to determine the provenance of the painting and this will create a cottage industry for art scholars," murmured Fiona. She stared at the changing surface of the canvas.

"Sergio must have made a copy and substituted the fake in his nefarious business dealings. The real Caravaggio was always hanging on my living room walls," Fiona said under her breath as she continued to examine the old painting as it emerged from the varnish.

"My Caravaggio!" a familiar voice grunted.

Fiona and Arturo looked toward the entrance and were shocked into silence. Count Volpe was standing by the door.

"You found it, my clever Fiona," he said in his rasping voice. The count was smiling but pointing a small pistol at her. He took catlike steps into the studio all the while holding the gun in a firm grasp.

"Let me see it. *Attenzione!* Careful, no sudden moves. I'm an old man with an old gun. Silly to have it go off and hit someone or damage the picture. Arturo, move into that corner so I can see you better."

Count Volpe moved to Fiona's side and looked down upon the scarred portrait. Another picture gleamed through, just a fragment, but unmistakably Caravaggio. The count beamed with pleasure, a smile illuminating his tanned face.

"Now, hand it over."

Fiona looked fixedly at Count Volpe and saw he was no longer smiling. "And if I objected …" Her voice trailed off and she made a gesture of disgust.

Count Volpe shook his head. "This is not negotiable." He lunged at her all the while pointing the pistol at her chest and forced the painting out of her hands. Count Volpe carefully leaned the Caravaggio against the wall. In a seamless motion, Count Volpe cocked the pistol, still pointing it at her chest, and snarled, "And that's not all. I'm sorry."

Suddenly, the door opened wider and another voice said quietly, "Count Volpe, attenzione! Stop threatening Fiona!"

Antonio Celesti marched into the room but made no attempt to disarm the count. Standing ramrod straight, he did not appear to be armed and was immaculately turned out in a bespoke suit with a colorful pocket handkerchief. He glared at the count and did not for one moment seem threatened by the gun.

The count's eye's flashed. "And if I …"

"Put that sorry excuse of a gun down."

The gun clattered to the floor and the count looked at Fiona, "It was worth a try. It's a toy gun but a good fake." The old man at least had the decency to add, "I didn't want anyone to get hurt. I had to get the Caravaggio to save your lives."

Fiona stared back at him, shocked to see Count Volpe had the nerve to wink at her.

"Thank you, Antonio," she said. "Your timing was perfect, but how did you know we were here?"

"I decided to have your apartment watched by some of my employees. I was worried someone would break into your home and kidnap you to ransom the painting. Anything could happen when dealing with the Camorra. It was only for your safety." Antonio moved closer to the worktable and stood over the painting to have a better look at the Caravaggio glimmering through the overpaint.

"I don't believe you," Count Volpe growled.

Antonio shook his head. "I will not brook any more interference. Take it or leave it. And that's not all."

"What do you mean?"

"What do I mean?" Antonio sneered at Count Volpe. "You will take your painting and leave Fiona and Arturo alone. Forever."

The old man bent his head. "Va bene, Tonino. I'll remove the painting now and be on my way. Will you let your people know?" Without another word, Count Volpe picked up the painting and made for the door.

"Wait!" cried Fiona. "All this work, this hunt through a maze of clues, and you're letting Count Volpe treat the Caravaggio as his merchandise? It's plunder for the Camorra! Antonio, won't you contact one of your friends in government to save it for one of our museums? The world deserves to see such a masterpiece!" Fiona was practically beside herself with pent-up anxiety and anger.

Antonio Celesti looked at Fiona with open admiration and said, "Brava. Well said, Fiona. What a passionate appeal to my sense of noblesse oblige." But his dry and cynical tone of voice told Fiona he was joking.

"I appreciate your courage and willingness to fight for the museums, for the people, but the Camorra will not relax their grip on you, Fiona, until their property is returned. Let Count Volpe negotiate with the Camorra. He can be responsible for returning the painting to the Knights of Malta. The important thing is you will no longer be involved with the Camorra. You inherited Sergio's mess, but now it's been resolved in an equitable fashion. It's not for me to decide who the rightful owner of the Caravaggio is. I'm not only protecting you, Fiona, but my family. Let the Caravaggio remain missing from the public. Perhaps it will continue to embroider the mystery, the myth of that sad painter's life."

There was something about the tone of Antonio's ultimatum that was final, Fiona thought. He'd brook no further argument. Something hard had replaced his avuncular manner.

Antonio gave a sideways glance at Count Volpe and shrugged his shoulders. The old man continued dragging the painting across the studio while Antonio Celesti stuck his head out the door and gave a small whistle. Antonio kept the door open long enough for the count to exit and promptly shut it firmly behind him. Antonio said, "On second thought, you're welcome to look out the door or the window as you'll notice the Knights of Malta are waiting for Count Volpe. I believe it's your old professor, Graham Hughes, isn't it? He's greeting Count Volpe now. Ah, I see another familiar face."

Fiona ran to the window and looked out to see Professor Hughes hoist the painting into the van. She also saw Count Giustinani sternly order Count Volpe into a waiting black limousine. Fiona recognized some of the uniformed guards from the Order as they roughly hauled the old man away. Professor Hughes suddenly jumped out of the van and looked into the window. When he saw Fiona, he doffed his hat and then whirled it up in the air. Professor Hughes caught it, spun to the front of the van and clambered into the driver's seat. He tooted the horn and drove slowly away.

Antonio turned away from the door, looked at Fiona and said in a quiet tone, "I see by your eyes you are not truly surprised to see me?"

"No, nor Count Volpe. How could I be surprised after decoding Sergio's cipher? I finally understood his code of dirty business dealings. The cipher indicated Count Volpe posed several times as the owner of the Caravaggio when the painting was leveraged for more and more transactions, more filthy lire into his pockets and to Sergio. I also know the count was duped as the cipher also indicated Sergio kept the majority of the profits and they were enormous. Count Volpe unwittingly acted as a banker to the Camorra and also to Sergio in all his deals, legitimate and illicit. This unholy consortium of thugs leveraged the Caravaggio to buy raw heroin to be processed in Naples and then quickly converted the finished product for distribution. The fire not only destroyed the drugs but also a fake Caravaggio, a forgery created by Sergio, which went undetected at the time of the insurance settlement. That's as far as the cipher reveals. Somewhat later, we all know the Camorra realized Sergio had double-crossed them. In fact, they belatedly discovered he'd been double dealing for a long time and the Camorra sought vengeance. They tipped their hand to Count Volpe by using Umberto. Am I correct, Antonio?"

"You're doing well so far."

"Just a moment, Antonio," interjected Arturo, "the Camorra contacted you, not Count Volpe. Now why would they do that?"

Antonio gave a sharp inhale of breath and exclaimed, "The Camorra reached out to me as I was such an old friend of Orazio Giustinani and I was his banker. But how on earth did you find out about Count Giustinani?"

"I read several biographies of Caravaggio yesterday while Fiona was examining Sergio's cipher," Arturo paused when he heard Fiona gasp.

"I never knew about the Venosa connection," she stammered.

"It was serendipity. I picked up an obscure volume, old and not well-used," Arturo smiled and continued, "I discovered an interesting nugget of history about the Knights of Malta. In the summer of 1607, two cousins of the Giustinani family met with the grand master. They offered the family property in Venosa, near Naples, as a fortress or naval center for the Knights on the mainland. The Roman branches of the Giustinani family were collectors of Caravaggio's paintings. They were eager to purchase more of his work. Perhaps they petitioned the grand master to accept the artist despite his criminal record. It is about this period of time that Caravaggio made his way to the island and became a knight. He then commenced all his late, great work. Perhaps the pope's two paintings secretly went to the Giustinani family. The paintings have been held within the Knights of Malta or under the protection of the Giustinani family since Caravaggio's death in 1610."

Antonio shook his head and then looked at Arturo, "You solved a great mystery. You also know that it can never be revealed?"

Arturo nodded.

Fiona hurriedly continued, "But was the heroin really destroyed in the fire? Was that switched too?" Fiona looked at Antonio, trying to determine not only his knowledge of the unsavory business but also the extent of his involvement.

"Brava, Fiona. You are quick. The factory blew up either from the chemicals being used or through arson. But Sergio had already removed the real Caravaggio and also hidden the heroin. May I have it, Fiona? I need it to keep you safe."

With a sigh, Fiona said in a resigned voice, "I realized I had too much rabbit skin glue in my studio. When I looked at my supply this morning, I had enough to last me for the rest of my working life and then some. I assume it is heroin?"

"Sì. The packages masquerading as rabbit skin glue are indeed heroin. Sergio was clever to hide it in your studio, again out in the open for prying eyes to see. I never thought anything of it as I don't paint. I thought you just ordered your art supplies in bulk."

Fiona looked at Antonio with a blazing anger in her eyes and tried to suppress the rage in her voice as she continued her questioning, "The furniture factory in Naples was really a heroin-processing plant? They brought the raw product in from Marseille and made it into street-grade heroin?"

"Again, I was not familiar with the progression of my son's climb up the Camorra ladder of drug distribution. I only found out after his death. I thought the fire in Forcella was an innocent work-related blaze. I believed it was Sergio's art restoration workshop and someone, a laborer perhaps, misused the solvents. After all, those chemicals used in furniture restoration were highly combustible. He had fires and accidents in the past, but never a major loss. I discovered through my contacts that Sergio had been operating a massive heroin-processing plant in Campania. Those illicit labs or processing plants are always exploding. Sergio was operating on a massive scale, so any malfunction would lead to a horrific accident. His systems failed, creating a huge explosion, burning the property to the ground. The physical remains of the genuine furniture-restoration business disguised the drug operation, but only for a while." Antonio stared at Fiona to estimate her knowledge and quickly realized from the expression on her face that she was not surprised by his tale.

"You're correct that the furniture-restoration business disguised the true nature of Sergio's business. No one in the Camorra sensed the enormity of his business prowess in the manufacture and distribution of illicit drugs. I only realized the truth of his business operations upon deciphering the cipher he used through a copy of Dante's *Inferno*." Fiona pursed her lips and let out a sigh. "It's hard for me to believe that Sergio successfully led a double life, but he really fooled me." Fiona's voice caught and she stood silent, watching her father-in-law.

Antonio tensed and said, "Where is the cipher? Where is the book?"

"Safe. If anyone hurts me or kills me, it goes to the world press, the anti-mafia team in the carabinieri and the FBI." Fiona stood silently waiting for Antonio's next move.

Antonio broke the long silence and continued, "I shunned Sergio once he decided to produce and distribute heroin. He no longer was my son. In my mind, my son was dead. I did not want his disease, his black soul, affecting my family." Shaking his head with disgust, "I want nothing to do with the filthy business of drugs. At this moment, a few of my men are outside waiting to take the heroin to Sergio's partners. As I said earlier, it's to protect you and also my family from the Camorra."

Antonio looked in the direction Fiona pointed and then opened the door. A slight man came in swiftly and waited for instructions. "I believe you know Mimo?"

Fiona's stunned gaze passed from Mimo to Antonio. Arturo put a hand on Fiona, trying to calm her. Antonio gestured to the hiding place, and Mimo quickly removed all of the small wrapped packages from a cubbyhole in a corner of the studio. He stuffed them into shopping bags stamped with a designer logo and left not making a sound.

"I'm truly sorry my son betrayed your trust, Fiona. He was a cheap thief. That's all there is to it," Antonio said as he ground his handkerchief into his hands. "Count Giustinani will return the Caravaggio to the Order. I imagine the painting will be kept in seclusion. I don't know and frankly don't care. Count Volpe will most likely survive the scandal as it will be minimized by Count Giustinani. And most importantly, Fiona, you'll be left alone by those Neapolitan thugs."

Antonio's voice suddenly grew hoarse with emotion and he violently cleared his throat to continue, "You're a lovely young woman and deserve much better, a better man and a beautiful life." There was silence as Antonio took measure of Arturo. Tension mounted in the room, but the two men maintained their silence.

Fiona stood there a moment as if she was thinking over everything Antonio had revealed. She had no illusions. Finally, Fiona looked at Antonio and replied in an even, sure voice, "I think when Sergio was young he learned a lot from you, Antonio. I'm sure he looked up to you as any son would and wanted to learn the family business. Being the oldest son of your branch of the family, Sergio participated in his share of the business, but he wanted more money, power and to spread his wings. Something like Icarus? You understand, *capisce?*"

Fiona gave Antonio a penetrating look but did not expect a nod or any acknowledgement of agreement from him. She continued, "Perhaps Sergio felt he learned all he could and looked elsewhere for advice and direction? Sergio thought heroin was the modern business venture as it promised so much more money and at a faster pace. The demand for the drug was endless. My late husband was not interested in the old ways of doing business such as prostitution, contract rigging and gambling – even banking. Have I named all of your dirty businesses? What have I overlooked? What other illegal activities do you and your family control?" She realized she was screaming. She choked back her words and fell silent, waiting.

"Basta! Enough! I don't expect you to understand, Fiona," Antonio raised his voice and said harshly, "Sergio left the family, my family, when he decided to distribute street drugs. He went bad after all he was taught: Loyalty to the family, tradition, building trust. I decided not to touch him, but turned my back on him. His association with the Camorra killed him. He's dead and buried. You're free now. Live your life."

Antonio nodded at Arturo and turned on his polished leather shoes. He left quickly, closing the door firmly behind him.

Arturo came towards her and Fiona found herself in his arms. His embrace enveloped her, keeping her safe, and she looked up into his blue eyes. Arturo no longer looked serious; his eyes twinkled and he whispered into her ear, "How about a long lunch?"

"Great! But what about the mysterious key? Did you ever find out about the key?" Fiona looked mischievously at Arturo.

Arturo replied in an amused tone, "Not yet."

Fiona took his arm and replied, "Then we have more exploring to do. I wonder what we'll find."

Acknowledgments

Writing *The Caravaggio Contract* has been a delight and the following people all have helped make it so. My heartfelt thanks to:

The St. Botolph Writer's workshop, because I never would have completed the manuscript without you. Special thanks to Stu Liss, Patricia Buddenhagen, Ann Russell, and Jenny Hudson, who became my publisher. Especially warm thanks to Ladette Randolph for her steady counsel and insightful advice.

My dear friend, Sue Ambrecht, an incomparable editor, who cheerfully agreed to edit and re-edit.

Nancy and Bobby Wibblesman, who worked diligently to help me achieve my ambition of becoming a first-time author and screenwriter.

Carol Lustig and Nick Bogard, extraordinary copy editors, who provided stalwart and timely support.

Nancy Clark, my Wheaton College roommate and good friend, for being brilliant at her job in editing, web design, and social media.

Russ Bubas, private investigator, and Randy Lamattina, former Boston Police Bomb Squad member and protection specialist, for providing a constant stream of information about DEA procedures and past arrests for illicit drug distribution. Let's plan a heist next.

Carolyn and Tom Loucas, Marna Fullerton, Laurie Erickson, Acklen Dunning, Geraldine Scotti, Queeney and Todd Weintz, Joan Burns, Pat Duggan, Suzanne Schultz, Mitch Plotkin and Tiffany Cant for their enthusiasm and confidence in me.

Patricia Francy for taking seriously all the different parts of the book.

Michael L. Giacalone, public relations officer at the Italian Cultural Institute in Washington, DC, for his gracious Italian translations and his kind introductions to the cultural institutions in Rome.

Thanks especially to the late Bernie Williams, who gave his and time and energy for so many hours.

The largest thanks goes to my husband, Arthur Bauernfeind, who has lived with this book for years. Arthur can take credit for the fact that I still have a sense of humor and a few marbles left.